Award-winning author **E.R. Fallon** has studied criminology and was mentored by a leading advocate for the family members of homicide victims. E.R. has published several crime and mystery stories that received widespread praise from bestselling international writers.

**Praise for E.R. Fallon:**

'…the kind of book we stay up all night to finish.' - Da Chen, *New York Times* bestselling novelist

'One to watch.' - Thomas Waugh

*Also by E.R. Fallon:*

Body in the Box

The Stealthy Heart

The Trouble Boys

Finding Him Again

# CARVED IN BLOOD

E.R. Fallon

ENDEAVOUR INK

AN ENDEAVOUR INK PAPERBACK

First published by Endeavour Press in 2016

This paperback edition published in 2018 by Endeavour Ink

Endeavour Ink is an imprint of Endeavour Press Ltd
Endeavour Press, 85-87 Borough High Street, London, SE1 1NH



ISBN 978-1-911445-90-6

Typeset by Ana Marija Meshkova

Printed and bound in Great Britain by

Clays Ltd, St Ives plc

www.endeavourpress.com

*For Scarlett*

# Contents

# Chapter 1

Sixteen years ago, my best friend and neighbor, Ben, was murdered by my mother. I was seventeen. She killed other boys in and around our small town, too. Some of them were boys I knew.

She was imprisoned. Alice Lane. My mother. Better known to you as the 'Lovely Butcher.' My mother, a beautiful woman with dark hair and light eyes, who had worked as a mathematics teacher at our local high school, confessed to Ben's murder and to those of the others. Mack, the detective who arrested her in our hometown, Freedom Village, became a mentor of sorts to me, but he and I hadn't spoken in a long time.

Alice's case was famous, partly because she came from a prominent family in the region, and because of the lurid nature of her crimes and her physical beauty. Fifteen years ago you couldn't turn on the television or open a newspaper and not hear or read about her. Ever since then, I've had an interest in murders.

I was an only child, and I didn't remember my father, but I'd seen pictures and videos of him, so after my mother was imprisoned, it was just me. I hadn't known how I'd survive. But I had. And I always would. At eighteen, I fled our town for the Navy. After that, I moved to the city to further disappear from my past. I did well on my own.

My name is Evan Lane, and I used to be called Evelyn Lane, but I *always was* Evan.

I didn't visit my mother, the killer, in prison, and I'd stopped writing to her when I changed my legal name to reflect my gender identity. Her prison wasn't close to where I lived but I also didn't visit her because I would have felt funny seeing her because of my job as the crime scene clean-up supervisor for the city of Seven Sisters.

I was paid by Seven Sisters to supervise the city's very first official crime scene clean-up crew, where we mostly dealt with murders committed under ordinary—and sometimes strange—circumstances. I didn't get into my line of work because I was fascinated by grisly crimes, because of what my mother did. Part of my ambition *was* to make good, because my mother couldn't do that herself. But really what I enjoyed most was the act of getting rid of the bad things, of cleansing homes and businesses, and other places, of all that despair, and bringing in good, clean hope.

My girlfriend, Sammie Bai, was the reason the city decided to pay for someone to clean up the aftermath of its constant stream of crimes, which increased as the weather got hotter and more people walked its gritty streets.

Sammie had retired early as a narcotics detective and ran a non-profit organization for the families of crime victims. She'd retired because she had difficulty hearing in her right ear after being present when a meth house exploded during a raid.

Her younger sister was murdered by a home intruder while Sammie was away at college, and afterward Sammie decided she wanted to help the often overlooked victims of violent crime—the murder victim's family members, and those who owned the businesses or residences where the murders occurred or where a body was disposed of. Sammie didn't like that often it was up to the victim's family members, who sometimes also owned the places affected by the death, to have to arrange and pay for the cleanup. So, she petitioned for change and accomplished it. In the process the city ended up paying for the tidying up of *any* place affected by a messy crime.

They paid for the cleaning after the body's or bodies removal to the morgue. And because of that I met the love of my life, thank God. At the time, I was working for the city's medical examiner's office as a technician. It was a job I wasn't very good at, apparently, since the ME suggested I apply for a positon with Seven Sister's new clean-up crew, where she implied I'd be a better fit. I never was diagnosed with OCD, I think, but I was obsessed with getting places spotless. And the ME? It turns out she was right. After a couple years with the clean-up crew, I was promoted to supervisor.

Something was troubling me. I hadn't discussed it with Sammie but it kept me up well into the night. Several young men had been murdered in the Seven Sisters area in the past two months. The other day we'd done a clean-up near the high school, where a boy's body was discovered in an empty, weedy lot behind the school's main building. The young man wasn't a student, and the case had received merely a small mention in the media because the victims were nameless street hustlers and addicts. In comparison, Alice had murdered average boys in our town.

I was chatty with a few cops in the city but they hadn't revealed a lot of details about the deaths. I did know first-hand that the crime scenes had been pretty neat. Sammie was friends with a few of the homicide detectives but she hadn't talked about the case to me. We sometimes chatted about work in bed late at night. But I could tell the murders had been on Sammie's mind like they'd been on mine, and I wondered whether she thought like I did: My mother couldn't be abducting and killing the boys from deep inside her cell, so, then, who was?

Sammie had already left for work when my phone rang. Paige, our elderly dachshund mix, waddled up to me for her morning belly rub. Sammie had fed the dog before she left. We didn't get to kiss each other goodbye that morning because I wasn't out of bed when she left. Sammie liked to rise early. Sometimes she nudged me to wake up and kiss. That time, she didn't. And I wondered what that meant.

I saw the call was important and set down my coffee cup to answer the phone. I was in my pajamas, it was early in the morning, and we already had to cope with a scene. I spoke to Chief Gilani on the other end and he explained the general scenario. I rarely got to hear the top secret details but I received the basics: a body had been found in an apartment in one of the city's new luxury buildings. The fact that it was an upscale building wasn't surprising—gentrification had become a trend in the city. What was odd was the fact that Gilani had said the manager stated the apartment was vacant, with the rent being paid by someone who didn't reside in the country.

"Be discreet at the scene," Gilani said. "The manager gave us a lot of shit about *this* and *us* making his building look bad. He's a real piece of work. I said, listen pal, things could be worse, at least you aren't the dead guy. Anyways, he wants you in and out of there fast."

"He's lucky he doesn't have to pay for anything." I gave a dry chuckle.

"I know, right? The city's footing his bill. The lucky bastard."

Gilani gave me the address, which I entered into my phone. Then I pushed him a little because I knew I could. "Was the body male?" I asked. By the time my crew arrived, the bodies were removed from the scenes. "A street kid?"

Chief Gilani's silence told me *yes* and *yes*. "Are you notifying the homeless youth in the area?" I asked.

"We've told our foot patrol units to spread the word," he said. "But you know how those kids never stay in one area for long so it's difficult to reach them all."

"Not surprising when your guys are always busting them for loitering," I said sarcastically. "It's odd to find them—the bodies—this fast, isn't it? It's been a little easy."

"Maybe she wants them to be found," he said.

My throat burned but I hadn't sipped the coffee in a while. "She?"

"Or he. But my hunch is our perp's a lady."

"You have leads?" Chief Gilani often told me things if I pushed him hard enough, and for long enough.

He sighed on the other end. "The CCTV cameras near the scenes didn't capture anything relevant. But we found a note on the body at the apartment when we arrived on scene yesterday.

The coroner took the body away earlier this morning. The media doesn't know about the note so it goes unsaid that this information is between us."

Sammie and I hadn't watched the news the night before, and I wondered if the media had given the kid's death more than a few seconds' mention. No one missed those boys. Hell, most of their families hadn't bothered to file a missing person's report. So why should the general public have given a damn? "You got it," I said. "Where was the note?"

When the chief said, "On him," I gulped. "Carved into the body, right across the guy's torso. Rancid stuff." I heard shivering in Gilani's voice.

I was silent for a few moments. "A message for who? For you guys, for the cops?"

"Nah, for someone named Evelyn."

Evelyn. That was my birth name. It felt like my heart would leap out of my chest and I started to rise from the chair but my unsteady legs couldn't hold me for long and I sat down again. I rested my arms on the table and pushed the coffee away from me, for how could I drink that when I couldn't breathe? "Are . . . are you going to try to find them?"

"This Evelyn person?"

"Yeah."

"Sure, if we can, to see what's the connection to our killer."

"You don't think they—Evelyn—could be responsible for the deaths?"

He refrained from answering. "The handwriting on the dead guy was small, feminine looking, that's why I said that thing about our perp being a woman. Wipes the blood off the letters after she's done, like she takes pride in her art. She strangles them."

"Must be a strong woman. How? She uses her bare hands?"

"No. Some kind of cord, like an electrical cord. Easy to get at a hardware store. And we didn't find any prints. Not yet anyway. The lab's running additional tests for us."

"Maybe she's an electrician."

"An electrician? Anything's possible." Gilani laughed at the dark humor only years of police work could make someone appreciate.

But I breathed out in relief, because my mother had used her bare hands. Mack had said that conveyed an active, intimate rage on her part. Despite my mother being incarcerated, a part of me was worried. They'd never found my mother's prints, or fibers and hairs belonging to her, at the crime scenes or on her victims.

Ben's body had been discovered in the woods where kids went to drink or smoke pot behind the high school gym, and where we'd frequented together. Several people in the town had said they'd seen me near the woods on that day. I was interviewed by Mack early on in the investigation but never considered a suspect. But I knew I hadn't been in the woods with Ben.

In fact, they'd never found any forensic evidence tying my mother to the crimes. She'd been convicted based on a very detailed confession. Alice had known features of the crimes that only the killer would have known, like that on the day Ben was murdered, he'd been wearing a bronze ring with his initials that his father had given him. The ring was never recovered by the police, and my mother claimed she'd disposed of it in the river, which was dredged by the law but the object never recovered.

"What did the message say?" I asked. "You mentioned who it was addressed to but not what was written."

"You know I can't tell you that."

"Come on, I'm curious. I'm going to have to clean up the damn mess. I should at least know a little about the person who created it." I risked annoying him.

When I'd almost given up, the chief said, "The scene's fairly neat. Minimal blood."

"He cleaned up after?"

"No, it doesn't seem that way. It looks like it was just a dumping ground."

"Like the last few times. Any leads on where he's killing them? And his reasons for moving them to these places?"

"Not yet. *She's* tricky to pin down. No one here gets the motives, not yet anyways."

"You're so sure it's a woman. So, you do think he's—she's—a serial?"

"Another body—looks that way, probably, yeah. But, really, it's hard to pin down. The vics are being strangled and mutilated with the writing, but the dumping pattern is erratic. The media isn't paying attention, so, publicly, no one's connected the dots. Gives us some privacy to work on it."

I made another attempt. "What did the writing say?"

Gilani sighed. "Miss me, Evelyn?"

"*What?*"

"That's what it said: Miss me, Evelyn?"

A cold sweat broke out over my skin and I trembled. I dropped the phone to the floor and then quickly picked it up.

"What the hell just happened?" Gilani asked.

"Nothing. I dropped my phone."

"Evelyn. Kind of sounds like your name."

"What are you saying?"

"I was kidding, buddy."

"Oh," I said, and pretended to laugh.

"Anyway, that's what the message said. Same as the first."

"You're saying the first body had the same thing?"

"Yep. She's leaving the bodies so that they're found. She's proud of what she's doing. She's mocking us. Must be a real sick bitch."

My mother had been more discreet. I admired Gilani's ability to keep his cool when confronting injustice. A vulnerable sense of guilt over what my mother had done inundated me every time he said *she*. "The first body had those exact words?" I asked for the sake of saying something.

"*Yeah*, Evan."

I breathed out and didn't speak for a couple seconds. "Are the crimes sexually motivated?" I didn't believe my mother's were.

"You know I can't tell you that."

"A female serial killer's crimes almost never are."

"That's true. Sounds like you've done some research. Is this a topic that interests you?"

"Because of my work," I said quickly.

I waited for Chief Gilani to ask me more but he accepted my answer. "Listen, I got to go. Good luck with the clean-up. Tell the other guys I said hi. And remember to shut up about all this. Media's not really reporting on the cases anyway. It's just another dead junkie to them, you know?"

"I'll keep my mouth shut," I said.

I didn't tell him goodbye, and I dumped the remainder of my coffee, which now looked greasy and cold, into the sink. Sammie was the only person who knew the name I'd been assigned at birth, and I trusted her more than anyone in the world.

I texted my crew with the news that we had another job on our hands, and I got dressed. It was autumn, and chilly enough to need a jacket, so I put one on and left the house after giving Paige a goodbye pat.

I used to have my crew drive to a scene, but lately I'd been picking them up in the work van and taking them there myself. Not out of the kindness of my heart exactly, but because parking was limited in the city, and the last thing I wanted to worry about was where everyone would park once they arrived at the scene. A police escort and special privileges would have been appreciated at the time but hadn't seemed likely.

I hadn't showered. I did that when I returned home because even with wearing protective suits, sometimes a clean-up got messy.

The van we used for the jobs was parked in a municipal garage a few streets down from where Sammie and I shared our small apartment. I exchanged pleasantries with the guy who ran the garage's front booth and found the van at the back of the dim, cold space. Josh, my right-hand man, who had been with my crew the longest, had parked it there the other day after our last gig. The van was already loaded with our gear. Unfortunately, the number of engagements we had every week conveyed to me how unsafe the city I lived in was.

We weren't one of the most popular employees to the city, but the public liked us and that was enough for me to wake up with a smile on my face most days. Hell, some days you *had* to force yourself to smile when you had a job like that. When you had to see the horrors we saw.

I hadn't eaten, and after the details Chief Gilani gave me about the message, I hadn't felt like eating anything. Because it was early and Josh and Em both had kids living with them who needed their help getting ready in the morning, they often didn't have time to eat before meeting me at that hour. I swung by the donut shop and picked up a plain donut for myself just in case I felt like eating later, hot breakfast sandwiches for the crew, and three large coffees.

My hands weren't shaking as the smiling young woman at the drive-thru window passed me the warm bag of food and the coffees in a tray, but that didn't mean I wasn't alarmed by what had been carved into the victims' flesh. In my line of work it didn't pay to be fearful, so over the years, I'd built up a great wall of strength around me. I secured the coffees in the cup holders, tossed the bag of sandwiches on the passenger floor and the cardboard tray in the backseat, and paid the girl.

I headed out of the parking lot in time to encounter the morning commuters in the city's main thoroughfare and made my way toward Em's neighborhood. In the evenings Seven Sister's population thinned out considerably, when the workforce fled home to suburbia. Once people got to be a certain age they left the city for the leafy suburbs, except for a few die-hards, like Sammie and me. And Josh.

Em was only in her mid-twenties and still meshed with the city's vibrant, youthful scene. She lived in an industrial part of town, where old warehouses had been turned into artists' lofts. Em was a DJ who moonlighted with me because she needed the cash to raise her kid on her own. She reminded me often that she was working for me because she had to, but I liked to think the work would grow on her over time and she'd come to enjoy it, even if only a little. Em was a talented person from what I heard when I saw her perform at a nightclub once. She'd invited Sammie and me, and I'd told Em that she was so talented I, too, wished she would no longer be working for me someday, that she'd go on to better places.

I merged behind a city bus into the tense snarl of traffic and inched my way, along with the rest of the poor bastards, to the intersection. One thing that was decent about Seven Sisters was that the city was near the ocean and there was a regular breeze that pushed away the smog. Car horns blared behind me as I made a sharp left turn onto Em's street. I'd long ago ceased honking back at them.

I waited by the former warehouse's old loading dock with the engine running. A text pinged on my phone. From Em, who was running late. I didn't mind. She was a single mother and worked hard. I opened the bag of food. My nose twitched and I gagged at the smell of the sandwich meat. I took out the donut wrapped in paper. I was a vegetarian and had been ever since my senior year of high school when I read that my mother ate pieces of some victims, but not Ben. I had to read the morbid details in a sensationalized newspaper article, and when I spoke to Detective Mack about it, he gently told me the tabloid might have had some facts correct.

I signed up for the Navy before my mother confessed to her crimes, and I hadn't allowed her conviction to prevent me from honoring that commitment. After my service, I won a college scholarship to study chemistry, and while I was away at college, with my good friend Ben gone and my mother in prison for killing him, I'd lost touch with Detective Mack.

I didn't communicate with my remaining family. I became estranged from them during my mother's trial because of one simple fact: I'd believed in her guilt, while they insisted she was innocent. I suspected they were trying to protect their family's name and their money from her victims' families. I never got any of that money myself, and neither, as far as I knew, had the families of Alice's victims. It had been hard for me to comprehend that my mother, who had given me life, had taken lives, but I had accepted that fact.

I'd lost most of my high school friends during my mother's trial and every single last one after her conviction. Everyone either wanted to know too much about Alice that it became uncomfortable for me to remain close to them, or they chose to dissociate themselves from the lovely butcher's child. I didn't have anyone to turn to during that time except Mack. But I'd made a couple of new pals in the Navy, and then in college, where I finally figured out who, deep down inside, I'd known I always was. In college I was able to surround myself with people who supported me for who I was, and my happiness only increased when I met Sammie.

I slowly finished the donut. I put the radio on and drank some coffee, and spent a few minutes trying to convince myself the message from the killer didn't bother me. Not one damn bit. Okay, it scared the hell out of me. Although I thought about my mother sometimes, not about her crimes, usually, but about the sweet things she sometimes had done for me when I was a kid, I hadn't visited her, or written to her, in years. I still had friends at the ME's office but it would have looked suspicious if I rang them to see if they knew anything Gilani hadn't mentioned.

Em walked out from the building's wide gray door and approached the van. Her red hair hung damp around her pleasant, round face. She waved to me and made a gesture of drinking coffee. I mimicked the gesture to let her know that, yeah, I'd bought coffee. Em slid open the van's side door and hopped in. In the rearview mirror I watched her looking for Josh in the seat next to mine. I reached around and handed her a coffee and the bag with sandwiches. I pulled out of the parking lot with Em eating.

"Thanks for picking me up first, chief." She winked at me through her square-framed eyeglasses.

Em and Josh had given me the title in jest. Even Gilani, the real chief, had found humor in it. "Anytime." It had taken me some time to get used to the nickname, but ultimately I was okay with it. "How's Trent?" Her son.

"The sitter was late, but she showed, eventually. When I got out of the shower, she was there, thank God, but I didn't have time to dry my hair. Sorry I'm late."

"What were you, a few minutes late? Don't worry about it. I didn't even notice." I hadn't. "How's your son?" I asked again.

"He's doing well. We saw his dad last night."

I sat up straighter. "Everything okay? I thought you didn't get along with his father." A bicyclist cut in front of me and I swerved to avoid hitting him, an occurrence so common in the city that Em didn't make a sound from the back. She kept chewing.

"That's true. But I don't want Trent growing up to resent his mom for keeping his father away from him so I let him see his dad, when the guy's sober enough. How's Sammie? And you?"

"We're fine." How I never revealed more than a small amount of personal information about myself to Em and Josh was a running joke between them. It wasn't that I didn't trust they would do anything other than accept me, but given my job, I didn't want anyone besides Sammie knowing about my mother's crimes.

"What's the word on the scene?" Em asked. "Blood and guts aren't so hot on my stomach in the morning."

"Scene's not bad, according to the real chief." I smiled at Em in the rearview and picked up speed on the way to Josh's part of town. Even if we didn't end up cleaning away much blood, people liked that our presence seemed to cleanse whatever taboo death had left behind, however imperceptible.

"Another neat one. How odd." Em's gaze met mine in the mirror. "Is there any connection, I mean, to the kid at the high school?"

"Possibly. I can't say more."

"If someone's killing boys, it makes me worried for Trent." Em's voice wavered.

Nothing in the past had ever seemed to shake her that much, and I needed to comfort her. "You haven't a thing to worry about. Trent's a lot younger than those boys. They lived on the streets and not under the best circumstances." I hoped like hell I'd be right.

Josh lived with his wife, Martina, and their daughter who was in college, and the daughter's little girl, in a pleasant neighborhood with bungalow houses. Josh had a bad back, and he worried sometimes that I'd ask him to leave because of that. I'd assured him that he was out of luck because he'd never get rid of me. Lots of crew members had come and gone, but Josh was dependable. He'd moved to the States from Honduras a decade before, and had worked for the city in some aspect ever since then. Em was often the one I worried wouldn't stay.

I beeped the horn to let Josh know we were parked by his house. I gulped my lukewarm coffee. Josh, a big guy with a surprisingly smooth, elegant walk, was hard to miss as he exited his pink-roofed house that had a well-kept, gated front yard. A loud advertisement came on and I shut off the radio. Josh's curly dark hair and smiling plump face appeared at the passenger side window and I waved at him. He opened the door and crouched to enter. Although it had never been officially decided, Josh, who was with me from the very beginning, rode up front, while Em sat in the back. It had taken the city a few tries to find a second reliable employee after the slot had been vacated, and then Em came along.

We didn't wear uniforms, just jeans and t-shirts mostly, and shorts and tank tops in the warmer months, because it got hot under the hazmat suits. Without the suits on we looked like we were heading to bed instead of venturing to work. But we were comfortable, and elbows-deep in blood and gore, what more could one want?

Josh got settled, I indicated his coffee in the holder, and Em handed him a breakfast sandwich from the back.

"Thanks, chief," he said.

"Anytime." I'd bought food for them practically every day, yet every day they thanked me as though I'd bought them presents. Sometimes lunch, sometimes dinner, depending on the time we were on duty. We tended to work through most meals so we ate before the job. What we'd see on-site changed with any given job, and who'd want to eat after seeing blood and guts?

The first time I saw a dead body wasn't when I was in the service but when I worked for the ME. My face had turned so pale, apparently, the medical examiner had asked if I was sure I was in the right profession. But I hadn't vomited.

Em's face had looked that way, too, alabaster, the day of her first crime scene. I had her study crime scene photos online when she first came on board the team to prepare her for the real thing. Unlike me, people like Em and Josh didn't get into our line of work because it appealed to them for personal reasons. More likely, it was a job to them, an opportunity to earn a decent living, something they might have continued to do for a long time, but, still, a job. Eventually, Em became so accustomed to the rank, stinking, hard-to-look-at, gut-wrenching aftermath of death that she joked along with us as we worked. It might sound tasteless, but when you see so much death you get used to it, and it becomes an ordinary thing. So you laugh as you work.

I entered the luxury building's address into the GPS and pulled into the main street. "How's the family?" I asked Josh.

"Martina and me have been after Gina to enroll Isabella in preschool."

Em whistled from the backseat. "Isabella's that old already?" she asked about Josh's granddaughter. "I can't believe that. Seems like a few months ago she was born."

"They grow up too fast." Emotion thickened Josh's voice. He looked out the window at the passing traffic and the blurred buildings in the commercial district.

The sun poured into the van through the window and I flipped down the visor.

"Sammie's fine?" Josh asked.

Em barely hid her snicker. Whenever one of them asked about Sammie, I always replied, *she's fine*. "Shut up or I'll put you with the body bags," I teased them.

Body bags. We *did* keep a few of those in the van just in case a body was dismembered and someone forgot to pack up a part—or two, before our arrival. It did happen.

Em played along. "You wouldn't."

I glared at her in the rearview and she flipped me the bird. I didn't reprimand her. I wasn't a very strict boss. I laughed.

Josh stared out the window and chuckled. He turned and faced me. "Where are we headed today?"

"The Tower on the Cove. You know, one of the new luxury buildings with those fancy sounding names? The places that don't only look rich, they sound rich?"

"What the heck are we doing there?"

"A body was found there, and we're cleaning up. Didn't I text you with all this earlier?"

"I read your first text, then Isabella started having a tantrum and I got distracted. Never got around to reading the second one. Sorry, chief."

I patted his wide shoulder. "It's all good."

"The Tower on the Cove place?" Em said belatedly. "That's surprising."

"What kind of murder was it, some rich people thing?" Josh asked.

"No. Some young guy they already ID'd as a street kid, so no one gives a fuck," I said.

"That's messed up. Like the kid at the high school."

I let out a sigh. "Unfortunately, yeah." I reminded Josh to put on his seatbelt. He groaned and I said, "It's the city's rule. Besides, I wouldn't want to have to tell Martina something happened to you."

Josh relinquished. With one hand steering, I groped around for a red biohazard bag on the floor at my feet. I handed one to him to throw away the food wrappers and empty coffee cups.

"You should really clean the van, chief," Josh said.

"Sure, *we* can do it later."

"Sounds like fun," he murmured.

I used a more serious tone. "Remember, like I've always said, any of the details I tell you about a case that aren't mentioned in the press shouldn't leave the van, okay? They stay between us. You can't even tell your families. Gilani's risking his job by giving me some of this stuff, and I'm risking mine by telling you."

Josh saluted me. "Understood, chief."

"Won't tell a soul," Em said from the back.

And for some crazy reason, every time I made them swear on something, and they did, I felt they would keep their word, every time.

# Chapter 2

To uphold discretion, I'd been instructed by Gilani to park in the luxury building's maintenance lot. We changed into our rubber boots and disposable yellow hazmat suits. A guy rounded the building's corner and came running toward us from across the parking lot. The sun beat down on the asphalt and made it warm inside my suit and boots. My back and neck itched from sweat but a breeze from the rippling blue water cooled my face. The van doors were open, and Em and Josh sat on the rim of the opened back. One side of the van was pushed down from Josh's generous weight.

"What are you doing? You can't do that outside here!" The small, wiry man in a fitted gray suit reached us, and was out of breath.

Em pulled her long, now less wet, hair back in a ponytail, and she and Josh each gave me a look that said, *Who the hell is this guy?* I shrugged but had a hunch I knew: the manager of the building, the person Gilani had warned me about.

I quickly reached to shake his well-manicured hand in an attempt to disarm him. The man was smaller than me, and I wasn't a very big person myself. "Sir, we've been sent by the city—"

He stared at my glove, and even when I removed it, he wouldn't shake my hand. "I know who you are. I'm Phillip Arnett, the manager of the Cove. You can't stand around dressed like *that*, out here." He indicted our suits. "People will see you and be frightened. This is a high-end building, not some flophouse."

"With all due respect, sir, the body was found here, not at some flophouse, so . . ." I said. Behind me, I heard Josh and Em snickering. I stood in front of them like a papa bear, when Josh was large enough to protect himself and Em and me at the same time. "If you're not going to evacuate the building temporarily, and our chief said you weren't, there's a good chance someone inside will indeed notice us." Arnett grimaced at me and crossed his arms. He had slicked-back, very light hair, one of those tan, glowing faces that made it hard to tell his age, and he wore too much cologne. "Listen," I said. "We're already dressed. We'll be in and out of here fast if you let us get our equipment and head inside."

"You can't use the main elevators." From the look on his face, he was aghast at the idea of us trudging through his glistening marble lobby, which I'd seen through the glass front door when we pulled into the lot.

"How about we use the service elevator? After all, that's the reason I parked here, isn't it, to use the service entrance?"

Arnett smiled a little at my sarcasm and made a sweeping gesture to a bolted metal door at the side of the building. "Help yourselves. It's never locked."

"After what happened here, you might want to think about changing that; not locking the service door, I mean."

Arnett didn't acknowledge my comment.

"After what's happened, it'd do you well to take me seriously," I said.

Arnett winced, and he nodded fast. Then his arrogant exterior returned. "Apartment 102, the apartment needing a . . . thorough cleaning, is on the tenth floor and nearest to the elevator once you step out." I smiled at the delicate way he'd put what we did. "Don't leave the elevator until you arrive at floor ten, please. One of our janitorial staff found the . . . the body after tenants in the nearby apartments began complaining about a smell. It hasn't been easy trying to keep the news from spreading. I don't need you scaring our tenants. Some of them work from home."

"We'll exit the elevator on the proper floor. But if you're that concerned about someone seeing us, you might want to evacuate the building," I said.

Arnett laughed in disbelief. "I already told your superior I can't do that." He paused. "A lot of our tenants are at work this time of the day, but how long do you think it will take you to finish? I want you out of here before people come home from work or go out for the evening." He handed me a key. "This is for the apartment. I trust you'll keep the noise down?"

Em and Josh got up and stepped around to my side. "It'll take a few hours," she told Arnett. "We'll be gone before the day is over. Is the electricity on in the apartment? I know it's vacant. We'll need to have power for our equipment."

"There's electricity. Is there any way you could change inside the apartment and not walk through the floor wearing those things?" Arnett pointedly overlooked Em and spoke to me.

I gave him a blunt no. He stared at me for a moment, and then seemed to comprehend that I wasn't going to offer an explanation even if he demanded one. He walked away, calling over his shoulder, "My office is inside the lobby. I'll come upstairs to check on you to make sure you finish on time."

"What an asshole," Josh said when Arnett was out of earshot. I grunted in agreement. He crushed his coffee cup and dropped it into the biohazard bag, and then tossed the bag at the back of the trunk. I helped him and Em pull our heavy-duty cleaning gear out of the back.

We dragged our stuff through the barren service entrance, past a row of receptacles with festering garbage. The elevator, not as large as I'd assumed, was a tight fit, but we squeezed inside.

On the ride up to the tenth floor Em glanced at the glowing buttons to her right. "What do you think will happen if we get off at a different floor?" she asked.

"That dude will probably call the city and complain," Josh said. "Who knows, maybe he'll even sue the city."

I chuckled, but lawsuits had happened before, and for sillier reasons. The elevator dinged once we reached our floor. We kept our hazmat hoods down to look less intimidating and hauled and rolled the gear into the hall. The heavy cleaning equipment bounced along the floor and created a lot of noise, rattling the walls. Given the hour, there weren't many tenants coming and going in the hallway, thankfully, but a young man leaving an apartment across from ours gave us an interested glance.

He stopped by the main elevator with gold doors, the one we hadn't arrived on. Then he pressed a button and turned around. "Hey, are you guys here because of that body they found in 102?"

I thought about what to say, and then Em spoke for me. "We're a cleaning crew, sir."

"You aren't—really?" The guy touched his mouth. Our large, mitt-like gloves probably gave us away. He lowered his voice. "Was it a murder or something? I tried looking for some information about it online but didn't find much. So, you know what happened, right?" He didn't seem gleeful, just genuinely curious. The elevator arrived on the floor and the doors opened.

"We're just the cleaning crew," I said.

I motioned to Josh and Em to wait until the guy left before securing their hoods with the attached masks.

"Of course you are," the guy said. He tossed a final glance in our direction before stepping into the elevator.

"We actually *are*," I said, but by that time he couldn't have heard me.

Josh, standing at my side, picked up the large shop vacuum and breathed out. "Let's haul this stuff in," he said.

We flipped up our hoods and sealed them. The yellow police tape had been removed by someone. Arnett? He wasn't supposed to take it down but probably had, so as not to tarnish his building's pristine image.

The key got stuck in the lock and I had to jostle the knob a few times to open the door. "Funny that such a posh building doesn't use key cards," I said.

"Maybe they're trying to be quaint," Em remarked.

"I believe you're right." Then I said to both of them, "Let's not sing as we work today." I pocketed the key and entered the apartment first. Sometimes we sang while we worked because at times it was the only way to get through the visceral realism of what we saw on a daily basis, and also because we were so accustomed to the routine that we sang to pass the time as we cleaned.

"That's a given," Em said.

"Yeah," Josh agreed.

Em held open the door as Josh and I lugged in the shop vacuum, the steam equipment, the pressure washer, and the containers of robust disinfectants so potent gloves had to be worn at all times when using them. She shut the door once we'd put everything inside.

"Should I lock it?" Em asked me.

"Arnett wouldn't like that," I replied, glancing around the place.

The apartment looked as though it hadn't been lived in for months. A set of white stairs dipped down into the sunken living room. I folded a black body bag that had been left behind on a step by law enforcement and set it by the front door to take away with us when we left.

The long windows with no curtains allowed sunlight to fill the wide space. The hardwood floors shone in the living room, and were clean save for the shoe scuffs and dusty footprints the cops had left behind. With the ample light from outside, there wasn't a need to switch on the lamps. I scouted for wall sockets to plug in our equipment, and was pleased to find plenty in the open-floor style apartment. I stepped into a kitchen that looked small and out of place with the rest of the spacious apartment, but with new looking appliances, yet with dead flies crusty on the counters. Larvae. Flies.

The smells of a corpse still permeated the air in the whole place, a smell far worse than the worst thing you ever inhaled in your life. I didn't know all the details of the incident but the body must have been inside the apartment for a good amount of time for the air to have stunk like that even after the corpse was removed. I'd intended to get rid of the dead flies in the kitchen even if the building's manager was an asshole, because I prided myself in doing the best job possible.

But the kitchen wasn't where the body had been found. The source of the odor came from another, more distant area in the apartment. Em and Josh trailed me as I, led by my nose, followed the stinking remnants of the corpse's scent into the apartment's sole bedroom. The faster my nose twitched, the closer I knew I was getting to the source.

A large walk-in closet where the corpse had been, roomy enough to hold two of us, its doors open, had a faint dark imprint made up of blood and postmortem bodily functions on the white interior carpet. No matter how long I'd been in my line of work, without my mask, even I would retch at the smells the dead left behind.

From the faintness of the impression, the body had been wrapped in something but some blood and decomposition fluids had seeped into the carpet, creating a brown-red sketch of what looked like had been a tall, thin person. The body appeared to have been folded inside the closet but the outline of what would have been the torso and arms were long.

Josh patted Em's shoulder. "They don't even have to tell him where to find it. Man's got a nose like a bloodhound's," he said.

The masks we wore made breathing difficult, and although they filtered the air to protect us from contaminants—no matter how clean-looking a scene appeared, one never knew what you could catch—I never liked wearing the masks because they muffled the wearer's voice and made it difficult to hear someone. Josh and Em moved out from next to me and made a movement toward the door to collect our equipment in the living room.

I whistled at them and they stopped in their tracks. "You know what? Why don't you two get started in the kitchen first—you saw the flies in there, right?—and I'll get started in here." I wanted the bedroom to myself for a while so I could check things out before we cleaned up and got rid of anything that might have been there, like a clue the police had somehow missed.

"Sure thing, chief," Josh said.

Em gave me an unsure look over her shoulder as they walked out, and I gave her an unwavering smile, because I couldn't let them know anything was wrong, although I was certain something was. Very certain.

The closet was empty save for a few wooden hangers and a cracked dressing mirror shoved against the back wall portion of the interior. When I could barely hear Em's and Josh's voices in the other room above the ear-splitting roar of the shop vacuum—if noise concerned Arnett, I'd expected he'd show up any moment and complain—I reached up to the closet shelf and felt around, came up with a little dust on my fingertips but nothing else. The rest of the bedroom was empty, like the living room and the kitchen. No bed, television, couch, tables, or chairs, or personal items like photographs. Why was someone paying the rent to keep an empty apartment?

"Do you want me to bring some equipment in for you? You don't have anything." Em's voice came from the doorway at my back. Sometimes she was a bit more intuitive than Josh, who scrubbed and scraped in the other room, whistling to himself as he worked.

I gave her a pointed look. She held a UV light in her hand that we used to find stains that weren't visible. "I was just on my way out to fetch something. Thanks for checking." Had she seen the truth beyond my false smile?

"Do you want me to bring something in for you?" Em asked.

"No, thanks, I've got it." And I hoped my reply wasn't too quick.

"You're sure?"

I nodded in silence and avoided looking at her thoughtful face.

"Just trying to be a good assistant," she said softly, and backed out of the room.

Halfway into our cleaning, someone began to open the door to the apartment. I stepped into the living room and the apartment fell silent as Josh shut off the whirring pressure washer in the kitchen. It was so quiet I could have heard a pin drop. Even through the mask, the acrid smell of cleaning fluids burned my nostrils. Josh exited the kitchen followed by Em, who went toward the door as it was opened. I motioned to them that I'd deal with whoever it was, presumably Arnett coming to grumble about the racket we were making, or coming early to check on us. Until that moment, I'd figured we were in the clear since we'd made it halfway through and he hadn't come by.

Arnett had his fingers stuck in his ears when he pushed his way inside. He spoke before I had a chance to. "Should you be doing that to our wood floors?" He indicated the pressure washer.

"That won't damage the wood," I said, but even I wasn't convinced. "You can always re-polish it later."

Arnett frowned. "I wasn't going to interrupt, but you simply cannot keep making this noise."

He made a gesture to some of the equipment Em and Josh had unloaded in the living room. Arnett stepped over the body bag by the door. "I thought the police already removed the—the body." He didn't look at the bag but gestured at it.

"They did," I said. "They left a bag behind. Don't worry. It's empty."

"You look like Martians," Arnett said. "How can you hear me through those things?"

"We can," I said, but I removed my hood and mask and carried them in the crook of my arm. "As bad as this seems, the noise could be worse. We've made a point not to use all the equipment at the same time. You shouldn't be in here while we're working, Mr. Arnett. Who knows what we're kicking up into the air when we clean."

He gestured to my hood and mask in my arm. "You seem fine without all that."

I smiled tolerantly and started to put my arm around him to guide him into the hall, but then noticed his grimace and thought better of that. I motioned for us to step outside to talk so Em and Josh could continue working, but Arnett wouldn't budge.

He quietly shut the door and walked farther into the apartment. "We'll do this right here, thank you very much. I don't need my tenants being disturbed more than they already have, why, with the police blocking everything off and not letting people up into the building at one point, and now look at what you're doing. I want you to leave now. I'll clean this apartment myself if I have to. You don't even need to be here. I never would have permitted this if it wasn't for the owner of the building—"

I cut him short and held his stare. "If you'll let us do the job the city pays us to do for you, we'll leave." Arnett's breathing hitched. A look passed between Arnett and Josh, who was double his size. I watched Josh next to me. A vein in his neck pulsed. "Let us do our job, and then you can do yours," I said. My tone conveyed we weren't discussing the matter further.

"People aren't always glad to see us but more often than not they're grateful," Em remarked after Arnett left. "But not him."

"You got that right," I replied.

On that day, we worked straight through lunch. As I pulled out of the Cove's parking lot, Sammie sent me a text letting me know to meet her for drinks and dinner at Kelly's Pub, our favorite local watering hole, after I went home and showered. She'd already gone home after work and fed Paige and was now out doing some shopping. It was her turn to get the groceries. I'd gone shopping for us last week.

I dropped Josh off at his house and tried to avoid Em's questions on the way to her place. Em crawled up front to sit next to me, which was something new.

"Thanks for the door-to-door service," she said.

"It's no problem. It's my job."

"No, driving us home isn't part of your job description. Technically, we could've driven to the garage this morning and then after work you could've taken us back to the garage and made us drive home from there." She removed her eyeglasses and cleaned the lenses with her sleeve.

"The garage is far away from where the both of you live. It's easier for me to pick everyone up."

"That's what I mean—you're doing us a favor so we'll get home sooner. Thanks."

I avoided getting too sentimental. "You're welcome. Will Trent be home from daycare by the time you get home?" My clothes stuck to my skin from perspiring inside the suit earlier at the Cove.

"Yeah, my babysitter's picking him up. Can I ask you a question?"

Usually, the answer would have been yes, but from the way Em looked at her hands, folded in her lap while she talked, I felt I knew what she wanted to talk about; something I didn't want to talk about.

"Back in the apartment, when you were alone in the bedroom, it looked like you were trying to find something," she said. "I remember you asked us to clean out the kitchen first—"

My skin heated as I felt her watching me, and my grip on the wheel tightened. A few moments passed between us, with the sound of my increasingly heavy breathing filling the space around us. "I wanted to pay extra attention to the stain in the closet. I was worried we wouldn't be able to get rid of it by the time we were scheduled to leave. You know, there's still a faint outline there anyway. I noticed it before we left. I couldn't get it to come out all the way. I'm sure Arnett will notice."

"An outline of the body?" Em said. I'd succeeded in distracting her. "I've noticed that happens sometimes even when we really try to clean—I think fluids from the body stain the area it decomposes in."

"You're right. I've heard that, too." I scratched the beard I'd started to grow.

"We should invent something and sell it to the crime scene clean-up industry, then we could retire."

"You know, that's not a bad idea." I glanced at her next to me and smiled.

After dropping off Em, I drove the van to the municipal garage, thought about leaving the equipment inside the back of the van, and then decided to put it into the garage's storage room. As I put the equipment away, I hoped I wouldn't be unloading it again for a long time. Then I cleaned out the van, which was something I usually ended up doing myself. It took longer than I expected, and when I got home, I had just enough time to shower, dress, and take Paige for a walk before I met Sammie for dinner.

# Chapter 3

I spotted Sammie—tall, slender and refined—straight away, sitting at the bar, facing the entrance door, with a vodka with cranberry and a twist of lime, her usual drink, and the tall glass of beer she'd ordered for me, my usual drink. I waved to her and she motioned at me to come over.

With Sammie's dark hair, porcelain skin, and a statuesque build that was striking even when she was seated, she would have been noticeable anywhere, the kind of woman too beautiful to blend into the crowd, even in a bar that was packed in the evening. And she was all mine. I knew how lucky I was to have her.

We came to Kelly's for dinner a couple times a week. Sammie had managed to save me a seat at the bar, and I made my way through the exuberant crowd blocking the door to get inside. Kelly's wasn't the type of place to have a hostess or a set of rules, so if you had someone waiting at a table for you, or in my case, waiting at the bar, you could walk straight in.

The voices of everyone talking at once hurt my ears, and I caught bits of conversations as I walked toward the sleek, dark wood bar. Someone mentioned a news story they'd read about a murder, but as I listened more closely, I realized it wasn't any my team had handled recently. My mother's story had been played up in the press partly because the boys she murdered were ordinary teenagers from average homes. The young men being found in the present had no one coming forward to claim them so far. It felt rotten taking comfort in the fact that that aspect of the murders was different.

I touched Sammie's shoulder and squeezed in next to her at the bar. "Hello, gorgeous. I love you." I kissed the side of her face. "I hope you didn't leave the ice cream in the car."

"Hello to you too." She accepted the kiss but wouldn't look at me. "I didn't buy any this time, but the rest of the groceries are in the car."

"Oh." Usually, she bought ice cream for us, no matter the season. I put my arm around her and pulled her close to me. Was something wrong? I'd walked to Kelly's from our apartment and planned to drive back home with Sammie and help her unpack the car there. "How was your day?" I asked. We'd texted a little throughout the day and I'd told her about the new victim—I wasn't supposed to but since Sammie was a retired detective, I'd figured it was okay.

"Upsetting," she said. "But isn't it always?" She shrugged in a half-hearted way and I rubbed her back. "Yours?"

"Not that messy, surprisingly. Had to work through lunch to keep the manager at that place from breathing down my neck." I looked around the jam-packed room. "Let's order from the bar menu. That'll be quicker."

"That should be fine." Sammie hadn't touched her drink so I knew something was wrong. She waited a beat. "Are you okay? Seeing where these boys, it must be . . ." She touched my shoulder.

Sammie was the only person in my life then who knew about my mother. "It's not pretty but I'll manage." I smiled and picked up my beer and drank. Sammie lowered my arm, stopping me from downing the glass.

"What is happening now has nothing to do with your mother." Sammie spoke as though she wanted to reassure me, but from the quiver in her voice I wondered whether inside she felt like I did, that things were awfully similar to have been just a coincidence. She put her hand over mine and held hers there.

I pointed to her glass. "Don't forget to drink that or I might end up drinking it for you."

"Don't change the subject." Sammie frowned, and I looked into her warm brown eyes.

"I meant it when I said I'll drink that if you won't." I reached for Sammie's glass and she swatted my hand away.

"You've had one of those days, huh?" she asked.

I nodded, and I finished my beer while she drew on her bar napkin with a pen she took out of her purse. "Do you know what you want to order?" I asked.

"Yeah." She didn't look over at me and continued drawing on the napkin.

I reached over and slid the napkin to my side of the bar. Sammie had drawn a picture of a house with a slanted roof and a small garden out front. I had my own artwork to worry about, like the fact that someone had written *Evelyn* on those dead young men. My palms moistened, and I smoothed out the paper over the bar. It had been some time since Sammie and I had talked about buying a house and, possibly, getting married. Kids? The thought of being responsible for someone's life worried me. I figured Sammie wanted to discuss those commitments now, that it was on her mind, even subconsciously, and I attempted to make light of the drawing. "Are you trying to tell me something?" I said.

Sammie shrugged. "It's just a drawing."

Although what I suspected what was on her mind was on my mind, too— finalizing our relationship and thus our lives—I put down the napkin and slid it back toward her. My thoughts were elsewhere. "You know, on the victims there was the strangest thing," I said.

Sammie's attention to me turned magnetic, and a current of understanding passed between us. Sammie was the kind of woman who, when you were with her, everything else faded away. Being there with her made everything in the background disappear. My gaze drifted to her lips, full, round, and painted a burnt red. Anticipating she'd ask me a question, I waited for her to speak first. When she didn't, I stroked the defined edge of her face, her soft skin, with my thumb.

Sammie moved out of my reach, and I kept my hand suspended there in the air, halfway between us. "What were you about to tell me, about the victims?" she said.

I pulled my hand back and rested my elbows on the hard bar, the wood cool through my long-sleeve shirt. "Oh, it was nothing. The scene wasn't too bad, not really." When discussing my job with those outside the industry, I often left out the more grisly details of the work I did with my team. As a former detective, Sammie could have handled them, but I didn't want to bring the more unpleasant aspects of my job, the nasty, vile things I literally came into contact with on a daily basis, into our relationship. My moments with Sammie were the only pure things I had in my life.

Sammie got quiet and was hard to read, and this made me nervous. I ordered another beer. "Do you want another drink?" I asked her.

Sammie held up her half-finished glass but didn't speak. When she got in one of those moods, it meant something was on her mind and bothering her but she wasn't going to tell me what. Sammie opened the one bar menu we'd been given.

"I love you," I said.

She nodded. "Let's order."

"Do you want to split something?" Someone walking past the bar bumped into me and murmured sorry. I waited for Sammie to share the menu with me, like always, but she didn't.

"No, I think I'll get my own thing tonight." She didn't look up from reading the menu.

"Are you sure?"

"Yes." Sammie closed the menu and pushed it down the counter to me.

"Let me know if you want to pay separately," I remarked under my breath.

To my surprise, Sammie laughed, a full, genuine laugh. "That's not necessary, my love."

And I breathed out in relief that she wasn't *that* angry with me.

Our apartment building didn't have a garage, so after we left Kelly's, Sammie had to drive around our neighborhood a few times to find a space to park our car. We carried the groceries from the trunk of our car up the three flights of stairs—the building lacked an elevator—to our apartment, which we owned. Sammie waved to a neighbor in our hall and Paige greeted us at the door to our apartment with her tail wagging. She wove around our legs and sniffed the grocery bags in our hands when we reached down to pet her. Sammie and I carried the bags into the kitchen and put what she bought into the refrigerator and the cupboards.

Sammie uncorked the bottle of red wine she'd bought and removed two glasses from the kitchen shelf. She poured our drinks, took hers, and left mine on the table as she headed into the cozy living room. Paige followed her, like she followed her wherever Sammie went. The dog loved her more than me but I'd never held it against either of them. I picked up my glass. Dinner had been a few sandwiches and, still hungry from having not eaten much earlier in the day, I snatched a large bag of potato chips from the kitchen counter, and proceeded to join them on the couch.

When I had trouble opening the chips bag, Sammie grabbed it from me and opened it. She didn't take any chips and handed me the bag over Paige, who'd curled up between us, as though she, too, felt the tension thickening in the small living room.

Sammie swallowed the rest of her wine and set the glass on the coffee table. I sipped my drink, well aware of the warming buzz I already had from the drink taking over my body. I held out the bag of potato chips to Sammie, and Paige stuck her nose inside the bag.

Sammie laughed at Paige's antics and I smiled a little. I loved her laugh. I put my glass down on the table, gently scooted Paige over, and leaned in to kiss Sammie. Sammie looked away and I motioned for Paige to get off the couch. With the dog now in her bed by the TV, I moved close to Sammie and settled my arm around her shoulders. After a few moments of Sammie ignoring me and looking the other way, she tilted her head and rested on my chest, and I held her even more tightly. I gave her a gentle kiss and she kissed me back in a rougher, exciting way. Sammie moved and her soft, small breasts rubbed against my side. I could feel her body relaxing into mine.

"There's something I haven't told you. I've been keeping something from you," I said.

"I know you have been. That's why I've been upset. And I had a pretty shitty day at work. You know how it is." Sammie sat up and moved back to her side of the couch. The room felt colder.

Paige whined and cocked her head at us. She jumped up from her bed onto the couch and inserted herself between us, giving each of us a few nudges with her nose. She wanted to play the role of the peacemaker.

"I'm sorry about your day. I haven't said anything before but my days haven't been so good either." I waited to speak until Paige settled at Sammie's side. "The person who's been killing the young men carved a message into their bodies, into their torsos. It referenced the name, Evelyn." I pushed out the words slowly, watching Sammie as I talked, bracing for her reaction. Then relief calmed me, because I'd finally told her.

"I know." She breathed out. "I know what it said, Evan. I know the whole thing."

"You didn't tell me?" I stood up and walked to the window, where a streetlamp outside brightened the room. Paige snuggled into the couch and fell asleep. Her soft breathing filled the space.

"A friend told me. She's on the homicide force," Sammie said. "Everyone on the force is excited about the possibility of a genuine serial killer in Seven Sisters. You know how it is with those guys, it's a big deal to get a case like this and could further a lot of people's careers. Everyone wants a piece of the action. My friend said there's even talk of bringing the FBI in to help with the case."

I tried not to sound accusatory. "And you didn't say anything because?" We both had been hiding something from the other.

Sammie got up and put her arm around my waist. "I didn't want to frighten you."

She pulled me into her but I didn't face her. "You're the only one in this city who I've told my birth name to," I said. Then I turned to look at her and tears bloomed and shone in her eyes in the darkness. I hated that I'd made her cry.

Sincerity deepened her gaze. I'd thought we were close, but how close could we have been if she had a friend I didn't know about? I smoothed back her soft hair with my palm and pulled her in close to my chest. Sammie rested her warm face against the curve of my neck. Her heart beat against me in a slow, steady rhythm.

"She, an old friend on the force, told me something else—during the investigation they found that the apartment at that luxury place—what's it called?" Sammie said. "Do you remember?"

"The Tower on the Cove. After the trouble the manager gave me, how could I forget?" I looked at her.

"What sort of trouble did he give you?" she asked.

We hadn't talked about that part of my day. "I'm sorry I made you cry, sweetheart." I dried her eyes and kissed her face. "The trouble was nothing—not a big deal. Who's your friend?"

"Christy."

"I've never met her."

"You did once, at the city's Christmas party."

"Right. No, I don't remember her."

"You did meet her the one time. You probably forgot. When Christy told me about the name on the victims' bodies, I decided I needed to get to the bottom of what's going on. I managed to pull out of her that the Cove apartment's rent is being paid by someone living in *Marseille*, named *A*-something."

"Mars? Say what?"

Sammie pronounced the name slowly. "*Marseille*. It's a city in southern France. I looked it up on my phone."

I let out a long whistle. "Europe."

"Yes. The detectives working the case found out from Interpol. This person has an address where their mail is being forwarded to a post office box in Lamont, also registered to an *A*."

"To—where did you say again?" Lamont was the closest city to Freedom Village, which wasn't a great distance from Seven Sisters either.

"Lamont. It's—"

"I know where it is," I said, and we both looked at each other. "Have they found fingerprints?"

"I'm not sure." Sammie's lips tightened as something seemed to dawn on her. "Lamont. That's near where you grew up, isn't it?"

I nodded, went back to the coffee table, and drained my wineglass. I grabbed Sammie's empty glass and held it between my fingers next to mine. "Want another?" I asked.

Her voice got so quiet I could hardly understand her but I heard the words, "Yeah. I love you, Evan. I'm sorry about before." Sammie turned on the television and sat on the couch.

"I'm sorry, too." I gestured to the chips bag on the couch and Sammie shook her head, so I took it with me and walked into the kitchen with our glasses in my hands. Paige hopped off the couch and, oddly, followed me. It was getting late, and I supposed she wanted to go out for her evening walk. I spoke loud enough so Sammie could hear me in the living room. "Paige wants to go for a walk. I'll take her out after I fix our drinks."

"Okay."

The sounds of the evening news, commentary, and the weather forecast, played in the other room. I listened but didn't hear anything about the boys who'd been killed. No one cared. Except for a few cops, and Sammie and me, and my work crew. Sirens screeched outside and I jumped. The wine spilled out in a thin, slithering red trail on the white counter, and I wiped it up with a dishtowel before it dripped off the side onto the floor tiles.

The TV shut off in the other room. Sammie walked into the kitchen and set her hand on mine as I poured. "I'll come with you to walk Paige," she said.

"You're sure? I thought you wanted to watch TV." I turned around and handed her a full glass. I picked up mine and she bracketed me against the counter while we drank, watching each other.

My gaze dropped from her deep-set eyes to the inviting curves of her lips, moist and stained from the wine. Silence could pass between

Sammie and me for hours and there still would be a connection between us that charged the air. I felt that if I held up my hand I could almost touch the current circulating around us, something warm, comforting, and a little sensuous; something I could hold onto.

Paige nudged her way between our legs and peered up at us. Sammie smiled and leaned into me and Paige bumped into my knees. "What I want is to take a walk with my family," Sammie said.

*Family*. We'd never referred to the three of us as that before, and it scared me a little. But I liked what it stood for and that it offered the promises of everlasting commitment and support. Something I'd thought I had with my mother until she confessed to the murders, and something I'd only recently started to believe I could experience again, when I met Sammie and then we adopted Paige from a rescue. And what if someday, our family included children? Did I want someone so dependent on me?

Part of the idea of building a new family frightened me because the one my mother had created for us eroded so fast once she signed her confession to accept a plea deal and was imprisoned. Rightfully so, but she was still my mother and I'd loved her before then and had believed in her innocence up until her confession. Even later, I could never bring myself around to truly hating her but I despised her repugnant actions.

That she might be innocent had scarcely crossed my mind. She'd admitted in writing to killing those young men, and by that, her innocence seemed unlikely. Not a day went by, though, when I hadn't wish for her to somehow be proven innocent and be cleared of her crimes, because even though I'd already lost time and years with her and because of her, and could never get those back, I didn't want to walk around with the label of *murderer's child* stuck to my back if I didn't have to, if she wasn't really that.

"We can finish our drinks when we get back," Sammie said, and set down her glass behind me.

I reached out and pressed my fingertips into her slender waist. She curled her fingers around my arm and squeezed my muscle. Sammie kissed me slowly, pulling on my bottom lip in a tender but persistent way, a very alluring way to me, and she tasted rich like the wine. She slipped away and took Paige's lead off the coat hanger by the front door. I drained my glass, figuring I could always have another when we returned, then got my jacket and walked with them out into the hallway.

Later than night, I received a text from Em asking me, if we didn't have a job site to go to in the morning, to meet her for coffee at the diner. There was such a sense of urgency in her message that I answered back yes.

# Chapter 4

The next morning I arrived at the diner a few blocks from the apartment I shared with Sammie. Em wasn't there. The server poured me a cup of coffee and put a menu on the table, and I asked for an extra menu for Em for when she arrived. I slid her menu to the spot across from me where she'd sit once she came. I hadn't asked her why she wanted to meet with me but we were on friendly terms and I wasn't too concerned.

I texted Sammie at work to see how she was doing. I'd been somewhat relieved that she hadn't mentioned the word 'family' since last night, and we'd gone through our routine of walking Paige and reading the newspapers together, a routine we followed when work permitted us to have some leisure.

*I'm worried about Paige not eating very much this morning*, Sammie wrote.

I texted her back. *She's fine. Whoever gets home first will check on her. Don't worry*!

The dog had been treated for cancer last year, and so far the disease had stayed away. Now, any slight change in Paige's behavior concerned Sammie, whereas I tended to downplay things that worried me, to protect Sammie.

Em came into the diner about ten minutes late, looking flustered, and bringing in a warm breeze with her. I'd been texting Sammie until she had to resume working. I waved to Em from the booth.

"Sorry I'm late." Em patted a few pieces of her curly, red hair that had come out of her twist and brushed against her eyes. "Trent wanted to come with his mommy, and I told him he had to go to his preschool but he wouldn't have any of that. It took a long time to get him out of the house. I feel so awful about the whole thing. He really did want to come with me." I could hear the love she had for her son in her voice and the exhaustion of being a single mother. She sat down across from me and removed her coat, folding it in her lap. "Did you already order?" she asked.

"No, I waited for you," I said.

"Thanks, Evan." Her generous smiled accentuated her somewhat crooked teeth. "Are you okay? You look stressed."

"No, it's—I'm fine. Do you want coffee? I'll let the waiter know."

"Yeah, thanks." Em set her shoulder bag on the tabletop and took out her phone. She read something on the screen and let out a poignant sigh.

I made eye contact with our server and touched my cup and then pointed to Em to show him what we wanted. He came over with a pot of coffee, poured some into Em's cup and refilled mine. "Are you ready to order?" he asked.

"We need a few minutes," Em replied. She pushed aside the pitcher of milk the server had set on the table when I arrived. A woman with a young child walked past the diner window and I caught Em watching them, and I wondered if she wished she could spend more time with her son.

"Is everything all right with you?" I asked her when the server left the table. "You seem distracted." I picked up and opened my menu.

"Truth is, I am. Sorry." Em put her phone in her bag.

"What's going on?" I put my menu down. I already knew what I'd order, the same thing I ordered every time I came there—a *chocolate death* donut—chocolate cake coated with melted dark chocolate and topped with chocolate chips. And the nearest to heaven I expected I would ever get. I drank some coffee and waited for Em to open up to me.

"You really want to know?" she said.

There'd always been an unspoken rule of mine at work: those I managed shouldn't bring outside baggage into our occupation. But seeing the tension in Em's eyes and the worry lines on her young face, I knew I could make an exception for her. "Yes, I do," I said. "What's going on?"

Em released another sigh. "I asked you to meet me here because I needed someone to talk to, and you always give good advice."

"I'm not sure about that, but go on."

"I want to send Trent to this private school next year when he starts kindergarten, and I recently found out he didn't get the scholarship I applied for. The local, free school near us is dangerous. There's a lot of gang violence. A couple of kids were shot there."

"I didn't know that."

"Yeah, it happened last year. Yesterday, I'd written to the private school to ask if there was any way they'd change their minds about the scholarship, and just now they wrote to tell me they're sorry, but no. It's been such a terrible ordeal because Trent *was* accepted to the school but I can't afford the tuition without some kind of assistance. He's really smart but it's just the luck of the draw, you know?" She looked across at me and shrugged. Em opened her menu but didn't read it. "I guess I'll have eggs over easy and toast," she said.

I wanted to help her with Trent's tuition but I wasn't financially stable enough to offer her my assistance, and neither was Sammie. Em rested her hand on the table and I placed mine over hers, feeling the warmth and love she had for her son. "I wish I could help you—"

"Thanks, but that wouldn't be right. I could never ask you or anyone for something that big."

I tried to think of something to tell her, some kind of solution to her dilemma. "Do you have family who might be willing to help?" I asked.

"I wish." Em's tone was bitter. "They don't have much for themselves, and what they do have, they're keeping. They haven't made it a secret that they didn't approve when I got pregnant, married Trent's father, and then they didn't approve when we got divorced. I don't have anything to do with them, and that's the way they and I both like it." She shivered, as though reflecting on her family made her cold. I could relate. Not only did Em and I both prefer our coffee black, we had pasts we'd erase if given the opportunity.

"What about other scholarships, ones outside the school?" I asked.

Em shook her head. "I already looked into a couple of those but either we don't qualify or it's too late for us to apply."

"Trent's father's family—are they in any way involved in Trent's care?"

"I couldn't ask them."

Her answer had been so fast that I got the feeling she wouldn't even consider the idea and that I shouldn't ask why. Clearly, Em wanted to avoid discussing them, and probably for good reasons. I was at a loss for words.

"It's okay. I'll think of something," she said.

Defeated, I said, "Let me pay for this meal. That's the least you could let me do for you since it turns out my advice isn't so great after all."

"You're sure, chief?"

"It's, what, a few eggs? How much could that cost?"

Em laughed. "All right, I think I can let you pay."

"And if you or Trent ever need anything else, I—and I know Sammie does too—hope you know that we're here for you."

"Thanks, chief."

We ordered the food, and when Em's eggs and toast and my donut arrived, and the server had refilled our coffee cups and left, I said, "You know, before, when you said I looked stressed?"

Em finished spreading butter on her brown toast and the bread glistened with grease. She looked up and seemed eager to offer me her assistance. I didn't elaborate, and Em said, "I know it's harder for you to open up to someone because you're a guy, but I really do want to help."

Even with her encouragement and her sincere, open smile, I hesitated. But I knew I needed to talk to someone. Because of what had happened to Sammie's sister, I didn't like discussing anything associated with my mother's crimes with her, but Em was my colleague.

The words came out of me like a dry, hard nut was stuck at the back of my throat. "You were right. Something is bothering me."

Em set her knife on her plate. "Tell me. You were there for me a few minutes ago, and I want to be here for you now. I want to hear what's on your mind."

"I was hardly there for you."

"You tried," she said.

I cleared my throat. "It's about the boy murders that have been happening around here."

"Do you have an idea about them?" she asked.

"Not quite." A look of trepidation clouded over Em's warm eyes, as though I might be about to confess to those murders. Laughing it off seemed callous given the circumstances of the crimes, so I said, "Oh, it's not that, it isn't what you're thinking. It's that I've been considering something Chief Gilani told me about the bodies." I lowered my voice. "He said that someone put a message on them. It's been on my mind a lot lately, and . . ."

Em spoke quietly. "Why? Wait, the killer wrote something on the bodies, like on the skin?"

I'd nearly forgot that the revelation would be news to her. "Yes, but not with a marker, if you catch my drift."

She shuddered. "That's awful."

Despite what we sometimes encountered and saw on a daily basis, that such an act would be shocking to her wasn't surprising to me. We didn't deal with the bodies themselves after a crime. We dealt with what came out from inside them. Our job often eluded the public's thoughts. While the work the police did solving murders and catching bad guys had the public enthralled, we handled a component people overlooked, the tidying up of the aftermath of a crime. We scrubbed away blood, removed guts, bones, and flesh from a scene, but we didn't *see* the actual horrors a murderer inflicted on their victim's susceptible body, a horror like mutilation. We saw the remnants. A victim's hair and brains. Gunshot wounds to the head were the worst for those.

"Was it something this person—the killer—wanted the police to know?" Em asked.

"It's hard to tell, but I don't think the message was intended for them exactly," I said.

Em picked up her cup and brought it to her mouth, clinking it against her teeth, her fingers trembling around the china. I braced myself for her to drop it and reached out to catch it. She set the cup clumsily on the saucer, and I sat back in the booth. "What—what did it say?" Em spoke as though she wasn't sure whether she could stomach the answer.

"Miss me, Evelyn?"

Em's brow wrinkled and her gaze narrowed at me. "Huh?"

"That's what the message said."

"I don't understand—what does that have to do with what's bothering you?" I remained quiet and drank my coffee, and she said, "Do you know this Evelyn person?"

"That used to be my name. Before I started to transition."

"Do you mean . . ."

"Yes."

Em nodded, and at last, she spoke, "All right, I think I understand. It's none of my business, but you should know I don't have a problem with any of that. This person, the killer, is trying to get to you through the messages, they're trying to hurt you, is that it?" Her eyes brightened. "That's why you wanted me to leave you alone at the Cove. You were looking for something—did you find anything? Could the messages be, maybe, a coincidence?"

Em's sincerity amazed me if only a bit. Even in these modern times, I was accustomed to people's ignorance about my sexuality. The way I felt about it was that I didn't question them about their choices, so what right did they have to question mine?

"No, I didn't find anything," I said. "And possibly they're trying to get to me through the messages or it's a coincidence. I'm not sure yet." What I didn't say to Em was that I suspected someone wanted me to know they were killing because of me.

"Do you have any enemies?" She appeared genuinely concerned.

"Are you asking me if there's someone out there who'd want to destroy my life and reputation? Take your pick." I smiled. When Em didn't laugh, I said, "I was just kidding."

"Oh," she said, and laughed in a quick, nervous way.

My mother didn't hate me, I knew that much. She hadn't been caught by the police, she'd gone to them willingly and turned herself in without telling me first. Other than perhaps the families of my mother's victims who might have wanted to hurt her through me, I had no bad blood with anyone, not anyone that I knew of, at least. The families hadn't wanted anything from me for all those years, not even money, for which they'd unsuccessfully sued my mother's family.

"Does Chief Gilani know about your name?" Em asked.

I shook my head. "He wasn't really supposed to tell me about the messages but I found out from him. We've worked together for a number of years, and I trust you, but I can't stress enough that you can't tell anyone what I said about the writing on the victims. I'd like to keep my old name private as well."

"No problem. You can trust me not to tell anyone."

"It's very important that you don't say anything to anyone, not even to your friends or family. Telling someone—what was on the bodies—could get Gilani, me, and even you, canned. I also want to keep what I told you about me—"

"Keep it private, I got it."

Sammie knew the detail the police were concealing from the media, a detail that possibly only the killer knew; the killer's penchant for inscribing their twisted words on their victims was gossip among law enforcement, and Sammie was law enforcement, even if she was retired.

I wondered if Em would become like a sister to me, someone I could trust. I'd known Em for a number of years and never had an issue or a problem with her at work, had never had a reason to not trust her, but could I trust her with not only a detail that might make all the difference to the police's investigation but, also, inadvertently, with my past?

I hadn't divulged much of my life outside work to my co-workers, but I had trusted Em and Josh with a few small secrets over the years. But these were two very big secrets. Perhaps doubt had come too late on my part. I'd already spilled two secrets and would have to live with what followed.

"It's not like I have any family to tell, chief." Em's tone was wry.

"Right, of course."

The diner served the donuts warm, and I'd nearly forgot about mine, and bit into the dough that had gone cold from having sat ignored on my plate. Em speared her eggs and the yolk flowed in a thin yellow squiggle onto her toast. She picked up the soggy bread, which disappeared into her mouth in two bites. I swallowed down the donut with a large amount of coffee.

A silent agreement that our meal was done and we should get going passed between Em and I. Our server stepped over to ask if we needed anything else. We both declined refills of our coffee cups, and I asked him for the check.

I paid the bill and the tip, and grabbed my jacket off the back of the booth and put it on. "Next time—and we should do this again—feel free to bring Trent with you," I said to Em.

"Thanks, but I kind of like having some time to *not* be mommy, if you know what I mean. Thanks again for paying."

Sammie and I weren't parents but I could imagine Em's need for a little freedom from family life every so often. She put on her coat, picked up her bag, and we walked out of the diner together.

I held open the door for her. "Where to next for you?" I asked out on the sidewalk.

"I'm running a few errands before I have to pick Trent up from school. He has a half-day today, and I told the sitter I'd just pick him up if we didn't get called to a site. Fingers crossed we don't. Honestly, I'm always asking her to come at the last minute, and I think she was relieved I wasn't calling her for that."

I grimaced. "That must be hard. I'm sorry I put you through it and that I can't promise it won't happen again."

"Nah, I'm glad to have a job."

"And I'm glad to have you as part of my team."

Em blushed. She waited a moment or two, and then said, "About what you told me inside—both things—I won't say anything to anyone. I swear you can trust me."

"Should I ask you to place your hand over your heart?"

Em laughed. "I will if you want me to."

"Hey, I appreciate it but you don't have to do that," I smiled. "I will walk with you for a bit if that's all right. The weather's not bad. As you know, I don't live too far from here. Which direction are you heading?"

She pointed to the left. "I'm parked somewhere else but I need to go to the shops over there." Em skipped a beat. "It must be so hard for you." She gave me a sideways glance. "People can be so—I want you to know I'm not like that."

I felt the need to clarify why I wanted our conversation to remain private. "I didn't intend for you to get the impression that I'm ashamed of who I am, because that isn't the case." Heat pricked at my face.

"I know, I know, I completely get it. I think it's great. I know of some people who are . . . and I absolutely support them." She paused, and I could have counted to ten during the time. "What I mean to say is, it's no one's business but yours." The revelation seemed to have made her a bit anxious but she didn't seem uncomfortable with what I'd told her.

"Thanks, Em, for your support." A group of people brushed past us on the sidewalk and I lowered my voice. "But, see, the big thing here really is what Gilani told me about the inscription on the bodies—*that* can never be told. And I would appreciate you not telling anyone what we discussed about me. For instance, if the time came, I'd want to tell Josh before you did."

We picked up the pace and rounded the corner and Em stopped.

"You're going to tell him?" she asked.

"Josh? When the time's right, possibly."

"I understand completely."

"You know, I actually should check on the dog." I pointed to the right, where Sammie and I lived.

Em's smile faded. "Why, is Paige okay?" I'd discussed Paige with Em and Josh more than anything else in my life.

"Sammie's been worried about her. Lately, she hasn't been eating very much. But it's probably nothing. You know how Sammie worries."

Em shook her head.

"Well, maybe I never told you, but she does," I said. "Anyway, I'm sure it's nothing."

The way Em arched her eyebrow reminded me of Sammie's reaction whenever I downplayed something she deemed a crisis but which I felt wasn't a huge deal.

"I hope it *does* turn out to be nothing," Em said, and rubbed my shoulder. "Goodbye for now. I'm heading to the market, which is in that direction." She indicated the side street at our left.

"I hope I won't be calling you soon," I said.

Em frowned and her bag slid off her shoulder.

"What I meant to say was, I hope I won't have a good reason to call you soon, such as another murder."

Em fixed her bag, stepped forward and encircled me with her arms, drawing me close to her strong warmth for a platonic embrace.

"I'm not hitting on you, so Sammie doesn't have to worry," she said, and laughed in a subdued way close to my ear. The heat of her breath smelled like the coffee we'd had inside the diner. "You look like you could use a hug." She paused. "When you changed your name, how did you know?" she asked, her tone soft and thoughtful, standing close and holding me so tightly I was still.

I looked into her attentive gaze and smiled slightly. "You see, Em, I always knew—that's how it works. It's who I am, who I always was."

I didn't intend to become sentimental but a few tears stung my eyes, and I tried to discreetly wipe them away.

"You know, it's okay to cry once in a while. No one's ever going to think you're any less tough," Em patted my back and gave me a sympathetic look. She dug into her bag and handed me a tissue.

I laughed and thanked her.

"Catch you later, chief," Em stepped into the street.

"I sure as hell hope not," I grinned, and wiped my eyes. "I don't think I'll be calling you into work for a long time."

Em bantered with me as she waited to cross the busy street. "You think?" she spoke over her shoulder.

"I can't guarantee it but I'm pretty damn sure. I have a good feeling."

"I don't mind," she said. "I could use the money."

# Chapter 5

Around the same time I guaranteed to Em that things should be quiet on our end for a while, Gilani called to inform me that the police had discovered a young male who'd died in the same modus operandi as the others—death by strangulation and the same inscription on the victim's torso.

I had Em and Josh meet me at the municipal garage, and we drove to a budget motel on the outskirts of Seven Sisters. Gilani warned me ahead of time that my crew should bring our full gear because the scene was literally a bloody mess. The motel room had been the location of the actual murder and not a dumping ground, and the victim's body had been partly dismembered in the bathtub. No word on what the killer had done with those pieces of the body, but I'd willed for them not to have been discovered eaten.

We hadn't had such a bloody mess in a few months, and on the drive to the motel I braced Em and Josh for what we should expect to find on our arrival. No matter how much blood and body fluids and innards one encountered on a regular basis, you could never truly get used to something like that, or know how you would react in each instance. Some aspects of the job, like the cleaning and the smells, became routine, but not the visual carnage.

The motel rooms were accessed from the outside, and I pulled into the dimly lit parking lot, which seemed vacant except for a detective's car, what were probably some of the staffs' cars, and the vehicles of one or two guests. Over time in my line of work I'd learned the types of cars different people drove, and I also learned about various kinds of people; people who were mostly cruel, and a very few who were decent.

The room we were to clean was cordoned off by yellow tape around the small front patio and the door. I parked the van behind the detective's car. The place wasn't as dilapidated as Gilani had made it sound over the phone. From the outside the motel seemed plain and sparse but well-kept. This wasn't a place where someone paid for an hour to have a quick fuck in one of the rooms; rather, it appeared an ideal setting for the weary night traveler to pull into from the road and rest.

To our van's right was what looked like an office, well-lit, with a clerk inside talking to a tall middle-age man in a suit, who was a detective. In my line of work not only had I perceived the kinds of cars people drove but the people who drove them. The clerk, in a white collared shirt that was maybe a size too big for him, leaned against the desk but not in a relaxed way. He seemed quite distraught.

Although Gilani had informed the motel office when we'd be arriving, I left the van and stepped into the quiet office, without wearing my gear, to let the clerk know we'd be starting. Em and Josh stayed behind and unpacked the van. I also wanted to check with the detective that it was okay to remove the tape. Usually the police had finished long before we arrived on scene. I felt it would be smart to confirm that forensics had completed their tasks, collecting the evidence they needed, before we cleaned it all away in a mere few hours.

Both men turned in my direction when I opened the door to the office and let in the cold air. The detective had thick salt-and-pepper hair and a trimmed mustache. We introduced ourselves, and Detective Burke, who held a notepad in his hand—I had interrupted him interviewing the clerk—said to me, "I have to warn you, you have your work cut out for you in that room."

The clerk nodded in agreement, and his face paled, like he might have to excuse himself to go puke. He must have found the body in the room, the unlucky bastard. He looked fairly young, maybe a college student earning some extra money.

"You guys done, so my team and I can get started?" I asked Burke.

"Yeah. I just drove here to ask this guy a few more questions." He pointed to the clerk.

Detective Burke's phone rang and he took the call, leaving me to approach the desk to ask the clerk to confirm the room we were to clean. Most detectives were good people but they didn't think our job was as important as theirs, and indeed it wasn't as crucial. I often found the families of the victims, and the owners of the locations, knew more about where we were supposed to clean than the police.

Behind my shoulder Burke said, "Do you mind if I finish up here first? I just got another case assigned to me and have to leave." He had finished his call before I could speak with the clerk.

I nodded and gave them some space, stepping back and waiting by the front door.

Detective Burke opened his notepad. "Let me see where I left off." After a moment he said to the clerk, "Who was the room registered to, in what name?"

The office didn't have a computer and the clerk opened a big ledger. He put his finger on the page and moved down the list of what must have been the names of the guests. "Alice," he said, after a few minutes.

"Last name? Did they pay with a credit card?" the detective asked—at least I think that's what he said. It was somewhat difficult to hear them at that distance.

I'd stopped paying attention after the mention of the name, Alice. My heart thumped so much I thought it actually could burst through my chest. Alice, the killer I knew, was in prison, where the world was kept safe from her. So, how could this be happening?

The young clerk shifted where he stood and avoid looking at Burke. "I didn't get a last name from her. I do remember she paid with cash," he said.

"Did she leave an address? Here, let me see that." Detective Burke picked up the ledger and read it while standing. I waited for a sign that he'd found what he wanted but it never happened. He sucked his teeth and shook his head, and gave the ledger back to the young guy. "What did this woman look like? Older? Younger?" Burked rocked back and forth on the heel of his shoes as he waited for an answer.

It took the clerk so long to reply that in all honesty I assumed he would say he couldn't remember the woman well enough to describe her. Then he said, "She was in her mid-thirties, and I remember that she was pretty." He pointed at me standing by the door and I recoiled farther into the wall. "She had similar coloring to him."

Burke regarded me with a new interest. "Do you think you could describe her to our sketch artist?" he asked the clerk.

"Excuse me," I said fast, and went outside to get some fresh air before the situation could become more uncomfortable. I rested my back against the building's façade and rubbed my forehead. What the hell was going on?

When I looked up, I saw Em and Josh sitting in the back of the open van. They were upright workers who always waited for my okay before putting on our gear and heading inside. Josh signaled to me and Em gave me an expectant look. I shook my head and motioned for them to wait. Then I went back into the office to hear the clerk telling Detective Burke, "...I don't remember seeing the Alice lady with the dead guy. He must've waited outside or came to her room after."

A short while later, the clerk confirmed the room for me, and the detective pulled me aside before he left. I prepared myself for him to ask questions about the clerk's comparing Alice's looks to mine. My palms turned warm, and sticky with sweat.

"Listen, between you and me, we didn't find some parts of the body. The tongue in particular was cut out from the vic's mouth, and it was nowhere to be found in the room or around the motel. Anyway, on the small chance that you guys dig something up, let me know." He grinned. Up close, he had a scar on his face, a long, jagged line, like someone had cut him with a knife. His breath smelled a little stale and his clothes were wrinkled, but he'd been in and out of there all day and probably hadn't had the chance to return home and freshen up.

I breathed in relief, and my body cooled, and then the liberation of not being questioned dissipated when I processed what he'd said. "Maybe she's—the killer—feels silenced, that's why they removed the tongue." Detective Burke hesitated to agree with me but I perceived from his eyes that he did. "These parts, you really think they're missing?" I asked.

"I know they are."

I hesitated, and then asked, "Did the body have a message written on it?"

Burke put on a 'Who told you about that?' face.

As much as I didn't want to give him Gilani's name and possibly get the chief in trouble, given the insider information I had, I also knew lying could make Burke think I had something to do with the murders. "The chief might have mentioned it," I said.

"Ah." Detective Burke watched me with a contemplative gaze. "You know, the mother of the first kid who was killed ID'd his body at the morgue last night. I bet you didn't know that?" There was a glint in his eyes. Was he testing me? "She said he was addicted to drugs and ran away from home, and she didn't know where he was. Sad stuff."

"I didn't know," I said. "It is sad. I can refer her to an organization that supports victim's families. My girlfriend runs it."

"Is that right? I'll let her know if I see her."

"I don't have a card on me." I searched my pockets but knew I didn't have one.

"She can look it up online or wherever."

I gave him the name but noticed he didn't write it down. Then he said, "And to answer your question: Yes."

I knew he couldn't tell me more, but I assumed the message on the body was what had been written on the others.

"Let us know if you find them, the body parts," Burke said. "Seriously. Because we couldn't."

Judging by his tone, he wasn't kidding.

"I personally believe the killer ate the parts right off the victim," he said. "We didn't find teeth marks on the vic but some parts of the body had been cut right out."

"Ate them, without cooking them?" I said.

Way back when, the newspapers had said my mother roasted the parts of the victims she ate, like a witch, but I never noticed or smelled her doing anything like that in our kitchen, and Mack had told me the tabloid claims were bullshit. Mack said that just because some parts of the victims' bodies were missing that didn't mean the killer ate them, that my mother might have been what Mack called a collector, someone who fetishized their victims and kept pieces of their body, or entire parts, around. However, back in the day, they'd found nothing like that at the home I shared with her.

"What if the killer is simply collecting the body parts?" I asked Burke.

"Yeah, that's possible, or maybe she—if you know about the writing, then the chief must've told you our theory it's a female—prefers them *very rare*. Maybe she took the tongue home for later like a deli meat." He started to smile but ceased when I leveled my gaze with his—he was a good few inches taller.

Josh, Em, and I might have sometimes sang while we worked, but I drew the line at joking about the victims.

"I have to leave now, and it's about time you got started, unless you want to be here all night." He winked. "The bathtub's a mess. The whole bathroom is. It's got white walls, white floor tiles, and a white tub. Doesn't matter. Everything's red as hell now. The rest of the room's not so bad. That bathroom, though?" Burke whistled in astonishment. "It would've made your life a lot easier if our girl had put down a plastic sheet in the tub, but it's not like we could've asked her to do that, you know? Killed and then chopped up in a tub—what a way to go, right?"

"Yeah, what a way to go." I glanced at the clerk, who pretended to be busy behind the desk while he listened to us with his white ears burning red.

I strode out of the office with the detective, who hurried to his car—I was right about which one was his—and I made a beeline for Josh and Em.

# Chapter 6

I woke up to my ringtone playing on the bedside table the following morning.

"Who's calling you this early?" Sammie asked next to me. She had her head on the pillow but her brown eyes were open, wide and clear with sleep. She moved under the covers to pull me back toward her.

I gently pushed her away. On top of the bed Paige stirred at our feet. Em and Josh and I had finished cleaning the motel late last night, and now, half awake, I thought the call was Gilani notifying me that another clean-up was needed, that another murder had happened. Except the ringtone wasn't the one I used for the chief. I didn't recognize it because Josh rarely called me at home. It stopped ringing and I started to text Josh to see what he wanted before the phone went to voicemail.

A text from Josh suddenly appeared on my screen. *So sorry, chief. Want you to know I support you 100%.*

"What the hell?" I said.

Sammie sat up and read the screen over my shoulder. "What's going on?"

I motioned for her to wait a second and texted Josh back. *Ok, thanks, but what are you talking about?*

Josh wrote: *Blog post.*

*What?*

*Crime Man. But it's everywhere now. Got picked up by everyone. It's on Twitter now. Facebook. It was trending. You didn't know?*

*No. It's about who?*

*You.*

*Me?*

*Yeah.*

Somehow, I managed to explain to Sammie what was going on and asked her to get her phone and look up the website. She felt for her phone on the bookshelf adjacent to her side of the bed.

I sent Josh another text. *What is it, some kind of story about our work?* I almost jokingly asked whether it had gone global yet but I didn't want to know before I'd read what it was about.

*I don't think I should send you the link. It's a bunch of BS. You shouldn't worry.*

Sammie took in a sharp breath like her bare skin had made contact with something very cold. "Oh, fuck," she said.

I sent Josh a final text. *Sammie found it.* And she hadn't liked what she'd read.

Sammie hid her phone from me when I tried to peer around her shoulder to look. I dropped my phone on the bed and ducked around her waist and grabbed it from her. Paige leapt from our bed and paced nervously around the room. She hadn't gone out for her morning walk yet. I started to read the screen.

"Please don't read it. It's bullshit," Sammie said.

I ignored her and processed what had been written. The *Crime Man* blog was part of a notorious crime enthusiast website and moderated by someone who'd been dubbed 'Crime Man.' They also had a forum with members who acted as passionate online sleuths.

I tended to avoid visiting those websites because they were mostly filled with lurid crime scene photos and sensationalist speculation about famous and, sometimes, not so famous, murders. It was a more modern version of the kind of place that would have written about my mother and her crimes years ago. After dealing with the public onslaught my mother's case brought into my younger life and seeing crime scenes in real life on a daily basis, I'd already read and viewed enough of those sorts of things for my taste.

*Crime Man* also featured a section where they "broke" what they deemed to be impending major crime stories. And that morning they'd "broke" the Seven Sisters murders. And my life along with it.

I struggled to see the blog post's text through my tears, and I had to read the post twice to fathom that it was, indeed, about me. I wasn't prepared for this.

*BREAKING NEWS*!

*Seven Sisters city police hunt for serial killer in their city who leaves a message written into the flesh of the slaughtered: Miss me, Evelyn?*

*We received a tip that 'Evelyn' is the former name of Evan Lane, a Seven Sisters employee who heads the crime scene clean-up unit there. Coincidence or a troubling fact? After a little digging, we at Crime Man have discovered that almost two decades ago Ms. Lane's mother, Alice Lane, was a serial killer of young men and a cannibal. She was known as 'The Lovely Butcher.'*

I could only skim the remainder of the post. They called me Alice's 'daughter.' They hadn't referred to me as transgender but they had implied that, and they'd deadnamed me by using my birth name instead of my chosen name. They weren't blaming me for the murders, exactly, but the suggestion was there.

Sammie's phone slipped from my fingers onto the blanket. I swung my legs over the bed and my feet touched the cold floor. My chest quaked with each sob I released. I disliked getting emotional but I couldn't stop myself. Beside me, Sammie dangled her legs over the bed, too, and she seemed to be trying to figure out the best way to approach me. I don't think she'd seen me cry like that before. I reached to where I'd dropped the phone behind me, and Sammie slid more to my side and prevented me from grabbing the phone. She put her slender arm around my waist and pulled me into her soft hip, tucking my larger frame into her.

"Don't read it again," she said. "You don't need to see that crap."

"I didn't finish reading it. I need to read it," I said, my voice shaking with emotion. "I need to read it—"

"No. Because it's bullshit. I can't stand that someone's made you feel this way." From Sammie's voice, she could barely restrain her fury. "We *are* going to fight this."

Paige, who had been pacing the bedroom, her nails clicking on the floor, pressed her nose against our legs. "She needs to go outside," I said to Sammie. "Let's take her out."

Sammie dried my eyes with her sweater sleeve and then got up and pulled back the curtain at our bedroom window.

"What are you doing?" I asked.

"Making sure there aren't reporters parked outside our building," she said.

"Oh." I hadn't thought of that. "Do you think that's possible?"

Sammie peered at me over her shoulder. "If that horrid story is online, then yes."

I started to rise but Sammie read my thoughts. "Don't turn on the TV," she said.

At the other side of the bed, my phone received a text. I picked up the phone and Sammie hurried over to the bed. "It's okay," I said. "It's just Em asking how I am. She must have heard. Geez, is there anyone who doesn't know? Why don't you take the dog out first?"

Sammie gave me a worried look.

"Please? I need a few moments to myself, and I can also text Em back. I'll join you when I'm done," I said. We took the same route around the nearby park every time we walked Paige in the morning.

"I'm not leaving the phones with you so that you can read that dreadful muck of a story again," Sammie said.

I gave her a smile that would have been difficult to give anyone else under the circumstances, but Sammie wasn't just anyone; she was my love. "I need to text Em back so I'll need my phone. Please? Thanks."

Sammie eyed me like she didn't trust me. "Do you promise me you won't look at that shit?"

I nodded. "Are there any reporters outside?" Our address wasn't listed publicly, but if *Crime Man* had found out the information they had, then someone could have easily found our address.

"No. Not yet anyway. I'm going to wear a hat and sunglasses when I take Paige out, and I suggest you do the same."

She made me laugh in spite of everything. "You're kidding?" I said.

"Hell no." Sammie winked.

She sweet-talked Paige out of the bedroom, and when I heard her fastening the dog's leash and the door opening into the hallway, I began to read the *Crime Man* post again. But I stopped myself before I read farther than I already had. I didn't need to read it again to know what it said. Going behind Sammie's back hadn't felt right either. What had happened affected her as well as me. I loved Sammie, believed in her so much I trusted her with my life. I closed the website and texted Em to thank her for the support. I read her response three times before I grasped what she'd admitted to doing.

*I wouldn't have done it if I'd known how far they'd go.*

When I didn't reply, Em wrote more.

*I've been a follower of the website for years. I leaked the story to them because I needed the money for Trent's tuition so he could go to that private kindergarten next year. I was worried he wouldn't be safe at the free school. That neighborhood isn't safe. I'm so sorry. I never cashed their check and won't ever.*

I wrote: *You should take the money to help your son. It's already too late to change things.* I shuddered at my impartial reply, and an unfamiliar sense of composure and restraint overcame me.

I got up and set my phone on the dresser instead of flinging it across the room at the wall like I wanted to. Then I sat on the bed and didn't move or think about anything for a while. It wasn't until Sammie re-entered the apartment with Paige leading her inside, that I felt the weight of Em's betrayal pushing me down, a sensation so overwhelming and tremendous that I'd need someone to grab onto me and pull me to my feet or else I wouldn't move.

Sammie closed the door and called out to me, "You never showed up so we came back home. I hope you weren't reading that dreadful crap."

Once loose, Paige galloped happily into the room, jumped up onto the bed and wet my face with her kisses. I rubbed her soft ears and gently eased her away. The dog's leash clinked when Sammie hung it up in the other room and then Sammie stood leaning against the bedroom doorway with her arms crossed, watching me. She had an expression on her face like she was confident we'd get through the ordeal and be okay. I wasn't as positive and was glad I had her on my side.

I remained seated. Paige sat between us on the floor. I spoke calmly considering the situation. "Em leaked the story. That was why she texted me, to confess."

Sammie's tone bordered close to brutal anger. "She can't—she can't just do something like that."

"She did. That's what she wrote to tell me just now, while you were out with Paige. She sold the story to that website. She wrote to apologize."

Sammie ran over to the dresser and snatched my phone. After a moment I realized she was reading Em's texts. "She can't get away with what she did to you. There has to be a consequence . . . I didn't know you told her about private stuff."

"I opened up to her when I met her for coffee. We've worked together for a while now. I thought I could trust her. I couldn't have been more wrong. The most fucked-up thing is I can't bring myself around to hating her." I chuckled at the lunacy of what I'd said. "She needed the money for her son. I know what it's like to be broke and desperate."

"I've always been sympathetic to her situation, but, I'm sorry, I don't care how desperate she was, she must have realized how much doing this would hurt you. You don't do that to someone's life, you just don't, not if you even remotely care about them."

"I'm not sure about that. I can't say that if I was in her situation I wouldn't have done something similar. She was afraid what might happen to her son if he attended a school with a high crime rate. She was trying to do right by him."

Sammie faced me and gripped my arms, and it took her a few tries but she lifted me to my feet. "You're too good of a person sometimes to see when someone's wronged you. But I'm going to tell you, she has."

"I don't need to be protected."

"Seems to me you do if you feel sorry for the person who did this to you."

"This thing, whatever happens, will pass. I'll deal with it and move on." I went to the window to check outside. "I'm not going to make a big deal out of it if I don't have to."

Sammie approached me and looked out the window too. "You might have to. You could get into trouble for telling her what you did about the messages left on the victims. At the very least you certainly won't feel comfortable working with Em after this."

"I might not have to. She could get fired," I said.

"And rightly so."

"I could be fired also."

"What? No, they can't do that."

"Don't tell me the possibility hasn't crossed your mind?"

Sammie looked at the floor and reluctantly nodded.

Not only had I lost my privacy, I'd also lost a team member, and the nauseating tension of all of that hitting me at once was almost too much to bear. I swayed and leaned forward, and it felt like my legs could give out and I'd crash through the window and tumble to the sidewalk below. Sammie supported me in her arms and walked with me to the bed, where she sat me down and took a seat with me.

She sounded eager to get me to focus on something else. "We haven't fed Paige her breakfast yet," she said. "I hope she eats this morning."

"At least then that will lift some of the burden," I agreed. "I can feed her, or you can go feed her now if you'd like. I'm fine here."

Sammie didn't move from her place beside me. "She can wait a moment. I'll feed her in a bit. I'm not leaving you. You can't be alone."

"With this crap out there, this story, it'll change things for us." I waited for her to concur with me. "People will know certain things about us, about me, and about my mother."

"We won't let it change us. We are going to fight this thing, we'll fight it to the death." The determination in Sammie's voice inspired me.

"Do you think that can be done?" I asked.

"I know so. After everything you've been through and we've been through together, this whole thing will be a small dent in our life. We won't let it be anything greater than that." Sammie pressed her lips to my forehead, with her words warm on my face.

"I'll go feed Paige," I said, getting up.

I didn't get far because Sammie held onto my shirtsleeve. "You're not walking away from this," she said.

I sat down again and wrung my hands. "I'm not walking away from anything."

"You were walking away from me just now."

The sun filled our bedroom with a soft, joyous yellow light that contradicted the mood. "I was going to feed Paige." I looked from my hands to her.

Sammie gave me a reproachful look, and then smiled. "That was your excuse. I already said *I* would feed her."

"Okay, you win." I managed to smile.

An hour later, after I'd dressed for the day, Gilani rang me. Em had sent me a few more texts, one where she asked me what I planned to do with what she'd confided to me, but I hadn't written her back.

"You've read it, then," I said to the chief.

After a pause, Gilani said, "I heard about it from someone in the precinct and, yeah, then I read it. I need you to come to my office to talk with me. I don't want to do this over the phone."

I considered he might have been firing me.

"I don't want you to think I'm harassing you because, you're, you know," he said. "This is not about that."

I waited in silence but I was certain that, yes, I did *know* what he meant.

"I need to see you because certain aspects of the case were mentioned and that could harm our investigation," he said. "So I have to talk with you, in person."

"I understand. I'll come in to speak with you. What time do you want me to come in?"

"I'd like to see you now." He didn't sound as friendly as he had in the past, but he didn't sound angry either.

"I take it this is pretty serious," I said.

"It is. Can you come in?"

"Yeah. If the traffic's not too bad, I should be there in a few minutes."

"Good. When you arrive, come straight to my office. Whoever's at the front desk will be expecting you."

Sammie had called into work and asked for the day off. "Do you want me to come with you to city hall?" she asked, handing me my jacket at the door.

"No, it's all right, you stay here and be with Paige. She'll be frightened if any reporters come knocking on our door." I took the jacket from Sammie and she watched me put it on. Paige hadn't eaten again when Sammie fed her.

"Are you sure?" Sammie asked.

"Yes," I said, tucking my arms around her sides and kissing her. "I'll be fine. Don't you worry about me, okay?"

Sammie nodded slowly. "I *am* worried. I'm worried about you, and I'm worried about the dog. What did Gilani say to you?"

"Are you asking me if he's going to get me fired?" The question had been there in her tone.

Her eyes widened and her lips parted. "Are they going to?" Then she answered her own question. "How can they? You weren't the only person who knew about the writing on the victims. Others did. I knew."

"They didn't used to be named Evelyn, and their mothers weren't notorious serial killers."

"What are you saying, do you think he considers you a suspect?"

"Possibly." I shrugged my arms into the jacket's sleeves.

"Are you going to tell him about Em, that she sold them the story?"

"I've considered doing that, but it's not my place to tell, it's up to her, and I think she will."

"You have too much faith in her," Sammie said, with a distant look in her eyes.

"Someone has to." I gave her a quick peck on the cheek and left.

# Chapter 7

Sammie and I often kept our car in a garage a few blocks north of our apartment building. Living in a city with easy access to pretty much everything, we rarely drove the car except for trips to the stores or to travel out of town.

That morning I rode a taxi to the city police's main headquarters. I'd wanted to walk to clear my head, but the risk of running into members of the media put an end to that wish.

About twenty minutes later, I arrived at the five-story red-brick city hall building and paid the driver. I half expected two cops with handcuffs to be waiting to arrest me as I got out of the taxi and headed for the steps. The guard at the front desk, who oversaw the goings-on in the lobby, and who I somewhat knew through work, nodded at me.

The inside of the expansive building was as noisy as the street outside. People waited for elevators to arrive in the marble-floored lobby. I entered the police headquarters on the first floor and made my way through the rows of police administrative workers at their desks, who made little effort to conceal their murmurings among each other and the interested looks they shot my way, to Gilani's private office at the back of the area.

I'd visited his office once before, for a meeting at city hall, when I was first hired by the city. At that time, the chief had told me, the young and eager crime-scene-cleaner-to-be, that although the city expected him to manage us, he didn't have time to babysit the team when he had families who wanted those responsible for their loved ones' deaths caught and locked away, but that if I had what I thought was a *very important* question, I should feel free to ask him. And I felt he'd be there for me if I needed him. I'd refrained from bothering him, and had done fine, until now.

I stared at the lettering on the frosted glass window of his closed office door and knocked. "It's Evan Lane," I said.

"Come in." I couldn't read his emotions through his voice. He sounded somber and confident, but, then again, he typically did.

Chief Gilani didn't get up from his wide desk to greet me. He looked up from reading the paperwork he had in front of him and gestured to an office chair in my path. I removed my jacket, hung it over the back of the chair, and sat down.

"I'm really sorry about all this." He stacked the papers and set them aside. "First off, I want you to know that you aren't a suspect right now. I know the kind of person I hired and I trust you."

I breathed out, but my breathing hitched a little at the *right now* part of what he'd said. "I appreciate that."

"But I am going to need your word that you won't leave the state," he said.

I didn't hesitate. "You have my word."

"I'm sure the leak was internal, but in light of what was written on that . . . that website—I'm not going to give it the dignity of calling it a news site, because it's not, it's junk—I don't think you gave anything to them. Regardless, it isn't good that certain information about the mutilation done to the bodies is now known to the public. I've been bringing in anyone who had access to that information for a chat. Is there anything else I should know about? Is there anyone you might have told?"

Sammie knew, but I had the feeling Gilani meant outsiders to law enforcement. I uncrossed my ankles and sat taller. Now was the time. "I'll admit I did tell one of the people who work for me, Em Gregory." I didn't let him know that she'd confessed to telling *Crime Man*. I reckoned I'd leave that decision to Em for when she was ready. And if she didn't, then at some point I would have to tell.

"I see." The chief set his hands on the desk and made a steeple with his fingers. He lowered his head and touched his forehead to his hands. "I'll have to call her in to speak with her also." He raised his head and stared at me, seated across from him. "But don't tell her I'm going to do that."

Had he thought Em might refuse to come in, or that she would flee the city to avoid speaking to him? "I won't, sir. You have my word," I said.

"I know I do. That's what I've always liked about you, Evan. I feel I can trust you. I hope I'm still right."

"You can. I'd feel terrible if I disappointed you. I consider you a friend."

"And I consider you the same, and while I don't like that you told Em, it would be two-faced of me to hold it against you, considering that I broke the rules by telling you in the first place."

Gilani didn't bring up my birth name, although I didn't get the impression that he was intolerant, rather I sensed he was quietly aware of the fact and it was the unspoken question in the room, a question he didn't plan on asking.

"Are you going to ask me to step down?" I said.

The chief shook his head.

"You're going to *tell* me to step down?" I asked.

"Not at this time, but now that I know you disclosed confidential information to Ms.

Gregory, information you weren't authorized to have told, or even authorized to have known, I will have to recommend that the city suspend you, temporarily, so pay won't be an issue. As for Ms. Gregory, I'll know more after I've spoken with her." He paused. "It doesn't matter if you personally didn't give information to that website. Of course, there will be repercussions for me as well, given that I've admitted to discussing undisclosed evidence in the case with someone outside the force. You'll also have to attend a hearing."

"All right," I said, and swallowed air. "I'm sorry how this has affected you."

The chief gave me a rare smile. "It's affected you more, and I'm truly sorry about that. I wouldn't want you to think we're—I'm—blaming you because . . ."

Even if others inside law enforcement knew enough details about the recent murders to sell them to *Crime Man*, I was an outsider and not given the same professional courtesy.

"I don't think you are, sir," I said. "I consider who I am to be a fact, not an issue."

"Right, then. The city has support staff, counselors and the like, on hand if you feel the need to talk to someone during your time off—"

I hurried to cut him short. "I won't need to do that."

"All right, but it's a city requirement that I let employees know that."

"I understand. I don't need anything like that." I tried to laugh it off but that appeared to escalate the chief's concern that I talk with someone.

He sat back into his chair and furrowed his brow. "Are you going home after our meeting?"

"I don't plan on jumping off a bridge, if that's what you mean," I said.

Gilani shook his head and gave me a reluctant smile. "Take care of yourself, all right? Someone from my office will be in touch about the date of the hearing."

"When will it be?" I stood up and put my jacket on.

"It should happen within a week from today. Mine's before yours."

"I'm sorry, chief." I genuinely was.

He nodded. "I'll have someone call you to let know."

"Thanks."

I got to the door and opened it, but before I could leave, Gilani said from his desk, "Evan?"

I stopped and turned to look at him. "Something else on your mind, chief?"

He hadn't mentioned Alice in our meeting, but from his body language, that was what he wanted to ask me at that moment. "No. I'll have someone call you with the date of the hearing. Take care of yourself."

"I can't say I'll look forward to that call, but I appreciate your faith in me." I didn't mention Alice either. I figured Gilani had enough resources at his disposal to research my mother if he wanted.

Outside city hall I blended into the large number of people walking on the sidewalk and I texted Josh before I got a taxi back to the apartment. I wanted to let Josh know that he would be heading the entire unit by himself until further notice and that Em and I were out, for now.

*Call the real chief with any questions*, I wrote. *I'm not authorized to answer them for the time being.*

*Sorry to hear that. You'll always be our chief*, was his reply.

Tears burned at the corners of my eyes and welled up. In the meantime I poked around the web and found out that the *Crime Man* post had indeed gone viral and people were making death threats against me online, but there was support for me too. I stopped looking, and my fingers shook as I texted Josh back thanks. Then I looked for a cab.

Although I wasn't a suspect at the moment, there wasn't anything preventing me from becoming one eventually. I knew what I had to do before that could happen. I had to return to Freedom Village and see my mother.

# Chapter 8

"I can't believe you didn't tell Gilani what Em did," Sammie said to me that night. "If she doesn't confess to him soon, then I'll tell him. And you can't leave, not like this. It's crucial that you stick around to fight this thing and not look like you're running away, which you are right now. What about the hearing, Evan, how are you going to attend that if you're in another state, tell me?"

I packed a suitcase on our bed with my back facing her. Sammie grabbed my arm and turned me around so I'd look at her.

"I don't know," I said. "What I do know is that if I don't leave now to figure this thing out, I could be in a whole lot more trouble later on. It's worth the risk. It's happening again, and my mother is locked away so it isn't her, and this time it's happening because of me, someone is killing to get to me. I need to know who."

She held me. "I can't believe this is happening to us. How could this have happened? And I could kill Em, I really could," Sammie said.

I rubbed away her tears. "No, you couldn't."

"Why?"

"Because you're a decent person."

"Let me come with you." She gripped my arms. "I can take the time off from work. We can drive there together."

"I need to do this on my own. It's hard to explain but that's what I need. Besides, Paige needs someone to stay with her and make sure she's doing all right." I disentangled myself from Sammie's embrace to resume my packing.

"Paige can come with us. We'll bring her along. She enjoys car trips. The car needs gas. Why don't I go and fill it up and then I'll return to pack, does that sound good? Do you want to leave tonight or tomorrow morning?" She spoke as though she hadn't heard me.

"Sammie, I need to do this alone, I'm sorry."

"I'm not going to say I'm okay with that."

"I'm leaving tomorrow morning. I can take a bus if you want me to leave the car here with you so you'll have it."

"I want you to take the car."

"I'm not sure I would feel safe if you're here without a car. What if you need to take Paige to the vet's?"

"We'll be fine. I can carry her there if that happens, which I hope it doesn't, and most taxis accept small dogs these days. I want you to take the car. We hardly use the car here. Your trip will be more comfortable if you do take it. You said once how rural your hometown is. How will you get around when you're there if you don't have a car?"

I closed my suitcase. "So, you're okay with this, after all, with me leaving?"

She went into the bathroom and came out with my toiletries, handing them to me. "No, but I know how stubborn you are and that you'll leave no matter what I say, so I don't have a choice, do I?"

I opened my bag and struggled to find room for what she'd handed me. "Thanks for remembering these. How would I survive without you?" I gave her a smile.

Sammie didn't return my gesture. "You're so stubborn, I'm really not sure how you *would* survive. You have to call me when you arrive so that I know you made it there safely. What's the name of the hotel where you'll be staying?"

"I'm not sure where I'll be. I don't have a reservation with any place."

"Are you saying your plan is that you're going to pull into some place when you get there and hope they'll have a room available for you?"

"Something like that." I closed my suitcase and picked it up to set by the front door to take with me when I left in the morning.

Sammie took my suitcase from my hands. "What if there aren't any free rooms? What will you do then, sleep in the car?"

"Oh, they'll be plenty of vacant rooms. You know, Freedom's only got one hotel. 'Least they did the last time I was there."

"One hotel? No, I didn't know that," Sammie said. "One hotel. What makes you think they'll have rooms available?"

"We've never visited my hometown, so you wouldn't know this, but no one goes there. It's the kind of place people leave; they don't go there for a visit."

"And when were *you* there last, when you were in high school? Places change. For all you know it might be a very popular place to visit now and you'll end up sleeping in the car. It isn't summer anymore. You'll be cold at night."

"I doubt I won't find a room."

"You're so confident sometimes, I could just kill you." Sammie gave a wry chuckle.

"You can kill me, but don't kill Em." I grinned at her.

"Very funny. I want you to call me whenever you stop and when you get there. I need to hear how you're doing. I also need you to ask how I'm doing, for my sake. Are you leaving early in the morning? I want to say goodbye before you go."

"I won't leave without giving you, and heck, maybe even Paige, a goodbye kiss. Now, can I have my suitcase?" I held out my hand.

She held the suitcase behind her, out of my reach. "Not so fast."

"What, why?— "

Sammie gave me a dark, half-lidded gaze and set the suitcase on the rug in our bedroom and pulled me down onto the unmade bed with her. She pressed me onto the bed with her body and unbuttoned my shirt.

*

I'd intended to wake up before Sammie and quietly get ready, then rouse her to take Paige for a walk together so I could say goodbye to both of them properly. But I awoke to Sammie resting on her side, halfway under the covers, watching me.

"Good morning," I said.

She put her arm over mine when I started to sit up. "Please don't do this," she said.

I rolled on my side to face her again. "After we talked about it last night, I thought that you had accepted my decision."

"I wasn't thinking clearly. There was a lot going on at the time. I thought about it some more during the night. I hardly slept, I was thinking about it so much."

I had felt her moving next to me in the night. "I know, I heard you tossing and turning during the night."

The bed smelled of Sammie's perfume. I attempted a smile but stopped when I noticed something had wet the area of the sheet by my hand—Sammie's tears. She blinked her eyes to prevent more from falling. I leaned toward her to dry her eyes, and she buried her face in my hand. I made strokes on her soft cheekbone. "I won't be gone forever," I said.

"I can come with you. Paige and me, we both can."

"It'll be too hard for her on the road. And I'm so sorry, darling, but I need to do this alone. Can you understand that?" I gently touched her face.

"I've never visited your hometown once even though it's only a few hours away," Sammie said. "Do you not want me to be around that part of your life, is that it?"

"No, you don't understand. They don't know me as Evan there. No one from back there knows I'm transitioning. Them, that place, isn't my life anymore, and there are good reasons for that."

Sammie's need to protect me came through her voice. "Then you'll need me there to be with you, to support you. You know how people can be, I don't want you getting hurt."

"They can't hurt me. I won't let them. They might've known me as having the name Evelyn but I've always been Evan. Just because my name changed, doesn't mean my soul has. I'm as tough as ever." I didn't know whether I spoke the words to comfort Sammie or myself. "I haven't decided whether I'll even bring up Evelyn," I said.

"You're right, they don't need to know. Maybe you shouldn't bring up the other name. After all, you *are* Evan."

"I'm not going to hide if I don't have to," I said. "I've worked hard to accept who I am, and I'm not going to pretend to be someone else so others will feel more comfortable. Fuck that. I still have the same soul."

"I know, but people can be awful sometimes."

I knew all too well. And Sammie did, too. I'd had people scream in my face that I was a freak and we'd had them spit at us. Someone once had thrown a cup of hot coffee at us when Sammie and I were walking home from brunch, right there in our home city, because they thought we looked 'funny.'

"Yes, but we can't let them stop us from living our lives," I said.

I sat up and made another attempt to get out of bed. Sammie held onto my shoulder and wouldn't let go. Paige, who was still sleeping, stirred at our feet. She lifted her small head to peer at us.

"Sammie," I said, touching her hand. "You have to let me go. I'll call and text, and I want to hear from you, too, okay? Get in touch whenever you want and I'll answer. I'm going no matter what, and I don't want to leave on a bad note."

"You're running from me?"

"I'm not running from you but, rather, to solve something."

"Then why are you running from this, from what's happened—happening— to you?" she asked.

"It's affected you, too," I reminded her.

She looked away from me and didn't seem to want to confront the pain the situation had caused her. "What do you plan to do there? How do you think visiting there is going to stop what's happening here? It's not your fault, Evan. You have to move on from what your mother did. She's not you. You're a completely different person than her."

I turned away from her. "I'm not running from anything, I'm running to find answers."

Sammie glanced at me and pried her fingers off me one by one. She sat up, hugging her knees under the covers. The position made her look young and fragile. Paige waddled on her short legs over to Sammie's side of the bed and stopped in front of her, looking at Sammie and then at me. I sat on the edge of the bed with my feet touching the floor. Sammie got up and Paige followed her into the bathroom. Sammie slammed the door shut and I rose to make coffee for us.

I left the apartment two hours later, after showering, dressing, and waiting for Sammie to return from walking Paige—I hadn't been invited—so that I could say goodbye to them. Sammie gave me her cheek and wouldn't let me kiss her goodbye on the lips.

I sighed and carried my suitcase with me to the garage where we'd parked our car, around the corner from our building. There was a train service to Freedom Village and its surrounding areas but I wanted to get there as fast as possible.

Having packed light, I could easily carry what I had with me as I walked to the garage. It turned out Sammie and I had forgot to pay our monthly bill for the garage, and after I got that matter sorted, put my suitcase in the trunk, and finally started the car, I needed to stop for gas straight after leaving the garage.

I left Seven Sisters later than I'd desired, but I avoided the morning commuter traffic and headed out of the city with a full tank of gas. I'd checked my phone at the gas station and sent Sammie a text to let her know I was only then departing. I deleted the numerous apology texts from Em—Gilani had asked me not to communicate with her—and waited for Sammie to write back, but she never did.

*

I used the GPS on my phone to navigate my unremarkable journey to Freedom Village. Along the way I stopped for coffee at a roadside café, a rundown place off a quiet dirt road surrounded by cornfields that swayed in whichever direction the wind took them. Before I got out of the car, I saw that Sammie had written me back. My phone was also inundated with requests for interviews.

Somehow journalists had obtained my number. I deleted them and read Sammie's message.

*Have a safe trip. Don't forget to keep in touch.*

I smiled knowing Sammie and I were on good terms once again. I quickly wrote back that I loved her.

I shut off the engine, left my sunglasses on, and went inside. The other patrons didn't so much as turn my way, and I felt safe enough to remove my glasses for now. The people who sat on the red vinyl stools at the coffee counter looked like members of the local farming community on their lunch breaks.

Before stepping inside, I'd planned to get a cup of coffee to go, but once there and smelling the delicious aromas, I sat on the only free stool at the counter, the vinyl seat still warm from the last occupant. I grabbed the stained menu that was already on the counter when I sat. A woman a few stools down from me lit a cigarette and shook the ashes onto her finished plate, and nobody acted as though she couldn't.

I ordered a grilled cheese sandwich and a cup of coffee from a waitress wearing a yellow apron. I wasn't a local resident, but no one seemed to particularly pay attention to me, other than a few glances my way. They drank their coffee, ate, and chatted among themselves. I wondered if strangers passed through there often given the café's location close to a road that was an offshoot of the main highway. I discreetly downed my pills with my coffee. My doctor had switched me over to a pill form of testosterone because the injectable kind hadn't agreed with me.

The waitress, a pretty young blonde with her nails painted red, set my wonderfully greasy sandwich on a plate on the counter. She smiled warmly.

"Do you know how many miles it is to Lamont?" I asked. Lamont was the closest city to Freedom Village and a destination point most people in those parts would have known about. I could have just as easily checked the route on my phone, but travelling in the car had made me lonely and looking for a chat with someone approachable. So I took a risk and started a conversation with her.

"I'd say you're about sixty miles from there," she said, refilling my coffee with a grin. A streak of red lipstick stained her gleaming white teeth.

"Thanks." I'd already driven close to seventy miles.

"Are you going there for business? Or maybe visiting family? Most folks who stop in here on their way to Lamont are traveling for business, but you don't look like a businessman." She looked me over carefully from behind the serving counter. I wore jeans and a long-sleeve shirt. She spoke in a soft drawl, her body language a little too welcoming, and her blue eyes shiny with interest.

Even if I hadn't had Sammie, the server was too young for me to have been interested in her, but I said in a polite tone, "Business, even if I don't dress the part." I grinned. Then I uttered the first career that came to my mind, "I'm a journalist." Because I'd decided in the car that was how I'd get access to my mother in the correctional facility. I'd say I wanted to interview her for an article I was writing. But I'd need someone like Detective Mack, who, according to a Google search, was still very much alive and still a detective, to get me through the gates.

"Like for a newspaper?" the waitress asked. She seemed vaguely impressed. I could tell she stood on her toes to get a better look at me.

I nodded, not wanting to give too much away, like my home city. I'd been tempted to look at social media to see how far the *Crime Man* story had disseminated since I last checked, but the potential emotional setback of that prevented me from venturing to what could be dark places.

The waitress didn't ask me which newspaper. "Are you staying around here overnight?" Her interest in me deepened her voice.

I loved Sammie and didn't want this girl to get the wrong idea. "No, I'm passing through," I bluntly said. "Soon as I leave here, I'm back on the road."

"Oh." The waitress frowned. Then she seemed to remember I could be leaving her a tip. Or not. "Enjoy your lunch and have a safe trip,

Mr. Journalist," she said. Flirting until the very last moment, she beamed at me, and I avoided returning her gaze but watched her heading for another customer farther down the counter.

I finished, paid the bill and did leave her a generous tip, and also got a large cup of coffee to go. I stopped frequently along the way to text Sammie and to get more coffee, and, then, dinner.

# Chapter 9

I made it into Freedom Village around 10:30 that night, and I figured I had less than an hour to check into the town's sole hotel. Despite gentrification in areas nearby, the town hadn't changed much since I'd last been there almost twenty years ago. I quickly found the hotel, which *had* been renovated into a quaint chalet style building that spread out behind the main street, tucked between the hardware store and the pharmacy, and across the street from the butcher's. I drove around the corner and pulled into the nearly filled parking lot at the rear of the building. Perhaps I'd underestimated the popularity of the hotel, and of the town.

In case they hadn't a room available and I'd have to spend the remainder of my night searching for lodgings on the outskirts of town, I left my suitcase in the car. Sammie would have said, I told you so. I texted her as I walked to the front entrance and into the softly lit lobby, letting her know I'd arrived safely and to see how she was, and how Paige was.

The lobby was painted a neutral tone and resplendent with vases of long-stemmed orange and white flowers. A dark-haired woman at the front desk, who was around my age and wore a white dress shirt and a slender gold necklace that glittered faintly in the light, greeted me with, "Hello."

The burnished floorboards squeaked as I approached her. A laughing couple exited the one elevator in the lobby and walked past me at the door, out into the night, and I smelled the woman's spicy perfume.

"Welcome to the Freedom Lodge, sir," the woman at the desk said. "Do you have a reservation?"

"Not exactly. I was hoping you'd be able to squeeze me in somewhere, but now that I've arrived, I'm wondering if I should've planned ahead." I tried to persuade her with a smile.

I didn't want to begin a discussion with her about how surprised I'd been to find the lodge overflowing with business, in contrast to my youth, because I didn't need her asking questions about my identity. I didn't need everyone in town knowing that Alice Lane's kid was back home; everyone, because if I told the front desk attendant it was inevitable she'd tell someone else, and so on.

She squinted down at the computer screen and typed something on her keyboard. "Let me see. We are crowded."

I waited for her to tell me no.

Then she said, "But I do have a small room available, if that'd work for you. It's *very* small." She smiled warmly, and I recognized her as someone I'd known in high school, someone I had hung around with a little, Rebecca—Becky—and I couldn't recall her surname. She didn't seem to recognize me, though.

"Yes, that's fine. Anything will work." I could waste hours if I had to seek out accommodations outside the town. Growing up, there hadn't been places to stay outside of Freedom, and driving up there I hadn't seen that any new hotels had been constructed.

"I'll get you checked in, then." She typed on her keyboard.

I'd had top surgery but not bottom, and I had the scars to prove it. The process of changing my legal name hadn't been simple, but I'd made it happen with the help of my physician and an understanding lawyer Sammie knew through her work. My identification, including my credit cards, had me as male. Regardless, I paid for the room with the cash I got before I left Seven Sisters, and I gave the woman at the desk a different last name, Samuels, a play on Sammie's name.

"Do you know where I could get breakfast around here tomorrow?" I considered asking her whether the diner was still there but that would have revealed too much. "Is there a restaurant here in the lodge?"

She stopped typing. "I'm afraid not, about a restaurant being here, that is. I do know the owner is considering opening one here in the lodge. We do offer a continental breakfast every morning in the lounge. I recommend the diner for other meals."

"The diner by the library?" I said.

"Yes. How did you know?" Her smile widened. "Have you visited before? Or are you from around here?" Now, her face glowed with curiosity.

I thought of something fast to say. "No, I passed by it on my drive into town."

"Oh." After a moment of silence she said, "It's the best place to get breakfast around here. Everything's homemade, and the new chef there, well, he goes beyond the usual fare. They have pancakes but with a gourmet twist."

"Sounds great. I'll have to try it in the morning sometime. Do they serve anything that's vegetarian?"

"I think so." I sensed she wanted to ask me more about that but held back. "Tell them Tawny sent you and they'll give you a discount." She pointed to her nametag.

The writing was very small and I had to squint to read it. She had the palest skin even on her hands. I watched her very white throat as she talked. So I'd been wrong about her name. But I'd known her in high school. She was one of the girls in our school who had a thing for Ben. A lot of years had passed since then, but I remembered Tawny had stopped being friendly to me after my mother's arrest, which wasn't entirely heartbreaking because most of my other classmates had acted the same way. The large number who had been cruel to me? *That* had been heartbreaking. I was relieved she wouldn't know who I was, and I had no intention of telling her.

"The chef's my boyfriend," Tawny spoke as though she was telling me a secret.

"When I stop in there, I'll let them know you told me to mention you," I said to end the conversation.

The moment lingered as we smiled at each other. I got a text from Sammie about Paige, who hadn't eaten her dinner. My mood sank. I frowned down at my phone.

"Is everything all right?" Tawny asked, concern darkening her gaze.

I replied, to hurry things along and get back on track, "I'm not sure how many days I'll be here."

That seemed to veer her off course. "Oh. Do you have any idea? Are you here to tour the vineyards, or are you visiting someone, or—"

I hadn't known Freedom had vineyards. Times had changed. I gave her the safest answer. "I'm here on business. I'm a writer." I spoke before she could ask me what kind of business.

"So, you aren't here for the winemaker convention? Or are you writing about that? That's why we're so crowded—it's normally not like this here. Even being one of the very few hotels in the area, we're lucky if we get enough business at peak season to pay *some* of our yearly costs."

I ignored her question about whether I was covering the wine convention and smiled. "About how long I'll be staying, could we work something out, perhaps I could let you know the day before I plan to leave?"

She bit her lower lip. "I'm sorry but we don't really do that. I'd ask my manager but he already left for the day." She peered at the clock behind her. "My shift's done in a few minutes. Then the night desk guy comes on. He's not supposed to check people in, unless he really has to. But I guess what you asked would be okay. I'll leave a note for the manager for when he comes here in the morning."

"Great. Thanks, Tawny."

She grinned at my using her name. "You're in room 11, on the second floor," she said. "It's right after you get off the elevator." She handed me the key to my room. "We don't have electronic key cards, sorry. You're lucky, you just made check-in time. Check out is at eleven, that's *eleven in the morning*, but we don't know how many days you'll be staying . . ." She beamed. "Do you need someone to help you with your luggage? Everyone's gone home for the night but I could help you."

"That's all right, I only have one bag."

"Okay, then. Enjoy your stay."

I pocketed my key and went to the parking lot to retrieve my suitcase from the car. I paused to text Sammie.

A few minutes later, I saw Tawny leaving work for the evening. I'd parked next to her. I waved to her and told her to have a safe drive home.

"If you find you need anything, Kurt, the night desk guy, will be right downstairs," Tawny said. "Normally, I don't leave before he gets here but he let me know he's running a little late. I feel safe getting into my car with you here in the parking lot. It's so dark, you never know who's going to be waiting out here. My boyfriend likes me to text him as soon as I lock my car door. We have plans for tonight—my boyfriend and I—so I need to get home. Romantic plans." She blushed. "He was away supporting his father during a medical crisis and he returned this afternoon. I haven't seen him yet. I wanted to go with him to see his family but there was no one to fill in for me at work."

"Have fun," I said. Then I asked, "The town is dangerous at night?" Had something changed in the past twenty years?

"No, but you never know, right? Maybe my boyfriend and I have seen too many scary movies." She laughed. "Between you and me, the police caught a serial killer here, but that was years ago. I was friends with her daughter—the serial killer, that is, was a woman. Management asks us not to tell guests *that* part of the town's history but you seem trustworthy enough. Please don't tell anyone I said anything to you. Lots of people who visit here ask the locals about it."

"What happened to her daughter after?" I'd asked Tawny, to see if she cared what had happened to me.

She shrugged. "I'm not sure. I hope she's okay."

I was at a loss for words because that wasn't what I'd expected.

Before I departed Seven Sisters, I'd looked at the Freedom Village town website and found that Detective Mack still worked on the town police force. Right then would have been an ideal time to bring up Mack to a longstanding resident like Tawny, and ask if he still lived in the same house. Detective Mack had been a fixture in the town. I'd checked online and he wasn't listed in a phonebook. I assumed that was because of his work. "You have my word I won't tell," I said quietly, and closed the car trunk.

"You're a nice guy, good-looking. Do you have a wife back at home? I would think so, a catch like you. I love the name of your home city." She spoke like she was sighing, "Seven Sisters."

She had taken down my home address when I registered at the front desk. "I have a girlfriend," I said after a moment.

"She's a lucky woman." Tawny stood with her car door open and I wondered what kept her from going inside. "You look a little familiar. I thought so when you first came into the lobby but didn't want to be rude and ask you right when you came in. Have we met before?" She looked at me closely.

"I don't believe we have. In fact, this is my first time in the town." The lie burned in my mouth when I spoke it. She had warm eyes and I wanted to trust her, but I knew I couldn't. "So I don't see how we could have met before." She leaned against her car door, and I moved to hold it open for her so she'd be on her way.

"I could've sworn." Tawny kept staring at me as though she didn't believe my answer.

"You must be mistaken because I know I've never met you." I'd raised my voice without realizing it, and regretted it afterward. Tawny might have been inquisitive but she'd done nothing to deserve my temper.

"Okay, then. I'm sorry. I must be wrong," she said softly.

A moment passed before she got into her car, and I considered telling her I'd known her in high school.

"Tawny," I said, my tone gentler.

She waited for me to continue.

"Have a good night," I said.

She shut her door and through the car window I saw her texting her boyfriend.

I carried my suitcase into the quiet lobby, and no one had taken Tawny's place at the desk. It seemed the other guests had turned in for the night or were still out. I took the elevator up to the second floor and padded down the carpeted hall to my room.

I hadn't seen any of the other rooms in the lodge, but going on its size alone, room 11 had to have been the tiniest there. The room had a claustrophobic ambiance; a small bed pushed against the wall to accommodate a large television set, and a writing desk and chair in front of a window overlooking the parking lot. I couldn't see the main street, or the rest of the town for that matter, from the room, but it would do for my purposes.

There I was, back to where my old life had ended and my new one began. I texted Sammie to let her know I'd made it up to my room and to check on Paige's status. Sammie wrote, telling me to get some rest and that, no, the dog hadn't eaten. I gave her the name of the hotel again and asked if there were any reporters outside our building.

*A few. But I chased them away.*

I laughed only a little because I knew Sammie was serious.

*

In the morning I woke up late and peered down at the parking lot from my room window. The number of cars had thinned out as people had left the hotel for their day at the wine conference or wherever.

There were packs of instant coffee in the room but no means to boil water. I couldn't get the tap water hot enough, so rather than drink the watery muck I'd created, after I'd showered and dressed, I started out to the diner.

As one of the few guests who hadn't already left for the day, I stood out in the lobby. I waved to the older man at the front desk, someone less pleasant to look at than the petite, green-eyed Tawny.

"Are you the gentleman in room 11?" he asked before I could walk outside.

"I am. How'd you know?" I forced a smile.

"I'm the lodge's manager. Tawny left me a note about your stay, with a description of your looks. She was um . . . quite detailed about how handsome you are." He cleared his throat.

Heat imbued my face. "Yes, she mentioned she would leave a note for you. She was very helpful."

"I'm delighted to hear that. She is one of our best employees."

"That makes sense, then."

"I beg your pardon?"

"That she gave me good service is what I meant." After I spoke, that sounded a bit lewd and so I said quickly, "Nice to see you. I best be on my way—"

"Very good, sir." His smile weakened. "When you have an idea of how long you'll be staying, we're here to help." The manager handed me his business card and I politely put it in my pocket. "We want you to feel at home so there's no rush, but we'll need to know at some point." He emphasized the second half of the sentence, so I knew he was serious.

Their general willingness to accommodate me caught me by surprise. I hadn't experienced small town hospitality in a while. But as a man, I'd never liked how people tended to treat me better than Sammie, a woman.

"Off to spend the day in the town?" he asked. "Tawny mentioned you were here on business, that you're a writer?"

"I'll probably get some breakfast. I had a late start to the day." I laughed it off. "I'm a newspaper writer."

"Which one? I'm an avid reader. Perhaps I've read something you've written. What brings you to Freedom Village, a story? Are you covering the winemakers' convention? If so, you're a little late this morning, if you don't mind my saying. They've already started for the day." He looked at his wristwatch, and his questions seemed genuine.

I weighed my answers. I could tell him I wrote freelance for a few places, or I could name a specific newspaper and risk him looking into me. I could say I planned to visit the local women's prison for research for a story or for a book I was writing.

Instead I said, "I'm writing a story on the tourism industry," and I didn't name an employer. The idea sounded ludicrous to my ears because Freedom wasn't exactly a flourishing destination, but it worked.

The guy's mouth practically hung open. "Will you be writing about the lodge?" he asked.

"I just might be. Actually, I wanted to get some work done while I was here, but there isn't much space in my room." It wouldn't hurt to use his concern to my advantage.

He straightened his necktie, suddenly seeming to care what I thought of his appearance, and the lodge's, for that matter. "Let me see what can be done about that. I'm sure I can get you a better room, sir." He spoke fast, and grinned widely, revealing slightly stained teeth.

"I thought there were none available?" I knew what he was getting at but for the sake of politeness wanted to seem flummoxed.

"It's no problem, we'll get you into a better room. Would you like us to move your luggage for you while you're out? I'll give you your new room number and your key upon your return."

"How . . ." Did I want them in my room?

He stepped out and around the counter, toward me. "It's no trouble at all, sir," he said. "Would you like us to move your things for you? What would be most convenient for you?"

I didn't have anything in my room that could reveal my relation to Alice Lane. "That would be terrific, thanks."

"Wonderful, sir. And if you find you need anything, *anything*, during your stay here with us, however long it is—and please don't feel rushed to give us your check-out date—do not hesitate to contact me. There's a phone number and an email contact on the back of the card I gave you." He pointed them out.

In turn, I sensed he'd expect the lodge to get a decent mention in my 'story.' If they followed up after I left, I would have to tell them the newspaper decided not to run the article after all. I expected they'd be disappointed or pissed off, both probably.

"Do you need a suggestion for where to get breakfast?" he asked.

"Tawny recommended the diner."

"A great choice." He smiled. "Do you have directions?"

"Yes, she gave them to me last night," I lied.

"Wonderful. Enjoy your meal. We'll have your room all sorted out for your return."

I texted Sammie as I walked to the diner. We'd discussed my plans before I left Seven Sisters, but she didn't know that I intended to visit my mother in prison nearby under the guise of a journalist covering a story. The less Sammie knew, the better, for her sake. I didn't want her to come under scrutiny by the law if my plan backfired.

I didn't plan to reconnect with any old friends while in town. I intended to seek out Detective Mack and get a prison visit pass through him. Mack was the one person in law enforcement I felt would help me if he could. Mack had said I should feel free to come to him if I ever needed anything and that he wanted to help me. Although we'd lost touch over the years and he hadn't known about my transition, I expected his offer would still stand. Getting his support would be the quickest way to see Alice and get some answers, and then return to Seven Sisters to sort out the messes that I'd left at work and at home. I also felt that once I revealed to Mack that I'd begun my transition, he wouldn't spread it all over the town.

Someone from city hall in Seven Sisters had called me and left a message for a hearing I knew I wouldn't attend. Missing my hearing with my superiors had crossed my mind more than a few times as, at the very least, having the potential to taint my reputation. Or get me fired. But I needed to be here in Freedom Village, finding answers.

Some of the town's shopfronts had been remodeled or at least repainted in my long absence. While Freedom might never succeed as a true tourist destination, the village had overhauled itself over the years to make it more appealing. Yet, if it wasn't for the influx of wineries in the surrounding area, something I wasn't aware of until Tawny mentioned them, I suspected the town would have gone to shambles during the harsh economic times of years past.

The village was in a valley, and in the distance I could see fields of grapevines and the white rooftops of processing buildings. The winemakers were probably getting what they could out of the end of the season. Behind the thriving vineyards loomed the old prison: three multi-story, institutional, gray structures—one of which housed my mother—separated by recreational, small, cement courtyards, also bleak and gray. A very high barbed-wire fence outlined the entire property. The village couldn't escape how close it was to the crumbling prison. My mother had liked to garden. How could she have found any solace in the weed-filled prison yard?

But I had other things on my mind that day, like whether Ben would have accepted me as Evan. He'd been okay with me liking women, but would he have been all right with me being Evan and liking women?

Ben had been an only child, like me. Slim, with blond hair and golden skin, Ben was handsome, and into his garage rock band more than school sports. Girls had loved him despite him being a little shorter than most young men his age, and he couldn't get enough of them. Ben had been aware I loved girls, too, and accepted that part of me. He was the only person close to me who knew. Kids in our high school would whisper in the halls that we were more than best friends—since practically birth—and Ben had let them believe we were more, to protect me. He knew not everyone would be as accepting of me as him. Some of the girlfriends he had in high school viewed me as a threat to their relationships with him, and we'd laugh about the misunderstanding, but I never lost Ben's friendship. Until Alice.

A psychological profile on my mother? Why did she murder Ben and those boys? I'd never looked into most of the articles, books, or research papers that had been written about her. But I did ask Detective Mack directly why she'd done those crimes. Compulsion, he'd said. And psychosis. But there were few clues in her life or her childhood that would have predicted that. As far as I saw, she'd led a relatively normal existence with me, and her childhood had been ordinary with the rare dash of minor setbacks that everyone experiences at some point in their life. In other words, she hadn't been abused or neglected in any sense of the word.

At the time, Mack's diagnosis of my mother, given to him by her prison therapist, had sounded like bullshit to me. My mother was a compulsive killer, Mack had explained. Once she'd murdered Ben she felt compelled to kill another young man, and so on. She hadn't harbored an intense dislike toward men, and that fell along the lines of what I recalled growing up. She wasn't a hateful person; she was an ill person.

Ben had visited our home as a guest over the years and became a fixture in the household I'd shared with my mother. There'd been no inkling that she would someday kill him. Alice had suffered from depression on and off her whole life but no one in the town had seen the murders coming. She'd been an ordinary woman from a respectable family until the confession was signed and the charges were brought against her. Of course, there had been that business of her husband packing up and leaving when their child was small, and no one knew what ever became of him. Clayton Lane was his name. She'd kept his last name after he left, and I'd inherited it, too. Alice hadn't remarried after he exited our family but she had dated.

I'd thought about visiting Ben's parents, William and Susanna Palmer, when I was in town, if they were still around, but then I'd either have to give them my birth name or tell them I was a journalist visiting Freedom Village for a story about their son, but it didn't feel right to tell them I was a journalist. Also, they might not have wanted to speak with a reporter and lose their sacred privacy.

Even during Alice's trial, Ben's parents had never taken their anger toward her out on me. They seemed to have felt sorry for me because of my mother, not hate me. The parents, siblings, and general relatives of Alice's other victims never spoke to me. Their long, hard stares were enough to convey the abhorrence for my mother that they must have lived with every day, and their hatred of me, a blood and flesh representation of her existence. I hadn't faulted them. I didn't speak at Alice's trial but I'd attended briefly. I couldn't bear being there to see the thing play out in its entirety.

I paused in front of a café Tawny hadn't mentioned, a place I didn't recognize, and I read the menu posted in the window. Pretty overpriced considering Freedom was in the sticks, but they claimed to have the best coffee within a hundred miles. I'd had my fill of coffee on the drive up there.

Going with my original choice of eating at the diner, I strode in that direction, a few blocks north of the café. An older woman walked out of the library adjacent to the diner and said hello to me in the way one greets strangers. I ducked my head a little lower anyway, and I nodded at her as I passed by.

I stared through the diner's many windows at the few people sitting at the counter, their backsides hanging off the stools, and at the empty checkered tables in the background with a chair or two at each. Every table had a tall daisy in a clear vase. The diner appeared to be renovated since I'd left the town in an attempt to give it a trendier atmosphere. Since Tawny had recommended the place and she'd disclosed something about her boyfriend having trained at a fancy culinary institute, I reckoned I'd give it a try.

I had a late breakfast at the diner, and when I returned to the lodge, they had moved me into a large room on the top floor, with an expansive view of the vineyards. I spent the afternoon in my room except for when I ventured outside to get lunch at the same diner, writing down questions to ask Alice once I could see her.

I'd been chatted up by my loquacious server at the diner my second time there, once I let her know that no, I wasn't there for the convention, and gave her my journalist story. She'd promised to reveal to no less than the entire town that a journalist would be writing a travel story about their little village. Then I'd taken a chance and asked her if a detective with the name Mack lived in the town, and I hadn't been able to fool her about why I was asking.

"You want to know about Alice Lane, don't you, for your story?" she'd said. "Does something like that belong in the kind of story you're writing?" Suddenly, she'd seemed less friendly, as if she didn't approve of me portraying her town in anything less than a positive light.

When I pressed her, she'd reluctantly said, "In his younger years, Mack was the one who broke that case. He comes in here once in a while."

"I might mention the Lane case a little at the beginning of my article but it's certainly not the focus," I'd said to pacify her.

I hadn't wanted her asking me additional questions so I didn't bring up whether Mack lived at the residence I'd known as a teenager.

# Chapter 10

There was the off chance he worked nights, but that early evening I left my room at the lodge and headed to what I'd known as Mack's house, figuring he'd be home by then. I planned to grab a meal in the town after, and would most likely end up at the diner again. Perhaps Mack would join me.

When I'd known Mack he'd lived away from the more crowded main section of town, behind the railroad tracks. I took a chance and strode in that direction from the lodge.

Cars and trucks roared past me as I waited to cross the busy road leading to the outskirts. Every so often I could decipher a vehicle's blurred license plate. There were a lot of out-of-state places. People heading back to the lodge from that wine convention? I turned my gaze from the burning glare of headlights. Even after all the years that had passed, the town hadn't installed crossing lights.

I waited for a break in the heavy stream of traffic to sprint across the road. Most people in these parts drove to places instead of walking, even if they didn't have to travel very far. I was the sole pedestrian out on the street that evening but instinctively felt safer there, in a small town.

The sidewalk ended a few steps from the silhouette of what had been Mack's house, and what I hoped still was. I saw the faint outline of an unlit streetlamp in the dark and walked close enough to notice that the glass part of the structure was cracked. The lamp had always shone brightly when I left Mack's house late at night as a teenager, to better hide from the news reporters, who during the day, waited outside the home I shared with my mother.

I'd wanted to believe in my mother's innocence but her confession had me feeling helpless. To some people, her confession had made me guilty by association. There was a time when I wanted to confront her outside the courtroom during her sentencing and kill her myself. There was a time when I probably hated her more than the relatives of her victims had. I didn't act on those feelings, though, because that would have made me seem just like her. I never let my mother's actions define who I was. I did spend my twenties trying to convince anyone I met that I was a good person.

I had no plans to return to my childhood home during my visit, for standing outside, staring, would have brought attention to myself. I assumed whoever bought the house after my mother's family arranged for its sale after her conviction had torn it down and rebuilt.

The farm fields near Mack's house where owned by his neighbor behind him, as I recalled, and had become overgrown, as though the farm had been abandoned since I left Freedom. The area directly around Mack's house appeared well-kept, from what I could tell, as I approached the white structure in the dark.

I stopped in my tracks and contemplated trying Mack at his number—there was a chance he had the same phone number after all those years—to explain who I was before knocking on his front door. He wouldn't remember me as Evan, and the sight of a strange man on his doorstep in the evening might alarm him.

Through the closed curtains, there was a light on inside the home. But when I dialed the number I remembered, no one answered and a machine didn't pick up.

I took my time walking the length of the trimmed lawn, scattered with the red, yellow, and orange fallen leaves of autumn, to the front door. From afar the home had appeared well-maintained but up close it seemed to have deteriorated a little since I saw it last. The once-bright paint had peeled away, and the entrance steps were cracked in numerous places. Mack still hadn't installed a doorbell so I knocked.

Someone peeked through the curtain inside the house.

After a moment the doorknob rattled and a man stepped out of the house. "Who is it?" he said, and I recognized detective Mack's baritone. He kept his hand on his waist where his gun would have been.

I remembered visiting his house during Alice's trial because Mack felt sorry for me, or at least that was what I'd believed. Back then, I started to resent Mack's sympathy, but the years following I came to realize he had been genuinely concerned for me.

I stood on the front steps and I could see Mack clearly in the porch light: tall, with broad shoulders that had begun to stoop over the years, and a bit of a belly where his thin waist had been. Streaks of white stood out on his wavy dark hair. His light eyes in his fuller, tan face—when I'd known Mack, he'd liked to take his boat out on the lake on the weekends—narrowed on me, standing a step lower than him, which made our height difference seem greater.

He waited for me to say who I was, and when I didn't he said, "Can I help you?" He lowered his hand from the area around his waist, as though something about my appearance had disarmed him.

"Detective Mack, it's . . ." For a second I forgot he wouldn't know me. I noticed he didn't have a gun and I wondered if he'd reached for it instinctively.

"Yes?" he said.

"I didn't intend to show up like this," I said. "I tried calling you but no one answered."

"What's the number you have for me? I changed it recently." He rubbed his chin and watched me closely. "Who are you, anyhow?"

I recited the number I had. "I'm . . ."

"That's my old phone number. How did you get that number?" He frowned and crossed his arms in front of his chest. "What's your name? You never answered my question about that."

He was still the astute detective I remembered, but did he still have the big heart he once had?

"You didn't give me a chance to tell you my name," I said. "We've met before, a long time ago. You wouldn't remember me like how I look now." I indicated my body.

Mack backed up on the steps and stood in the doorway, like he thought I might be one of the few criminals the town had, and who he'd arrested, and I was now coming to seek revenge. He leaned against the doorframe and could have easily shut the door in my face and gone inside if he wanted.

"My name's Evan." I reached to shake his hand. "Sorry if my showing up here has frightened you." I smiled at him, which seemed to mollify him enough to accept my handshake.

"Evan, you're right, I don't remember you," he said. "In fact, I don't believe we've ever met. But I'm not scared of you." A spark of challenge shone in his eyes.

"You needn't be. But you might want to watch out for my mother." I attempted a smile.

He gave me a staggered look.

"Detective Mack, it's Evan Lane," I said. "I used to be called Evelyn?"

"You're pulling my leg," he said.

I looked up at him and shook my head.

"Evelyn Lane left this town years ago and no one's heard from her since," Mack said. "What kind of stunt is this? Did you do something to Evelyn, is that what you're trying to tell me?"

I'd known the detective to be a generous man with an open mind, but what if he didn't react the way I wanted him to, and what if, instead of inviting me inside his home, he chased me away? "There's no other way to tell you this," I exhaled. "My birth name was Evelyn, now I'm called Evan to reflect my true gender. Does that make sense to you? You've heard of that these days?"

Mack's eyes enlarged, and his jaw went slack as comprehension washed over his face. He nodded slowly. "I think I know what that is. It has been in the news a lot lately." His voice was softer, as though he was jolted but no longer afraid of my intentions in coming to his house.

With anyone else I would have left it at that but Mack wasn't just anyone. "I needed how I felt on the inside to be reflected on the outside," I said.

"There's no need to explain, I get it." He looked over my clothing, and at me, shivering where I stood. "Nice jacket. Not very warm, though. Do you want to come in?" I'd worn the leather jacket Sammie had given me last Christmas.

"If it's no trouble."

"It isn't. I was in the middle of making myself dinner."

Detective Mack had been a widower when I'd known him years ago. "Sorry to have interrupted you," I said.

"It's no problem." After a pause he asked, "Would you like to join me?"

"Sure, that'd be great."

Mack held open the door for me and I entered the warm house first, a welcome respite from the cold outside. Behind me he shut the door. A short walk down the hallway led to a cozy sitting room with a sleek, wood, coffee table, a plaid couch, and a stuffed reclining chair, also plaid, parked in front of the television. The TV set was tuned into the evening news and Mack walked over and bent down to lower the volume. I smelled something savory cooking in the kitchen.

"I didn't know if you'd be home or whether you'd be working tonight," I said.

At that moment, Josh sent a text asking me where I'd gone. I wrote back I was fine and not to worry, that Sammie knew where I was. I'd been ignoring Em's apology texts and voicemail messages, and there were a few new ones. I felt for her but also knew it would be better to not contact her, at least until the situation with Gilani settled down.

"Sorry for the interruption," I said to Mack, and put my phone away.

"It's okay. You're young, always on your phone, I get it. And, at my age, I don't work nights much anymore." He gazed over my face as though the change in me amazed him. "You really do look like, you know, a guy. They did a good job, whoever does those things. Did they change, you know, all of you?" He glanced at where my breasts had been and his face reddened. "I'm sorry. I didn't mean for that to sound . . . Heck, it's none of my damn business." He rubbed his hair and looked down at the braided rug we stood on.

"It's all right." I patted his shoulder. "I don't mind people asking me questions." When they didn't ask questions and rushed to judgment? *That* bothered me. "So, yeah, it's okay, Mack," I said. "And the bottom half of me hasn't changed." I took my hand off him.

Bottom surgery was something Sammie and I had discussed at length, and we'd both wanted me to go for it but my insurance company was fighting having to pay for the remainder of my surgery, and our battle against them didn't seem close to being done.

I assumed Mack would blush but he gave me a pensive smile. "You make a good-looking man," he said. "There, I said it, I told a guy he was handsome. I can tell it's you because of how you say my name. You emphasize the *k*."

"Thanks," I said quietly, both surprised about and grateful for his acceptance of me. Seeing him brought memories, some good and some bad, and I cleared my throat to stave off a tear. If Mack noticed my blooming emotions, he didn't give an indication he had.

"What are you doing back in town, after all these years?" he asked. "I was going to ask you when you explained who you are but there was so much to take in that the question slipped my mind. When you left for the Navy, you called me sometimes and then you stopped. You went to college after the Navy, didn't you? I thought you forgot about us and would never return. I figured I must've done something wrong."

I touched his hand. "You didn't do anything wrong. That's not why . . . It's hard to explain—I needed to get away from everything, away from being under constant scrutiny because of her, to find out who I am."

"I understand, kid." Mack squeezed my hand and gestured for me to sit on the couch. "That's not why you—because of your mother?"

It was a question I knew I'd be asked someday, but I wasn't prepared for it to happen right then, or for Mack to be the one to ask me. "No," I spoke firmly. "This is who I've always been, and who I would be regardless of what she did."

"I don't know much about it, and I apologize if I sound intrusive."

"It's all right. I prefer people ask me questions instead of coming to a wrong conclusion." I sat down and reclined into the lumpy couch.

"Are you married? Have kids?" he asked. Then he mumbled, "Again, I'm not sure how that works with you."

"It's possible," I said. "But no, no kids, and I'm not married, but I have a girlfriend, Sammie." I figured it would be safe to give Mack Sammie's name. If I couldn't trust my former mentor, then who could I trust?

"Good for you," he said.

"How about you? Do you have any—"

Detective Mack shook his head before I could ask the question. "I'm an old bachelor. Celeste—you remember I told you about her years ago—she and I never had children before she died." His wife had been murdered years before I met him, but other than that fact, I didn't know the exact circumstances of her death. "I'm glad you were able to carry on with your life after what happened. You're strong. I admire that."

"I wish I could say I felt strong." I struggled to navigate my sentiment to a place faraway, into some other compartment in my mind. "The reason I came here is because of her, because of

Alice. I have a few questions I want to ask you. And I need a favor."

Mack let out a low whistle and cracked a joke. "So you only come around here when you want a favor from me?"

I chuckled.

"Tell you what, I'll be happy to help you out," he said. "Can we talk over dinner?"

"You might not be as happy once I tell you what the favor is." Dinner was the ideal, casual time to push what I needed on him.

Now, it was Mack's turn to laugh. "Are you okay in here for a few minutes while I finish making dinner?" He pointed to the TV. "Do you want to watch that while you're waiting? I can turn the volume up. What would you like to drink? I'd invite you to watch me cook but I'm afraid you'd find me quite boring."

"Whatever you're having is fine. I'm good, you don't need to raise the volume." I held out my phone to show him how I'd occupy my time. "I can check my email and such. But I'd love to help you cook." I started to rise from the sofa.

Mack waved me back down. "Nah, you're my guest. Please, sit."

I sat. "What are you making? Smells fantastic."

"I should've asked—do you have any dietary preferences?"

He'd already started making the food, and I didn't want him to have to go out of his way and change his plans because of my vegetarianism. “None,” I said.

“Good, because I’m making steak. Do you have plans to see your mother’s family now that you’re in town?”

Blood warmed and throbbed in my ears. Mack must have not known about my—and my mother’s—estrangement from them. “Not this time,” I said.

He didn’t push me for answers. “Do you like your steak rare, medium, or well-done?”

I sat up, relieved to talk about something other than Alice’s family. “Well-done.” I couldn’t imagine staring at anything remotely gory on my plate, so the less blood the better. I could just cut up the steak and push it around and not actually eat it.

Mack nodded. “You got it.” He checked the time on the slim gold watch he still wore. “Shouldn’t be more than twenty minutes. I have to say that while you do look completely different, I do recognize you, in your eyes especially. I’ll come get you when it’s done. Hang tight. What did you say you wanted to drink, again?”

“I didn’t, but I’ll take a beer, if you have that.”

“Sure do. Is a can okay? I don’t have the bottled kind.”

“That’d be great.”

An arched doorway, the cracked plaster embellished with old carvings at the top, separated the living room from the area where the pleasant smells came from, what I assumed was the kitchen, and Mack walked through.

I answered Sammie's 'how are you doing?' text while I waited.

*Good. Visiting an old friend. You? The dog?*

*We're fine. No reporters. Stay out of trouble.*

I smiled to myself. *Okay. Has Paige started eating?*

*Nope. I'm taking her to the vet's tomorrow morning.*

*I hope she's all right. Thanks for taking care of her.*

*Who's the friend?*

*Someone in the town. Don't worry. They're harmless.*

*Cryptic much? Be careful. I mean it, Evan. I love you.*

I looked up from my phone when Mack re-entered the living room, carrying a can of beer in each hand. I put my phone in my pocket and accepted the beer from him.

Mack nodded at the pocket where I'd tucked away my phone. "Work related?"

"Girlfriend related." I smiled.

Mack chuckled. "Isn't it always?" After a second he asked, "What is it exactly that you do for a living? I don't believe you mentioned anything."

"I didn't. I work for the city—Seven Sisters—where I live. I used to work for the ME's office, now I'm part of the city's crime scene clean-up task force."

"It's unusual for the public to pay for that service. Do they?"

"Yes, they do. It is out of the ordinary. Sammie, my girlfriend, is a retired detective. She worked in narcotics. She retired younger, after being injured on the job. Now she heads an organization for crime victim's families. She's largely responsible for making the task force happen in our city. That's how I met her. We've been together for a long time. Her sister was murdered. I don't know why I told you that but, there, I said it."

"And she doesn't mind that your mother . . . "

I shook my head.

Mack smiled. "I always thought you'd become a cop."

"I considered that but in the end it wasn't for me."

"So your girl's a detective? Good for you, kid. Do you love her?" He spoke to me as I imagined a father would.

I nodded. "Yeah, I do, a lot."

"Then don't let her get away. I gave so much to my career, early on too, and after Celeste was killed, I wished I'd done things the other way around, I wished I'd given more of myself to her instead. I threw myself into work even more after her death because that's the only way I could get out of bed every day. My own wife killed in a robbery while visiting her sister out of town, and here I am, a cop, and I couldn't save her. Remember when I used to dish out advice to you when you came over here to talk? Anyhow, you aren't so young anymore, and you probably don't want me to go on like this, an old man like me, how boring this must sound to you—"

"No, I hear you, I get it. Thanks for the advice. I'm not bullshitting you. You were always helpful, Mack, even back then. And I appreciate that."

"You're welcome, kid. You're still a kid to me." He winked. "Sometimes guys these days don't want to listen."

It wasn't lost on me that he accepted I was a guy. I smiled to myself and pulled open the tab on my beer. The drink relaxed me but I needed to have a clear mind when I set out my proposition to him, so I drank slowly.

"I have to say," he continued. "I happen to be retiring next year and won't have anyone to spend my time with. My point is, don't let something like that happen to you. Remember your career is your livelihood but your girl is your *life*." His voice filled with nostalgia, and his eyes turned red with fast-approaching tears.

Mack rubbed the tears out of his eyes and shook the can when he finished his beer. I didn't want to make him feel awkward but some sort of responsive gesture, an embrace or a pat on the shoulder, seemed required on my part. Yet the years had opened a distance between us, and though I began to lift my legs, I couldn't get myself to stand up and proceed, or simply, move my arm. The television cast a dull glow on the white walls. Something burning in the kitchen wafted into the living room.

"I better check on dinner," Mack said, and trotted into the other room.

Fuck, I thought. I wished I'd said something to comfort him. I swallowed back the rest of my beer and set the can at my feet on the floor. I'd overlooked the coffee table. I considered getting off my ass to turn up the volume on the TV, then something occurred to me: the television was tuned into a national news station, and I wanted Mack to hear about the Seven Sisters murders directly from me. I stood up from the couch and shut off the TV set. Well aware that I wasn't an adept cook, I took the empty beer can with me and strode to the kitchen to see if Mack needed my help regardless of what he'd insisted.

The sight of him standing by the stove in a red chef's apron made me smile. The kitchen was warm from the cooking heat and smelled like home. And a bit like burned meat. Mack's house *had* been like a home to me during my mother's trial.

Mack looked at me over his shoulder. "Getting hungry?" he asked.

"Yes. Smells terrific."

"Is that your wife's apron?" I'd contemplated for a moment about whether to ask.

Mack blushed.

"You're sure you couldn't use a hand?" I asked.

"No, I'm all set. It's almost done. I don't have a dining room so we'll be eating at the table over there." He pointed with the spatula at a small, breakfasting-type of table pushed against the wall. There was only one chair. He noticed me looking. "I'll pull another chair up from the basement," he said. "Bet you can't tell I don't have many guests."

I smiled at Mack's humor but the sole chair at the table had exemplified his solitude. I helped Mack carry up a chair for me from the basement. He hadn't asked for my assistance but I hadn't given him a chance to decline my offer, and from the way he'd put his hand to his lower back on the walk down to the basement, he'd needed my help.

Mack dusted off the chair we'd retrieved and put a fresh cloth on the table. He slid our steaks—both well-done, his unintentionally—onto plates and grabbed some fresh greens and salad dressing from the fridge to put on the side. We sat down to eat our dinner with a few more beers. My idea of having a clear head had gone out the window by then.

By the time I cut into my steak cautiously, Mack was already halfway through with his.

He glanced at me from his side of the table between bites. "Is the food okay?"

"Yeah, it's good." He waited for me to eat the steak. I forked a piece and put it into my mouth, relishing the warm, juicy, and tender surprises. I hadn't eaten meat in years. I talked while I chewed. "It's great," I said, trying not to give away my secret. In actuality, the steak tasted wickedly delicious. And although I felt a little guilty, that didn't stop me from eating it. I'd thought about not being a staunch vegetarian for a while now. Sammie, who wasn't a vegetarian, would be delighted about my change in appetite once I returned home.

"Are you staying here in town?" Detective Mack asked.

"At the lodge. I must say, after the renovations they did, the place looks pretty good."

"It does look good. Did you make a reservation before you left home? Everything around here's all booked up because of the wine convention."

"I heard about that. I managed to get a room after I arrived in town. The woman who works at the hotel's front desk mentioned the convention was happening. I was surprised to hear vineyards took off so well around here."

"The economy was terrible for everyone for a long time but it hit these parts especially hard. Even a portion of the prison closed, and jobs were lost. When people moved here from the city with money to start the vineyards, it helped things some. A lot of people around here didn't like the new people coming in. But the smart folks rode the rich folks' coattails and started—or enhanced their old—businesses around the vineyards. That's why the lodge got renovated. Must've been tricky getting a room on such short notice. I believe your family . . . your mother's family recently acquired a vineyard for themselves to run. Did they tell you about that?"

Mack took a drink of beer. I hadn't touched my second can.

I murmured down to my plate, "I'm not much on speaking terms with them anymore."

"I assumed you were here visiting them and that you dropped by to say hello to me."

I shook my head. "I don't plan on seeing them during my time here."

"Do you write to your mother?"

"I stopped writing to her."

Mack touched his chin and paused for a few seconds. "What are you doing back here, exactly? This is your hometown, you're free to visit of course. But after all this time, why? I'm a cop so I tend to ask these questions." He grinned. "You're not here for the convention, are you? Surely you'd want to have brought your girl with you for that." He dug into his salad, which shone with oil and vinegar, and crunched.

"I'm not attending the convention," I said.

Mack put his fork down. "You aren't only here to see me, are you?"

"That's not the only reason."

He looked across at me and waited for my explanation.

"I'm here to visit my mother," I said, after a pause. "And I need your help."

Mack coughed and I thought he had choked on his food. I reached out to him to check that he was okay. He cleared his throat. "Are you going to visit her so she can see who you are today, or for closure?" he asked. "You're a relative and are entitled to a visitor's pass at the prison. You can apply for one—I can help you with that—it'll take a couple of days for you to get clearance."

I looked him straight in the eye. "I'm not planning on visiting her as a relative."

"How are you going to visit her, then? You won't get clearance unless you're a relative, law enforcement, a member of her legal team, or maybe the media, but that's harder and reporters might not be able to arrange anything over the phone. I believe they might have to visit the prison office in person to apply."

"The last thing, that's what I plan to try, to go as a member of the press."

"But you don't work for the media. How—" Then he answered his own question. "You're going to lie. I'm assuming your mother doesn't know about any of these changes." He gestured to my clothing.

I slowly nodded and then resumed eating. I wasn't going to demand his backing until I had to.

Just when I thought Mack would cut the conversation short, he said, "They won't arrange a visit for you unless you have a press badge, or credentials at least, which I assume you don't."

"They'll let me in with your help. I thought that you of all people would—would understand. That's why I'm here, asking you."

"Understand what? You know, when you used to come over here when you were young, I used to worry about you sometimes because you felt so much, almost too much. You haven't lost some of your heart, have you, or your morals?"

I looked up from my plate at him and tried to steady my voice. "No."

"Then why can't you visit your mother as you are? If you don't want her to know who you are, what could you possibly want from her?"

"I'm not sure if you've heard but the police in Seven Sisters believe there's a serial killer targeting the city."

"I hadn't heard. You know this because of your job?"

"Yes, it was a secret until . . . Have you ever heard of this website, it's called *Crime Man*?"

"If it's not a newspaper, I won't read it unless it has something to do with my work."

I explained to Detective Mack about how the chief told me about the messages left for 'Evelyn.' "Someone I know leaked the information to this website. And this person also disclosed my name used to be Evelyn."

"That's a petty thing to do. I'm sure you'd like to punch the bastard. I would, and I don't know them."

"The bastard is a woman who works on my team. At the time, I felt I could trust her, not knowing how dead wrong I'd be."

"What a fucked-up betrayal. And now you're in trouble for telling her and she's in trouble for telling the website?"

"Yes, something like that."

"Your chief should've kept his mouth shut. You're not on the run from the law, are you?"

"No, nothing like that. The site, *Crime Man*, 'dug up' that I'm Alice Lane's child. Apparently, it's been on the internet some—you know how fast those things spread."

"I wouldn't know. As I've said, I don't pay much attention to that online chaos, outside of what I have to notice for work." Mack shifted in his chair.

"Someone's killing young men and letting me know I'm the reason for what they're doing."

"But you're not a cop so how'd they know you'd see the messages?"

I shrugged. "I guess they thought that fact would be in the media at some point and I'd make the connection then, if not sooner because of my job."

"You're sure they're trying to get to you? The messages could be for another Evelyn, couldn't they?"

"No," I said firmly. "They're murdering young men and leaving messages—carving them into the victims' skin, I might add—using my former name. They're taunting me. I was told the police even think the killer's a woman, for Christ's sake. Like my mother."

"Perhaps more information someone on the law side of things shouldn't have told you. Lots of guys can't keep their mouths shut these days, blabbering on Facebook and all that claptrap."

I refrained from commenting.

He didn't gaze at me as though I bordered on insanity, rather he calmly stated, "That wasn't your mother's MO, by the way. She didn't mutilate her victims. There was the eating part, possibly."

Mack paused and the tension built thickly in the room, and I was relieved when he didn't elaborate on *that* detail. I'd always been more than aware how my mother might have consumed some of her victims, and didn't need a reminder. Then Mack seemed to ruminate to himself aloud.

"But *if* there's a copycat killer," he said, "and I'm not saying I think there is, why on earth would they want to target you? Wouldn't such a person want to please Alice? Surely targeting her child wouldn't make her happy. I hope you're not suggesting I put the wrong woman away all those years ago."

"No." I had long ago accepted what my mother had done.

"I can assure you our investigation was thorough."

"I know that. I don't know what's going on exactly but someone's killing these boys and letting me know they're doing it, to get to me."

"It could be the serial's twisted way of sending their support to you. But *how* would they have known you'd find out about the messages if you're not in law enforcement? The police often keep those kinds of details hidden from the public while they're investigating. Did you see the bodies? Typically, the crime scene crew arrives *after* the body's gone."

"I didn't see them, no. Perhaps they thought I'd find out eventually given my line of profession. Either that or they assumed it would be exposed to the public, eventually."

"Maybe the serial leaked the story?" Mack's face brightened like he enjoyed helping me find answers.

I shook my head vehemently. "No. I'm afraid I'm positive that my colleague I confided in gave them the information."

"It was worth a shot, right? It'll be tough for me to investigate this myself since these crimes are occurring in a different town."

"I'm not here to convince you to investigate these murders. I need your help getting into the prison to see my mother, as a reporter, so she doesn't know who I am."

"What will visiting your mother do? She's not arranging for someone to commit her crimes for her while she's locked up—has she been writing to you?"

I shook my head. "And I stopped writing back to her when I was in the service, and she didn't have my address when I went to college or for any of the places I've lived since. She has no means of contacting me and knows nothing about who I am today, so it'll be simple for me to pretend in front of her. She might know something. I can't allow this to keep happening."

"Solving it is the police's job. Who do they have working on the case? Anyone I know?"

"A detective named Burke. I don't know who else."

"Don't know him," Mack said. "You might want to leave the solving up to the detectives in your city, no?"

"They don't know Alice Lane like I do. They don't know how to get through to her."

"You always could reach her when she wouldn't let anyone else in, true. Seems kind of wrong to do this to her, to lie to your own mother, no matter what she did all those years ago."

"You never judged her, not even when she confessed."

"She has an illness, she can't help what she does."

"Is she on medication in prison?"

Mack shrugged. "I wouldn't know. Probably. Last I heard, she drifts in and out from being housed in the maximum security ward to being in the section of the prison for the criminally insane."

The food had ceased tasting good and so I stopped eating. I opened and drank another beer, which was warm by now. Mack rose to get some more cans from the fridge, placing a cold one in my hand.

"Here, this'll taste better," he said. He took the other beer from the table, drained the remainder into the sink, and set the empty can on the kitchen counter.

I popped open the new can and swallowed back some of the bitter, chilled beer. "Thanks."

He nodded. "Are you finished?" Mack looked from his fully cleaned plate to mine.

My eating the rest didn't seem likely. "Yes. I'm not very hungry tonight, but it was great, truly."

He gave me a short nod, and I wasn't sure whether he thought I disliked the taste of what he'd cooked. I began to rise to help him with the dishes but he stopped me. "It's okay, I'll take care of it."

Mack cleared the table and dusted off the top with his hand, depositing the crumbs in the trash receptacle. He scraped my uneaten food into the same receptacle, and put the dishes in the sink.

When he returned to the table, he brought with him another beer for himself. I waited to hear what he had to say before I pushed him again for his support. We drank our beers in silence for a while.

"Here's what I think," he finally said. "I think pretending to be someone else when you see your mother wouldn't be a good idea. I think you should return to Seven Sisters and work this thing out with the police there. I can call them and speak on your behalf, if you'd like. I don't think you, someone not in law enforcement, should be investigating something this big yourself. It could be very dangerous, and something could happen to you. I couldn't live with myself if I gave you permission to do that."

"I need to see her, and I need to protect my identity and stay anonymous. Freedom is a prison town. You know how most of the guards the prison employs live in the town, and that there'd be nasty gossip. Regardless of what you say, I still plan to try to visit her, and as a member of the press. In fact, that's what I've been telling anyone in town that's asked why I'm here. I can't go to the police back in my city. My fear is that they'll think I had something to do with the crimes if I don't find out the truth and explain it to them. People can be very—they can misjudge me, and they often do, and not only because I'm Alice Lane's kid but also because of my lifestyle. You're the only one who can help me."

"Christ, when you put it like that, do I even have a choice?" Mack put his hands to his face and rubbed his eyes. "You know what you're asking me to do, don't you? You want me to be part of your lie, and if I help you, then I'm an accomplice." He spoke through his fingers and sounded bleary.

"If you want to put it that way, then, yes, I am asking you to be my accomplice of sorts, but for the greater good, to get this person off the streets. The boys being killed are street kids mostly, hustling for drug money, and it's not like there's a lot of people out there crusading for justice for them."

"I hear you." He lifted his fingers off his face and stared directly at me. "When you put it like that, how can I say no? Us against the world, right?" He'd used that expression with me in the past and it'd always made me smile, but not on that day. Then I waited for him to say *but* and explain why he'd have to decline. "I'll have to think about it," he said.

"You'll consider it?" Hope lightened my mood.

Mack shrugged. "We'll see. You're staying at the lodge? Give me your number there and I'll call you to let you know."

"You can call my mobile," I said, reluctant to have calls made to my room at the lodge from someone known to the locals as a detective. I had to maintain my story as a travel writer, covering the town for an article.

"I'll call either way—yes or no," he said.

"Suspenseful," I joked, and he chuckled.

I considered hugging Mack before we left but we shook hands at his door instead.

# Chapter 11

Very early in the morning, I awoke in my much larger bed at the lodge to the sound of my mobile ringing. Sammie wouldn't have contacted me at that hour unless it was an emergency. I wouldn't have stood for it if those reporters had bothered her. By then, they would have been curious about why I hadn't made an appearance outside our apartment building. I sat up under the covers and didn't see any sunlight coming through the gaps in the window curtains. I flicked on the bedside lamp to get my bearings in the darkness.

From the area code, the number on my lighted screen belonged to someone right there in Freedom Village. I slowly picked up, and sure enough, heard Mack's voice. He'd said he'd ring either way. I clutched the phone between my fingers.

"Sorry it's so early. I've been up all night, thinking," he said, before I could say hello. The silence dragged on.

"Thanks for calling. I don't mind the hour," I finally said. "Have you made a decision? Whatever it is, I won't hold anything against you."

"That's good to hear. I'll do it, by the way, I'll arrange for you to visit Alice."

I breathed out and smiled to myself. "Thanks, Mack. I owe you for this."

"You do," he said with a chuckle. "I'll ring you again later this morning with more concrete details."

"You can't tell them I'm Alice's child—"

"Your identity will be kept safe," he assured me. "I'm going to make a call to a fellow I know who works at the prison, a high-up guy, and tell him a journalist happens to be in town and would like permission to speak with prisoner Lane. What do you think? I must emphasize to you how much I dislike doing this, but that I'm doing it for you."

My stomach rumbled. Remembering the meat I'd consumed last night without a pause made me feel nauseous. I threw the covers back and rose from the bed, shirtless and in my underwear. "Mack? Hang on a second."

I gripped the phone to my chest and ran barefoot across the soft carpet into the bathroom. I dropped the phone to the floor tiles and didn't have time to lift up the toilet seat. I got on my knees on the cold, hard floor and threw up into the bowl.

Mack's voice said, "Evan? Evan? Are you there?" from the phone on the floor.

I glanced at the yellow bile floating in the toilet water and reached to flush. The ringtone for a text from Sammie came through. It still seemed early to hear from her. I reached for a towel, wiped my mouth, and then groped for the phone at my feet. I croaked out some words to Mack, "Yeah, I'm here. It sounds good—what you said—it sounds fine. Thank you."

I put the phone on the medicine cabinet shelf to run the tap water and rinse off my face. I dried my skin and picked up the phone to read Sammie's text. I checked the time too. It was already six in the morning, later than my body felt it was.

She'd sent a photo of her looking as though she awoke recently, leaning against the headboard on our bed back home while holding Paige in her arms. From the angle it was clear she had snapped the picture herself, with her and Paige looking up at the lens. She sometimes would take Paige running in the morning—it wasn't my thing but I respected Sammie's need for fitness—but with the possibility of the media lurking in the shadows of our apartment complex, I couldn't imagine that happening. I wondered if she would be going to work. While Sammie could have taken some time off, she would have had to return at some point, and that point would have been soon. I started writing a reply.

"Hello? What's going on there with you? Should I be worried? What's all that racket? Should I ring the front desk at the lodge and ask them to come check on you?" I'd forgot Mack was still on the line.

I put the phone on the speaker setting so I could talk to him and type simultaneously. "No, I'm . . . Everything is all right. I had to use the bathroom." I refrained from disclosing my illness to him. Knowing Mack, he'd fret and insist on seeing me himself to evaluate my condition. He wouldn't take my word if I told him *not* to worry.

"Oh," he said in an awkward manner and cleared his throat. "In that case, I'll let you go, to finish whatever you're doing in the bathroom, that is," he said, equally as awkward. "You can expect a call from me later. It could take a few days for me to get clearance for you. What do you want your last name to be? I assume you don't want me to give them Lane as your surname."

"Samuels," I said, without thinking. I'd already started that lie so why not continue it?

"That was fast," Mack said, like he was on to me. "Okay. Talk soon."

I skipped the lodge's light breakfast that morning, walked to the diner, and ordered a cup of coffee, no cream or sugar, to go.

*

Detective Mack rang again, later in the morning, when I'd returned to the lodge, and surprised me with the news that he'd obtained permission for me to visit Alice Lane, prisoner 899, my mother, that same afternoon. He hadn't given me much time to prepare but I knew that would be the one chance I had to step inside the prison and face her.

I dressed in a suit jacket, which was wrinkled from my having left it inside my suitcase. I wore the jacket without a necktie. I put on jeans but I donned my best dress shoes for the visit, trying to look the part of the hip urban journalist. That morning at the drugstore near the lodge I'd bought an inexpensive pair of reading glasses that looked like the prescription kind, and now I put them on. I put the notebook and pen—which I figured would be easier to get past the guards than an electronic device—that I'd picked up at the store too, into a work satchel to make my occupation seem likely. I smoothed back my short hair in the hotel room mirror and felt I looked the part decently enough.

I wondered, should I have bought a gift to bring to her, something she could enjoy in her cell, such as a book? But journalists didn't bring gifts to strangers they sought to interview for a story. And I'd assumed the guards would have confiscated one anyway. That was another thing I hadn't pinned down: Once at the prison, would I play along with the travel writer story I'd created, as though Alice and the town were a tourist attraction, or would I say I was conducting research for a story on the murders in Seven Sisters, murders that were similar to Alice's?

Mack had arranged everything for me so that my check-in process at the prison would go as smoothly as possible. I'd never visited my mother in her prison—I didn't desire to associate those kinds of memories with her—but I'd researched photos of the prison online, and I'd studied and memorized the car route by heart over the years in case someday I decided I wanted to make the drive from Seven Sisters to see her.

Using the GPS app on my phone, I substituted Freedom Village for Seven Sisters as my starting destination, and the miles to reach my destination shrunk greatly. Freedom was a prison town, meaning a large number of the population worked at the nearby prison, the ominous, gray cluster of structures I'd seen beyond the vineyards.

I hadn't divulged to Sammie what my whereabouts would be on that day. My withholding a secret from her would have troubled her if she'd caught on—and she would have, because she always, inevitably, discovered my little secrets.

I loved Sammie but this had to be a secret for now. I turned on the radio, and classic rock came on, a big, loud sound, to drown out how much hiding something from Sammie bothered me.

I pulled my car alongside a guard in the booth at the entrance to the women's prison, rolled down my window and gave her my name. I wondered which ward my mother was being housed in right then. Mack had mentioned she'd been transferred in and out of the psych ward.

The guard at the booth, an older woman with short hair, wore a beige uniform and greeted me with a subtle nod. Her eyebrows were so pale I could hardly see them on her very white face.

"How can I help you today, sir?" she asked.

I lowered the radio volume and I repeated my name. "I'm Evan Samuels. I'm here to interview a prisoner. I'm a journalist. I believe a detective in town set everything in place for my visit?"

I sat up in my seat and could see her staring at a clipboard on her desk in the booth. "Samuels, right? I'm sorry but your name's not on here." She stared at me from her booth as if she was waiting for an explanation.

"That can't be right." I smiled. "A detective named Mack Boyle arranged for me to come here."

The guard looked at me and didn't smile.

I shut off the music. My shirt stuck to my back and I gripped my damp palms against the steering wheel to gain my composure. Had Mack somehow made a mistake and put me down as Evan Lane?

If so, there would be plenty of questions from the prison's employees once I got inside, assuming I got past the guard at the front booth. Surely they'd want to know if I was related to *her*, the lovely butcher, and then they'd go and tell their spouses, children, parents, and friends. And before long, the entire village would know about my presence among them. Children would stop me in the street and want to take a photo with me. But they wouldn't know I'd once been called Evelyn, at least not yet.

The Lane surname was notorious in Freedom, and although they were very strong people, I didn't know how my mother's family had managed to stay in the town and cope with all the attention they must have received. I couldn't ask them. I didn't want to see them, and I assumed they felt the same way. Alice's father was a respected surgeon in the area and her brother had followed in his footsteps. I hardly knew them anymore but they had been a resilient group and were probably faring well.

"There's been a mistake. I confirmed with the detective," I stated firmly to the guard. "Like I said, he arranged for me to see this prisoner. It's very important I see her. I'm a writer and I need to speak with her."

"Please hold on a moment." The woman spoke into the two-way radio protruding from her shirt pocket. I heard her say something like, "Samuels. He's on the list?"

I took in the outside of the facility while I waited for the guard to sort out the issue. I found the *Freedom Women's Correctional Facility* entrance sign that blended into the overgrowth of lush decorative hedgerows ironic. Freedom in a prison.

The guard picked up a clipboard from the narrow desk area inside the booth and held it out to me. "It seems there's been a smidgen of a mishap," she said, and I held my breath. "I've confirmed you *are* on the visitors list for today. I'm sorry about the whole thing." She finally smiled.

"No worries." I breathed more comfortably.

"Please put your name here, sir." She pushed the clipboard at me.

I saw she'd already written my license plate number on the piece of paper attached to the board and I scribbled the name Evan Samuels below it. The guard pulled the clipboard back into the booth. Only I seemed to notice my lie.

"You'll see a sign for the visitors' parking lot—Lot B—when you drive through." She stuck her arm out of the booth and gestured to the expanse of asphalt at the nose of my car. "A nametag will be waiting for you when you check in at the visitors' reception area. You'll need to put this in your car so you don't get towed."

She handed me a tag with the word *Visitor* and a number stamped on it to hang on my rearview mirror. I must have looked concerned because she added, "It's a safety precaution, sir." I didn't get the sense that she wanted to comfort me, but rather that she sought to have me on my way so she could attend to the person in the car that had pulled up behind me at some point.

I nodded at her and hung the tag on my mirror like she'd instructed. She raised up the wood bar painted white that had blocked me from driving straight into the parking lot. Crackling sounded from her walkie-talkie and she spoke into the device and waved me on through. I didn't move the car forward for a few moments, waiting until the very last second to face what I'd started. When I did move my vehicle, it thumped and lurched over a speed bump, rolling into the prison lot.

I parked in Lot B, a simple task since mine was one of the two cars in the section. I turned off the engine. As far as having no identification that named me as Evan Samuels, I'd hoped that having a referral from a respected and well-liked local detective would do. I assumed they'd search me inside so I left my phone and identification in the car. I made certain that the tag hanging from the rearview mirror faced the right way, then got out with the satchel and locked the car.

The sunny afternoon darkened, and it seemed inevitable that rain would be waiting for me on my way out of the prison in an hour or so. An hour seemed like a short time to obtain what I needed but I didn't know if I could lie to my mother for longer than that. She, the greatest deceiver of all, had always been terrific at calling out liars.

It was a shame that I hadn't brought the umbrella Sammie left in the car trunk for us to use when the weather required it. I felt terrible about keeping my visit to Alice a secret from Sammie and not including her in the loop like I'd promised, but when she'd confronted me as I packed for my trip she hadn't asked whether I would visit my mother, and I felt I could get away with not telling her something she hadn't sought to know in the first place. But I really felt awful keeping even that from her.

The entrance marked *Visitors* lay outside of the sky-high barbed wire fencing that made up the main part of the prison. Crows cawed high up in the sky and their ruckus startled me. I shouldered my bag and slowly headed for the entrance. Before walking into the building, I removed my notepad and pen from my satchel, to better appear the part of the eager young journalist there to interview the prison's most notorious inmate.

I took a deep breath and pulled open the door. A woman dressed like she worked in the prison's administrative offices was about to exit and I held open the door for her. She thanked me and I went inside once she was out of the way.

Two hulking male guards, with very short hair and muscles nearly bursting out of the shirts of their beige uniforms, stared at me when I walked inside. I waved to them. Would they search me themselves or merely run a hand-held metal detector over my body? I was a man and they could rightfully give me a pat-down before allowing me deeper inside the prison. I didn't see the kind of metal detector you walked through. I felt grateful I'd worn a padded garment to show through the front of my jeans that day.

I joined in on the 'manly' banter I overheard them having about women, something that I normally didn't encounter with Josh at work, for neither Em nor Sammie would have tolerated that behavior, and rightly so. I'd known first-hand all the shit women had to put up with from men.

"Were her tits really *that* big?" I said with a grin, in response to the crude remark the taller guard had made to his colleague about his date last night.

The taller guard had cold blue eyes and a deep tan. He had a repulsive phlegmy laugh that he demonstrated to me right then. "Let's say they were more than a handful," he replied, and I cringed inside.

I'd never understood why some men thought those types of conversations made them appear manly to each other. In my opinion, they had the opposite effect. I wondered about my mother's safety inside the prison's high, impenetrable walls. From what I'd remembered—I hadn't saved photographs of her—Alice Lane was a beautiful woman, and strong.

I played along with his unpleasant repartee to get on these guys' good sides, if they even had them. "You must've had a really good time, then," I said.

"Oh, yeah." The guard gave me a boastful smirk. "It was a grab and squeeze kind of night, if you know what I mean."

*Yuck.*

Thankfully, the shorter guard interjected. "Hello, how's it going today?"

He seemed embarrassed by his colleague's behavior, appeared a little older and looked as though he took his job more seriously than the other fellow.

"I'm here to see one of the prisoners. A police detective made an appointment for me. I'm a journalist."

I gave them Mack's name as my contact and Evan Samuels' name as mine, and the shorter guard, the one who seemed more in charge than the other, walked behind a computer at a standing desk and typed on the keyboard. Before they could ask me for identification—I assumed they would—I pretended to search my pockets and bag for my wallet.

"Okay, we have you down to come at three o'clock. You're a bit early," he said.

"Yes, sorry about that. Shall I wait here?" I pointed at the plastic chairs lined up against the wall to my left. They looked uncomfortable and

I couldn't imagine family members having to sit on them while waiting to see their loved ones.

"No, that's all right. You can go in early. It's fairly quiet here today."

"Yes, I could tell from the parking lot." I smiled.

He remained solemn. "Can I see your identification?"

"Will my driver's license do?"

"Sure, that's what we usually ask for." He held out his hand and, again, I pretended to check my clothing and bag for my wallet.

"Ah, fuck," I groaned and searched my pockets again. "I'm not from around here. I seem to have left my wallet back at the lodge. You know the lodge, right?"

"We do," the taller guard said. He eyed me with mistrust. Perhaps I'd underestimated him.

I addressed the shorter one. "A detective, Mack Boyle, set up this whole thing for me, for me to interview Alice Lane for a story I'm working on. I'm a writer, you see. I already said that, but, anyway, this has all been arranged by a detective from here, from Freedom. Why don't you call him to confirm?" I couldn't recall Mack's new phone number off the top of my head and I had no idea what I'd do if the guard asked for it.

After what felt like an extensive period of silence, the taller guard said, "That's okay. All the guys from the press who come here want to talk to her."

Perhaps my earlier bantering with him *had* won him over to my side, no matter how unpleasant it'd been for me. He handed me my nametag and I clipped it to the front of my jacket.

The other man interrupted. "We have to check him." He indicated for me to empty my pockets into the white bins on the counter the other guard leaned against.

I didn't have a watch or other jewelry to remove, and I didn't have anything in my pockets to declare. I put my eyeglasses in the bin. Then I took my satchel off my shoulder and set it on the counter. The more serious guard stared at my pockets and I patted them to show they held nothing. He quickly went from that to clearing his throat and nodding at the notepad and pen I still gripped in my hand. I set them down too. The guard at the counter set the bin with my glasses on a conveyer belt and moved it through a small metal detector. Then he opened my bag and dug through the contents as the other man ran a metal detector wand over my body.

He hunkered down to scan my shoes and the area around my legs. "Do you have anything on you that you need to disclose before we let you inside?" He asked, standing up to my level.

"No."

When he scanned my pockets, the metal detector beeped. "Please empty your pockets completely, sir."

"I don't believe there's anything else in them," I said.

He tilted his head at the bins on the counter.

I found that I had left a few coins in my pocket. I dropped those into the bin and they clinked. "Sorry about that."

He gave me a knowing look and then picked through the coins with his finger. Once finished, he nodded at me to put them back in my pocket.

"One second," I said. "Will I be in the same room as the prisoner? I presumed from what the detective said, that I'd be separated from her, from the prisoner, by a sort of partition. But you seem to be searching me as though I'll have direct contact with her." Could I have faced my mother without a wall, even a clear one, between us?

At my side, the younger guard smiled at me with gleaming teeth. "What's the matter, are you afraid she'll bite?"

His cheap joke wasn't lost on me but I didn't react. "No, but I'd like to know what kind of setting I'll be interviewing the prisoner in."

"Everything we're doing is part of protocol. You'll be separated from her," the older guard said, zipping my satchel closed. He handed it to me. "You're all clear to go in. You can take your bag in with you. You'll be talking to her through a speaker."

I put the coins away. He nodded at my notepad and pen, and I picked them up from the counter.

The taller, younger guard didn't move from his current place, leaning on the counter and resting his weight. The other one motioned for me to follow him through a bolted metal door painted green.

"I'll escort you to where you need to go," he said.

He opened the latch with one of the keys on the set that dangled from his belt. It was then I noticed he also carried a gun on his belt, and I assumed his counterpart had one clipped on him, too.

With my satchel hanging from my shoulder, I reluctantly followed him, walking one step behind the guard into a brightly lit hallway with its walls painted an institutional white shade.

"What's your name?" I said. "If you don't mind my asking."

"Bennet."

"That's your first name?"

He glanced over his shoulder at me and had a look on his face that conveyed nobody in my current position had asked him that very question.

"It's Karl," he said. "With a k, not a c."

I waited for him to apologize for his colleague's behavior. When he didn't I said, "Good to meet you, Karl." We didn't cease our walk and I refrained from offering to shake hands since it didn't seem appropriate under the circumstances.

He murmured a greeting I didn't catch, and I didn't care to ask him to repeat himself.

When we had made the journey to the end of the hall, Karl stopped in his tracks just in front of me. He unlocked—typing a code into a keypad on the wall—and led me through another door, and into a different, ill-lit hallway with gray walls. Karl stopped at a white door to our left and used one of his keys on his belt to open it. My mother couldn't have escaped easily.

Once more, the lighting changed, and I struggled to adjust my vision to the now more intense glare.

"Where is she?" I asked, fighting to see through the intensity.

"She's over there, sir," Karl said.

# Chapter 12

I peered at the woman, directly in front of me, a step or two away, so that if I walked in a straight line, I could press my hand to the translucent partition that separated her room from the one I stood in.

A banquet chair had been set out for me to use during the visit. My mother looked small and alone behind the clear partition, alienated from me. There weren't other inmates lined up at her left and right talking to their loved ones through telephone receivers like in the movies. Alice Lane sat alone.

I didn't know whether they were keeping her out of the general population on purpose for her safety. The lovely butcher. My mother. How could it have been that nearly twenty years had passed and I hadn't seen her?

Sammie and I had a terrible row once about how although my mother had taken lives, she was my mother, and I could never fully bring every ounce of myself to hate her. I knew where

Sammie came from and respected her take. Her little sister had been murdered. Every time Sammie's sister's killer was up for parole, she spoke in front of the board to prevent his release. She felt killers deserved no remorse from anyone, their own families included. Sammie's grief at her sister's sudden death was more violent than that of Ben's parents, who were quiet and held forgiving, religious views even towards their son's killer, unlike the families of Alice's other victims, who had made it quite clear that if they had their say, my mother would have been drawn and quartered in the town square. Alice Lane was a murderer but she was also my mother, and I could never bring myself to despise her with all I had.

Alice, once the town's most feared woman, looked vulnerable and breakable, like my hand could have pushed right through her if we hadn't been divided. She was older, rounder in the face, and her body filled out her red jumpsuit. Her exposed arms looked puffy and white. She'd been well-fed in prison and the lack of exercise and fresh air had gotten to her.

Alice peered disinterestedly from me to Karl. She always had liked playing things cool. She crossed her arms and gave him one of her sweet smiles I remembered all too well from my childhood. Alice hadn't been the kind of mother who baked or was overly involved in my life, but she'd been there for me when I needed her.

"My favorite guard. The nicest one," she said to Karl. Her voice had aged into a weaker, softer, sound.

He blushed and frowned.

My mother's voice made it seem like she wasn't capable of killing anyone, much less several people. How she had misled me as a child. How much she had misled everyone in her life. The newspapers had portrayed her as a cunning woman, someone who hid behind the agreeable schoolteacher persona she'd developed in our town.

Before she became a known predator, most folks in the town remarked how peculiar it was that a woman as pretty as my mother had chosen teaching high school math as her profession. Why, with her looks and family pedigree, she could have married well, she hadn't needed to marry a man like my father, who'd gone on to abandon her. But my mother wasn't a brilliant mathematician. In fact, she was far from that. She'd grumble to me when she came home from work that it was all a great big ruse and there wasn't a day that went by without her doubting she knew what she was doing.

"You're my favorite," she spoke again to Karl.

He ignored Alice's goading and said directly to me, "You'll have an hour for your visit. I'll come collect you when the time's up."

"Is it possible to have a bit longer than that?"

"One hour." He moved his fingers over a large orange button on the wall. "Press this if you need me to come earlier." Did he think Alice might possibly hurt me through what seemed like a bullet-proof divider? When I didn't acknowledge his instructions, he tapped the button.

"Should I be worried?" I asked.

"I don't think she can hurt you from inside there just by looking at you." But he didn't sound convinced.

Alice nodded at me and talked to Karl through the speaker in the partition. I'd anticipated she and I would have each had to pick up a phone to converse through the glass, but, alas, no. The sound of her voice was fainter than it would have been if I was sitting in front of her. "Who the hell is that man?" She squinted at my visitors' badge but my name hadn't seemed to register.

"Evan Samuels." I extended my hand to her but we couldn't touch through the glass. She peered at my hand, and, from the gleam in her eyes, viewed my gesture with amusement. "I'd like to speak with you, if that's all right," I said, stepping closer, my voice raised, so close I could have pressed my nose to the partition's surface if I wanted. I knew my mother and how strong she could be, and I knew that straight away I would have to make it clear I was in charge if I stood a chance of leaving there with what I wanted. A part of me had been worried she'd recognize me somehow, but I could tell from her defensive stare that I wasn't familiar to her.

"Who said you could come here?" she asked. "My lawyer? And don't try to trick me with some line that you're my new lawyer because I know you aren't. Are you a fan? How did you pull the strings to get in here? All the guards told me was that I had to come with them to see someone right now."

"A detective," I started to say, and she pointed at the speaker like she couldn't hear me and wanted me to use that to communicate with her. I bent down to talk through it. "A detective in the area arranged for me to visit you."

"You're not law enforcement," she observed.

"It's that obvious?"

She didn't smile. "A detective you said? Was his name…Mack?" Alice's voice faded as a memory seemed to come to her.

I nodded.

"He was nice to my daughter," she said.

I took a seat in front of her while she continued to talk.

"Of course, this would have been years ago. My daughter stopped communicating with me a long time ago." She seemed so unassuming that it wasn't difficult to see why her confession had shocked so many.

Despite my awareness of her crimes and how much suffering she'd inflicted on others, tears of guilt at abandoning her in that place, that prison, pricked at the corners of my eyes. I held the tears back and quickly thought of how to explain I knew Mack, because she would inevitably wonder. "A colleague of mine put me in touch with him. I'm a journalist, and I'd like to interview you for a story, if you'll give me a few moments of your time."

She giggled. "Time? Listen, handsome—may I call you that?—in here all I have is time." I smiled at her, and her tone morphed into something less friendly. "You want to write about me?"

"I want to include you in my story, yes."

"Then you should know it's a rule of mine not to speak to reporters anymore. Your lot mostly prints trash about me. Too bad you weren't just a fan."

She stared at me for such a long time it made me uncomfortable. Did she recognize me?

"You're not bad-looking for a short guy," she said.

I breathed with ease. "I won't quote you directly in my story."

"I'm sorry but I can't trust you'll remain true to your word." Her manner stayed clipped and to-the-point.

"Have you been burned before?" I asked, though I recalled she had.

My mother paused, and then said, "When the news of my arrest first broke, I tried speaking to journalists in hopes they could spread my message that my family, my daughter, were victims too, in a sense, and people shouldn't blame them for something I'd done. But when my lawyer shared with me what they'd written, I saw they'd twisted everything around and made me look like a monster."

I recalled how the families of her victims hadn't liked her speaking to the newspapers. And rightly so. They hadn't wanted Alice to have a voice when their murdered loved ones couldn't speak for themselves.

"And you aren't a monster?" I said.

Serial murderers were sociopaths or psychopaths, from what I'd researched on the topic after her arrest, but for years I'd sought to hear an answer from her directly, all the while comprehending that she most likely wasn't capable of *admitting* the depravity behind what she'd done. Those like her—serial killers—almost never were.

"I'm sure someone like you would like to think of me as that," she said.

"Not necessarily. I consider myself to be a fair journalist. I stick to the facts and don't embellish the truth." I liked to think I did that regardless of my true occupation.

She looked at me like she found my answer, and me, amusing.

"You've had the same lawyer for all these years?" I asked, something I was ashamed not to have kept track of or cared about.

"No. The first one retired. I have a new one these days. He's a little man, like you, but his gumption makes up for that shortcoming."

"You have a sense of humor," I said.

She replied, "One has to have a sense of humor to survive in here."

I hadn't heard Karl leaving but he must have sneaked out because when I checked, he was gone. And I was alone with prisoner 899—I noticed the number had been stitched onto her jumpsuit—also known as my mother. I hadn't heard him locking the door but I assumed he had since he'd insinuated that only an official could escort me in and out of the room, something to do with that orange button.

"Which newspaper do you write for?" Alice asked.

I knew she was well-read and I didn't know what kind of access she had to newspapers in there so I chose my words carefully. "I'm freelance." I adjusted my eyeglasses. They were too small and squeezed my nose.

"I see. Did a newspaper assign the story to you, or did you come up with the idea yourself and then pitched it to them? Which newspaper? Usually, freelance writers work for a couple newspapers at once. I won't speak to just anyone these days, you know. Lots of media people want to gain access to me. However, most of them don't know friends of detectives who worked on my case. Maybe you'll get lucky, handsome."

I should have known she'd be too clever to outwit easily. "I plan to shop my story around once it's been written. I have a few places in mind." I hadn't corrected the guards or Alice when each presumed she would be the focus of my story. "It's not you in particular I'm interested in for my story, if that's your concern."

"I'm disappointed." She smiled. "Isn't that unusual, to write something without pitching your idea to them first?"

"That's what I've chosen to do."

"Fair enough. If you aren't here to talk only about me, then what's there to discuss? The weather? Tell me, what's it like outside, before you came into this concrete wasteland, what was it like?" She tapped on the partition and I jumped in my chair.

"I would have thought touching that glass would set off some kind of an alarm," I said.

"You overestimate the prison system," she laughed softly.

I regained my self-control before she could see how much she'd startled me. "They don't let you outside?" I asked in a neutral way.

"If you can call being allowed out of my cell for a half hour once a day to take a shower or walk in a circle around the barren courtyard being outside, then yes. In reality, they buried me along with my victims."

I looked directly at her and didn't blink. "No. It isn't the same. You're alive and they aren't."

"True. I'm buried in here to keep the world safe from me." She moved her hand over another speaker built into the concrete wall at her shoulder. "See this right here? This is so I can call the guard early in case I want to leave. All I have to do is press this button and they'll come get me. I'm going to call him. Lovely to have met you."

I thought of something fast, to stop her. "You wanted to know what it's like outside? It's all right outside. It's getting cooler this time of the year. There wasn't much sun when I came inside. It looked like it could rain. You aren't missing anything."

Alice seemed to stare right through me into my soul when I spoke to her. A small smile played at the corners of her full, pale lips, and she gradually lowered her hand from the wall. "That's easy for you to say, handsome."

The repartee between us felt strangely normal and casual, like we were at home years ago having a parent-to-child chat.

"You look good," I said.

She cocked her head and narrowed her gaze at me. "Compared to?"

"I've seen old photos of you in the press." I breathed faster.

"You must have been quite young when my case broke." For a moment, I fretted she would question me. "You aren't so bad after all. I think I kind of like you. I think I'm going to allow you to stay. " Alice patted her dark hair, which was much shorter than it had been. " . . . possibly."

"You'll speak to me, then?" My breathing somewhat returned to normal.

She shrugged. "Oh, why not?" Then she said, "For a little while," as though she wanted to put me in my place.

I cut right to the chase. "I'm here to talk with you because I'm from a place where murders are occurring."

That got her to pause, and her silence lasted for so long I feared she'd changed her mind.

"You aren't from around here," she said, looking me over. "I thought you were a local, because what you mentioned about your friend knowing that detective. Where are you from? No one forewarned me that you'd be coming to see me. Judging by your clothes, I'd say you are a city fellow. Those are expensive looking shoes."

I uncrossed my legs. "I live in Seven Sisters."

"A big city. It's not too far from here but I've never been there myself."

"What do you do there?"

"I'm a freelance journalist."

"Oh, that's right." Alice slapped her thigh and her laughter thundered out. "For a moment I thought we were old friends. Funny how it feels that way, when we've never met before, or have we?" She tilted her head and smiled, her teeth shiny and wet.

Emotion drove me to silence, and I didn't look at Alice for a moment or two but could feel her gaze on me. I set my notepad on the small counter in front of me and leaned in to write down our interview, but throughout the visit I rarely looked at the questions for her that I'd composed. Once I was there with her, I didn't need reminders of the questions I wanted to ask.

I found it strange she hadn't asked questions about the murders in Seven Sisters. "Aren't you going to ask me about the murders I mentioned?" I said.

"Is that a trick question?"

"No."

"I'm not committing them, if that's what you're getting at. Trapped in here, how could I be? What's this got to do with me? You want my expert opinion? You want to work together to solve it? I don't know who is doing it, that's my damn opinion." She gave a dry laugh and looked very pleased with herself.

I didn't overlook how she'd referred to the murders in the present tense. "The murders are similar to yours, that's why it should interest you." I'd abandoned the travel writer bit entirely.

"It's not every day I get visitors. Thanks for stopping by," she said.

I was determined to leave there with answers and didn't rise. "I'm not going anywhere."

"Fine. You stay, then. I'll go." Alice started to move.

"You're not as intimidating as I'd thought you'd be," I said to challenge her.

"In which ways are they, the murders, the same?" she asked. On the other side of the glass, her presence didn't appear as meek as it once had.

Serial murderers enjoyed hearing the grisly details of fellow killers' crimes, and I didn't want her getting off on a victim's demise. Blood pounded relentlessly in my head and burned my ears. I reminded myself that I was a new person and had shaped a new existence with Sammie, but there were moments in my life I doubted I'd ever overcome, and I held on strongly to the memories of them, for they'd become as tangible a part of me as loving Sammie was.

Alice Lane had uprooted me in my early years and stolen Ben from me, the one true friend I'd had in life before I met Sammie, and I never forgot her crimes and who she was to me. My mother, yes, but a monster too. A monster both to the outside world and to me, and an unimaginably cruel being with a hankering for flesh, blood, and bone. It struck me then that I'd never really *known* my mother. Even with me she'd feigned being someone other than her true self, or could a person have had two detached sides to them: Loving mother and sadistic killer?

Alice's pink tongue darted around the corners of her mouth like her appetite had been whetted. I longed to push my hand through the glass panel somehow and slap that smile off her face. Had Alice Lane wanted to murder me, what she'd seen in front of her right then, a young man, a stranger to her? But didn't she, my mother, deserve to smile? Perhaps she wasn't hungry for flesh and blood but content at having a visitor. That begged the question, did a killer have the right to be happy when their victims no longer could experience the same?

A promise I'd made to myself before I journeyed to Freedom Village had been that, if I got to see Alice, I wouldn't view her as my mother, and no matter what she said or did, I'd view her for what she was: a heartless killer. One doesn't often associate those words with one's mother, but it was the only thing I'd felt I could do to prevent myself from breaking down in sobs and telling her how I'd missed her over the years, and that I loved her.

"I can't give you details of the crimes," I said.

"No problem. I'll have my lawyer bring me a newspaper and find out that way. What do I need you for anyway?"

I maintained my composure despite her insolence. "I'm privy to details the press wouldn't know."

"How come?"

I didn't wish to give too much away so I explained, "I have a friend who works with the police."

"You have very beneficial friends," she remarked. "What details did your friend tell you?"

"I can't say."

Alice sighed. "Then what am I supposed to get in return? You want to hear my opinion but you want me to ask for nothing in exchange. Doesn't seem very fair to me, considering I'm in here and you're free."

How manipulative she could be; a sweet-looking lady with a steely core.

"I promise to portray you in a fair light," I said. "I won't intentionally make you look like a ghoul."

In Alice's presence, I'd completely dropped the idea of being a lifestyle writer. Locked away in prison, how could she have known what I'd told the townsfolk? And on my way inside I'd only mentioned to the guards something about being a journalist, not what kind of journalist.

Alice leaned toward her means of escape, the call button by her shoulder. "That's still not a fair trade."

"Then what do you want, a gift?" I kind of wished I'd bought her one.

She toyed with the button.

"Stop," I said. "I've come this far. Tell me what you want, and I'll . . . see what I can do."

"I want you to get in touch with my daughter and tell me how she's doing."

I restrained a gasp. It would have been so easy to declare right then, "I'm your child," but I said casually, "What's her name?"

"Evelyn. Last I heard from her, which was years ago, she was not married, so her last name's probably still Lane. We lost touch."

"I'll try. Does she live in town?"

"No, I don't think so. My lawyer said she didn't. My baby stopped writing to me years ago. It breaks my heart."

How could she not have recognized my eyes or my smile? "I'm . . . " It was on the tip of my tongue, and I'd almost revealed my identity to her.

Alice looked at me, waiting for me to elaborate.

"I'm sure I'll find her," I said to appease her. "But it could take some time. In the meantime—"

"Why should I do your favor before you do mine?"

"Finding your daughter's whereabouts will take time. It's not like I can walk into town, grab her, and bring her here to you. You said so yourself that you don't know where she is."

"You're going to bring her to me? That's wonderful. I would have settled for hearing how she's doing, but I like the sound of her visiting me in person better."

I'd dug myself in deep but couldn't renege then. "*If* I can find her, and *if* she wants to come here."

"There is no *if*. Now that you've mentioned it, I expect you to keep your word, and I'll do the same. I'll make it worth your while, believe me."

"What you're asking for is more complicated. Besides, you might not have the information I need. I could be wasting my time here."

"And you might not find my daughter and could be wasting my time. Ask me what you want to know and then you can see if you feel the same way, that I might be 'wasting' your time."

"Do you receive letters from anyone?" I asked.

"You mean, from the media?"

"No, but *has* anyone from the press tried to contact you lately?" I wouldn't have been surprised if Alice answered yes, given how far the *Crime Man* post seemed to have spread.

"Besides you?" She had a 'got you!' glimmer in her eyes, and I wondered if she was onto me, if I'd slipped. "No, in the past few months, there's been no one except you," she said.

"You've mentioned you have fans. A fan of your work has tried to contact you, perhaps?"

"I'm insulted you think I'd help out an amateur."

"Did you work with a partner?" I said. Although that was unlikely, it had occurred to me.

"Even if I had, what makes you think I'd tell you that?"

"How about someone who you're . . . instructing?"

"Are you suggesting that I'm giving orders to someone from inside this place?" She twisted around and knocked on the cement walls surrounding her. "That'd be a pretty *hard* thing to do, don't you think?" she winked.

I didn't laugh at her joke. "No. I was thinking more along the lines of a copycat, someone who has reached out to you in admiration, and who is trying to replicate your murders in my city, possibly to please you."

"Why on earth would anyone want to do that?"

"I don't know your kind. You tell me what they're like."

"I wouldn't have an answer, either."

Her statement caused me to pause.

"No one like that has been writing to me," she said. "The few letters I get in here are from my lawyer and hate mail telling me I'm an awful kid killer and will rot in hell." She glanced around at her steel and cement surroundings. "Seems like I already am rotting in hell." Alice yawned and covered her mouth, a habit I recognized from my youth. "Excuse me, I'm a little tired. The hate mail's thinned out over the years."

"Your family doesn't write?" I'd been estranged from the rest of our family and wasn't aware whether they were in contact with Alice.

"My daughter doesn't write to me. I think she hates me. It won't be easy getting her to come here to see me, but if anyone can do it, I know you can." Her eyes held a naïve admiration for me, then I grasped that it wasn't appreciation of me but for herself because she'd managed to trick me. I'd consented to assist her if she spoke to me, which, in theory, she had.

She'd dodged the real question, the one I'd asked about our family in general. But she wouldn't have expected a small-time journalist, like I pretended I was, to know who our family encompassed. Yet, if I pushed her, it could make her vanish into her apathetic shell again and I'd never get a taste of the answers I sought.

"Thanks for having so much faith in me," I said bitterly. "But you can't do that, you can't give me so little and expect more from me than you give me in return. I won't help you unless you give me more."

"I said I would talk to you and I am. That was our deal. You liking what I have to say *wasn't* part of our deal. You have to carry out your end of our bargain, that's how it works. I told you no one like that's been writing to me. I'm not even considering telling you anything else until you can give me your word you've found my daughter."

"I'm not going through the trouble of bringing her here if you have nothing significant to tell me."

"I didn't say you had to bring her to visit me right away, I said I need some kind of indication you've located her and then are able to bring her here *when the time comes*."

"Why do you want to prolong seeing her?"

"Mind your own business," she said, and I swore she shed a tear.

My mother loved having the last word, and that hadn't changed during the years we'd been separated. Time might have changed me but it hadn't moved her. It must be hard for a prisoner to advance inside a place where time often remained still, a place that never moved despite the world constantly evolving outside its doors. Alice might have seen her lawyer's smart-phone but she'd likely never held or used one herself.

But I was grown, and I couldn't let my mother have the final word. "If I agree to do that, will you talk to me some more now?"

"I'm going to need your word you're working on finding her, which obviously you aren't at the moment, so, no, not until you leave and get cracking on finding my daughter, will I tell you anything else. You can come back when you have something about her, then we'll continue this conversation." Her gaze lifted to the clock at my back. "It's almost time for dinner in here, and if I'm not in my cell by the time they're serving, they won't leave a tray for me." The word *cell* gutted me into inertia, and before I could reply, she'd pressed the button to make the speaker at her side work. "Guard, we're done here," she said. "We're done. We're done." The repetition made her sound like the madwoman she evidently had always been except through my younger, too-trusting eyes.

A female guard came to collect Alice on the other side. Alice waved to me when she was being led out.

The door opened behind me and Karl's friend, the other guard, entered the room. I stood up.

"How did you know I was finished if I didn't ring you?" I asked.

"I happened to be near this wing." He touched the two-way radio clipped to his belt. "I was notified that the prisoner was being removed and I came to collect you. I didn't think you'd want to stay in this pit a second longer than you need to, or am I wrong, do you like it here?" He gave me a sly grin. I avoided his gaze. "How did your chat with the resident cannibal go?" he asked. "You get enough stuff for your article? Just what is it that you're working on?" He stared at the notebook I held. "I might not look like much of a reader but I am. I also happen to know the guy who helped you get in here—Mack?"

Could it have been that I'd taken his presence too lightly? "What's your name, again?" I asked.

"I never gave it to you, but it's Eddie."

"They should make you wear nametags," I said. Eddie grimaced like he didn't fancy the idea, and I sensed neither of us favored shaking hands. "By the way, I'm a travel writer."

Eddie lifted an eyebrow. "And you were here to do an interview because you're writing about the serial killer tourism industry."

It took me a moment to gather he wasn't kidding. "No, I'm writing about Freedom Village in general and also the surrounding vineyards."

"Then why are you here, in the pen? Why aren't you at the wine convention?"

"That type of event is a little too obvious for my taste. Alice Lane is a big attraction."

He nodded in agreement. "I might look dumb but don't be fooled: I'm not." Eddie stood a good foot taller than me.

Feeding him more lies would have intensified an already deteriorating situation. Giving him a grain of the truth, that I was digging into a series of new murders, could have opened a Pandora's box of shit I wasn't prepared to manage. I opted to ignore him, for I didn't owe him an explanation. If this fellow knew Mack like he claimed, I trusted Mack would have my back and cover for me if Eddie inquired about my identity.

"I'd like to go to my car now," I said. "I believe that's what you're here for, to escort me out?"

Eddie cleared his throat and held still for a bit. He made an elaborate, servant type of gesture at the door. "After you."

I touched my nametag. "What do I do with this?"

"Keep it," he said.

"You're sure?"

"Yep."

"Good, because I might return."

I felt somewhat horrid acting like an elitist to him, but he wasn't a decent guy himself. I shoved my notepad into my satchel and strode into the hallway after him.

The rest of the walk consisted of me following Eddie in silence. Karl wasn't inside the area where they'd searched me when I arrived, and I continued out to the parking lot without uttering a word to anyone else. Distraught at the reunion with my mother, I wouldn't have been able to speak even if someone had wanted to talk, or there had been somebody to speak with.

Back in the car, I texted Mack.

*Do you know a guy named Eddie who's a guard at the prison?*

I'd been wrong about the rain and the sky had cleared while I was inside with Alice.

A minute passed before Mack wrote.

*I take it your visit went well. Eddie said he knew me? I wouldn't say I knew him. Arrested him for DUI last summer. Guy cried like a baby in the backseat.*

*Thanks. Had a bit of a run-in with him.*

*You ok?* Mack asked.

*Couldn't be better.*

My hands shook as I started the car.

# Chapter 13

That night I sat at the counter in the diner in town, eating a solitary dinner of gooey blueberry pie, and plenty of coffee. Tawny came in a couple minutes after I began eating.

She stood by my shoulder. "Hi, Evan."

I turned in my counter stool to greet her. "How are you?"

"I'm pretty good, thanks. Are you enjoying your stay in Freedom? I'm glad to see you're in the best place to dine around these parts." Whenever I saw her, she was smiling, and I wondered how she managed to find so much contentment in her life. "My spies tell me this isn't the first time you've been in here. I take it you like the food?"

I chuckled. "Your spies are right. The food's terrific. Please give my compliments to the chef."

"I'll go tell him myself." She smiled again.

From where I sat I could see the kitchen, and Tawny went back there and spoke with the chef, her boyfriend. The diner began to fill up as people left work for the evening. Soon every stool around me at the counter had someone sitting on it. Tawny pointed at me and I waved to acknowledge the young chef, who shouted his thanks.

My server gave me a fourth refill of coffee and I put the cup to my lips. The ringtone I used for Sammie jingled away and I set the cup down on the saucer before I could take a sip. Sammie almost always texted first unless she had something very important to convey to me, such as something wasn't right. I answered, my skin burning with anger and my throat closing in, certain she would tell me the press had started to hound her outside our building or, worse, that they'd somehow managed to get inside the building and found our front door.

"Are they bothering you?" I said. "Because if they are—"

"Is who?"

"The reporters."

"That's not why I'm calling you." She released a long breath.

"Are you all right?" Then I thought of the dog, who hadn't been eating and might have been ill. "Is it Paige, is she—"

"That's not it either. She's fine. Still not eating but okay otherwise."

I sighed. "Are *you* okay?"

Sometimes it took Sammie a while to get the truth out. She didn't like anybody being worried on her account. This seemed to be one of those times.

"I am. We are," she said. "Someone broke into the apartment. I wasn't here when it happened. I was at work, actually. Paige is fine, though. They didn't hurt her, and she didn't get out through the door."

"*What?* When the hell did this happen?"

"When I was at work," she reminded me.

I didn't know she had returned to work, and, normally, the fact that she hadn't told me would have wounded me, if I hadn't been so distraught over the news of a break-in. Visiting Alice in prison had been anything but uplifting, but I'd found comfort in the fact that I'd believed Sammie and I were on agreeable terms again. "Are you okay? Is Paige okay?"

"Yes. I just said we were. Are *you* all right?"

"I don't know if I am. I need to ask you a few questions before I know whether I'm all right. What did they take from the apartment? Did they leave a—"

"I already looked around for a note. There's nothing. I found nothing. It doesn't seem like they took anything. They moved around a few things but didn't take anything."

"What things did they move around?"

"Some photos."

"The TV's still there?" To my ears, I sounded astounded. "People just don't break into apartments and leave empty-handed, unless they didn't find what they came looking for."

"Like what?" she said.

"I'm not sure yet. Or they wanted to scare us, let us know they could enter our home without our knowledge."

"Who would want to do that? All the people I can think of who would want to do something like that because I helped put them away are all still in prison."

"Maybe it's not you who they're trying to frighten. You need to dust for prints."

"Are you saying that maybe they're trying to scare you?" Sammie's voice reverberated out of my phone and the people seated closest to me stared. "Me dust for prints? I'm no longer with the force."

"Hold on a second." I jumped off the stool and left my pie half-eaten on the counter.

Tawny ducked her head into the dining area from the kitchen. "Evan, is everything all right?"

"Yeah, I'll return in a second to pay," I replied over my shoulder, and then ran out the door. "Sorry about that. I was in a crowded diner," I said to Sammie.

"You're dining alone? I thought I heard someone talking to you just now." Sammie's voice held misgivings. Did she think I would stray from her that easily?

"I'm alone. The diner is crowded. There's a lot of people talking inside. Someone from the hotel recommended the diner. It's right in the town, close to the hotel." I didn't elaborate that the *someone* was a woman. Sammie got jealous easily, but I was loyal to her and she needn't have worried. "Have you called the police?" I asked.

"I don't want to because you missed your hearing," she said. "Gilani told you not to leave the state. I'm afraid they'd ask me questions about where you are."

I winced. The chief had left me a voicemail message saying he wasn't my goddamn babysitter and I should have made an appearance.

"They would," I said to Sammie. "You should check for prints. I know you kept a lot of your old equipment. Tonight, if you're feeling up to it, dust for them. One more thing—how do you know the apartment was broken into if nothing was stolen?"

"They busted the lock."

"If you can't get someone to come fix it tonight, I want you to go to a hotel with Paige. I don't want you staying there by yourself if you can't lock the door, do you understand?"

"Listen, macho man, I can take care of myself, okay?" I detected a smile in Sammie's voice.

"With your training, I have no doubt you could. But you no longer keep a gun in the house."

On the sidewalk in front of the diner, the constant quietness that enveloped the town compared to my bustling urban home startled me.

"And I know that you are aware that bad things can happen," I said to Sammie. "But I need you to promise me you won't turn your back if you're inside our apartment without a lock on the door. The person who broke in could return to finish—"

"To finish murdering me, is that what you're saying?"

"It's possible. You might have startled them when you came in."

"The kitchen window was open. I didn't hear anything when I entered but I guess they could've easily jumped the distance to the sidewalk from the fire escape. It isn't too far down from there."

"Someone must have let them into the building. Most likely by accident they held the door open for the wrong person."

"You want me to notify people that some creep got into the building?"

"No. That could scare someone into ringing the police. We don't need anything getting back to Gilani and then having him asking you questions about me. Has he called you?"

"Yep. He wondered whether I knew where you are. I said we'd had a fight and that I had no idea where you went after you left. I said you hadn't called me."

"He believed you?"

"He must have because he didn't contradict me."

"Did you tell him I took the car?"

"Nope."

"Thanks for that."

"What's a lover for if not to lie to the police for you?"

I chuckled. Even then, Sammie had a sense of humor and I loved that about her. "What are we going to do if someone in the building heard the noise of the break-in or saw something?" I said. "Heard Paige barking?"

"She isn't much of a guard dog. No one has said anything to me, and no one from the force has shown up here. The people here tend to keep to themselves. You know how it is in a big city, people mind their own business."

We'd appreciated that aspect of city life. Our apartment building was old and didn't have security cameras. "Right, that's true. Sometimes too true. Unlike where I am." I looked around the quiet streets. "Hey, you can sway the cops if they do show up."

"With, what, my charm? Oh, you mean because I use to be one of them. Sure, why the hell not, I'll give it a try if the time comes."

"That's my girl."

Sammie became quiet for a few seconds and then she let out a big sigh.

"What's going on, Sam?" I said.

"I thought you might like to know that there have been no new murders here—in Seven Sisters—since that website, well, you know what they did."

"I do want to know that so thanks for telling me." My gratitude was genuine. Then I spoke with sarcasm, "And that means there have been no new killings since I left. I hope no one else, like a certain police chief you and I both know, thinks of that."

"Evan, you can't think that way."

"But they can. And they might if I'm not careful."

"Don't say that. I believe in you."

"Then that's all that matters to me," I answered truthfully.

"How are things going there? Have you been able to get some answers?"

Sammie knew my past more than any other person in my life, but I'd managed to withhold my visit to Alice. "It hasn't been easy," I said, painfully aware of what I held back from Sammie.

"And? What have you found out, or have you not found anything yet?" she spoke softly.

"I wouldn't say that." I spoke quietly despite the lack of pedestrians on the sidewalk. "I visited the detective who worked on my mother's case."

"How did it go?" Sammie knew a little about Mack, the little amount I'd opened up to her regarding his involvement and supportive presence in my life at one time.

"Fine. It went fine. I don't know how much he can help me, but . . ." Reining in the truth from her felt like pretending I didn't love her. But at the time I felt that not mentioning Alice would simply be better. I sighed in frustration at the growing problems I faced, not all of which Sammie knew. "I just want them to let me return to work."

"I know," Sammie said. "I understand how much your job means to you. Don't you wonder if you should have stuck around here for the hearing? You ran off—"

The conversation was veering into less comfortable territory and made me want to tell her I had to take care of something and hang up. "I needed to—I had to—I had to come here and try to find some answers, and if I don't, I can say I tried. I can't explain it."

Sammie murmured and I didn't catch what she said, whether it was words of support or displeasure at my choice.

"I don't like you and Paige being in the apartment without me nearby," I said.

"I'm a big girl."

"I have no doubt you're capable of kicking someone's ass, but do you want me to come home early?"

Sammie's silence on the other end lasted for what felt like an eternity, because that was what she'd wanted to hear me say—that'd I come back—but it seemed like my offer to suddenly return prompted her into inaction because she didn't want me to resent her if she said yes, come home.

"No, I'll be fine, we'll be fine," she finally said. "Are you sure everything's okay with you there?"

My throat tightened and my longing to return to her seeped through my voice. "Yeah. Listen, call me when the lock's fixed. Do it tonight. Don't forget."

"I won't."

"Love you," I said, but she'd already signed off.

I stepped inside the diner to finish my meal. Despite the crowded atmosphere, I'd never felt so alone in my life.

*

I rolled out of bed late the following morning. With some coaxing and pleading on my part last night, Mack had arranged for me to visit Alice a second time. I'd have to lie to her that I'd somehow found information on her daughter overnight. Mack had wanted to meet me in person again to discuss the whole situation but I'd managed to avoid that, for now. I'd told him I hadn't gotten what I wanted the first time and needed a second chance. After some pushing on my end, he'd reluctantly surrendered.

A text from Sammie appeared on my phone screen and I questioned whether I was still asleep and dreaming. I'd mistakenly fallen asleep last night without having received word from her that our apartment's front lock had been fixed, and now I panicked. Had something happened in the middle of the night and I wasn't aware?

*I'm in the lobby.*

My breathing returned to more of a normal pattern, but, wait. Sammie was in the lobby, my hotel lobby? My fingers worked swiftly to formulate a coherent reply. I eyed the half empty bottle of cheap whiskey on the table by the window. It'd been full when I brought it up to my room last night. I'd picked up the whiskey at the liquor shop on my way to the lodge from the diner. How much had I drunk last night? I'd consumed it straight from the bottle, sans glass.

*Where are you*? I wrote.

*Hotel.*

*The lodge*? *Here*? *In Freedom*?

*Yep. I brought Paige along.*

If what she wrote wasn't part of some sort of half-awake dreaming state that I was in, was I really okay with her being there?

When I didn't type a response, Sammie wrote.

*Can you come down and get me*? *I don't think they'll let me up to your room unless you confirm you know me.*

*They're giving you a hard time*? I texted back.

*Not yet. I'm explaining to them now.*

*I'll be right down.*

I put the cap back on the whiskey bottle and tossed it into the trash receptacle in the bathroom, but the bottle's neck stuck out in such an obvious way that I removed it and then hid the bottle in the closet.

I started to ask Sammie if she'd spent all of the previous night on the road but stopped when I recalled I could ask her that in person in less than a minute. I put on the jeans I wore to the prison yesterday and left on the rumpled t-shirt I'd slept in last night. I wondered if the manager was downstairs. I hadn't given him my check-out day yet and had avoided him earlier. Perhaps he wouldn't ask for one if I continued to make him believe my journalist-on-assignment story, but would he or Tawny allow Sammie, an unregistered guest, to stay in my room? I wasn't sure about the lodge's policy on those matters.

I went into the bathroom and splashed cold water on my face. In the mirror above the sink my eyes looked bloodshot. If someone didn't know me very well, then maybe they wouldn't have noticed, but Sammie knew me better than anyone in the world.

I shut my room door and jogged down the stairwell instead of using the elevator, hoping it might somehow clear away the dreadful headache and ringing in my ears.

Sammie carried Paige in her arms and was speaking with Tawny at the front desk. Sammie turned when I came in and frowned when she saw me. If I looked as bad as I felt, then I wouldn't have been able to disguise my boozy night after all. Sammie would have crossed her arms if she hadn't been holding Paige.

"Evan," Tawny said. "Mr. *Samuels*," she corrected herself.

I acknowledged her with a nod.

Sammie took me by the arm and pulled me aside in the lobby. Paige wagged and I rubbed her head. "There's a discrepancy. They seem to have registered you under a different name."

I explained to her my reasons for doing that.

She grimaced. "I guess I blew your cover, huh?" Paige snuggled into Sammie's chest.

"Probably, but that's okay. You couldn't have known." I hoped to hell that I was right and everything *would* be okay. I tried to read Tawny's body language behind the desk. She wasn't smiling at me like she usually did when I'd see her around the lodge, but she didn't appear suspicious either. "Did you drive through the night to get here? Is the lock on our door—"

"Yes, and, yes, of course, it's fixed. I left right after he was gone. I wouldn't have left without doing that first."

"I would have come home, you know, if you wanted me there. You didn't have to come all the way here. What about your work, are they fine with you not being there?"

"They'll be fine if I miss a few more days. They don't know what's going on exactly, just that it's a family thing, and that is true, you are my family, Evan, and I'm yours. I decided I want to be here for you, to go through this with you. I was worried about you. You sounded so—I don't know—hopeless—when I called yesterday."

"I love you," I said.

"I love you too."

"Did any cops come around the apartment?" I asked.

Sammie shook her head. "And I don't think anyone's been watching the place. Are you okay with us being here?"

I thought over her loaded question and then concluded, "It's better you're both here because then I know you're safe." I paused and Sammie seemed relieved. I kissed her cheek. "With everything that happened, I forgot to ask, how did Paige's appointment with the vet go?" I said.

"And I forgot to tell you. He didn't find anything wrong with Paige. She's still not eating, though."

I sighed. "I feel guilty about the whole thing, like we're putting her health on the back burner."

Sammie squeezed my arm. "Don't feel bad, Evan. We're taking care of her the best we can. I should mention I did check our apartment for prints and found nothing unique."

"That's odd."

"It is, but I compared the many prints I found around the house with the prints we have on some personal objects. I found no prints besides our own. My guess is that the intruder wore gloves."

"Have things been, you know, pretty quiet, back at home?"

"When I left, there were no new murders. I mentioned that to you?"

I nodded. "No new murders since I've been gone. Terrific. I wouldn't want to see anyone else get killed but this is not looking good for me."

"Don't be ridiculous. Chief Gilani never said they suspected you." Sammie raised her voice and Tawny gave us an officious look. "What's on your schedule for today?" Sammie must have seen me react physically from the anxiety her question caused me because she said, "You do your thing, and I'll stay with Paige. You won't even know we're here."

I was scheduled to meet with Alice again at the prison that afternoon, something I'd kept hidden from Sammie, but I answered, "It's no problem, but, yes, that'd be great if you could watch her. You two come with me and I'll deal with the desk person. Let's get you settled in. You must be tired and should rest. Do you have luggage? How did you get up here anyhow if I took the car? The bus?"

"I rented a car. I drove through the night."

Sammie stood next to me at the front desk. She had set Paige down on the floor by then and held onto her leash. The dog walked around us in circles.

I explained to Tawny who Sammie was to me. "I know you're pretty full here." Then I said to Sammie, "There's a wine convention happening outside town if you want to check that out later. I'm sure you can carry Paige around inside." I spoke to Tawny again. "Can they be squeezed into my room? I thought I saw a sign posted somewhere that you accept pets."

"For an extra fee, yes, we do allow them, on a case-by-case basis," she said.

"I see. Paige, our dog, is very well-behaved, and as you can see, she's also very small."

That caused Tawny to smile. I tensed when she didn't speak, and I waited for her to ask me why I had two different surnames and who I was in relation to Alice Lane. After a minute she said, "I'll have to ask my manager. He's coming in this afternoon."

"I won't be here in the afternoon. I have a meeting. Is there any way we could speed things up?" I leaned on the desk and grinned at her.

She didn't return my cordiality. "She can bring her luggage to your room, but I'll still have to ask my manager how I'm supposed to go about charging you, since your room's a single and not a double occupancy."

"That's fine," I said. "And the dog, can she come up?"

Tawny nodded. "I'll add the pet fee to your room bill. Do you have a better idea of when you'll be leaving us?"

"I'm working on that."

"Very well, sir. Let me know if there's anything else you need." She'd turned cold seemingly overnight, or even that morning.

I walked with Sammie out to her rental car to help her carry her luggage inside. Sammie took

Paige over to the grassy section of the parking lot so the dog could do her business.

"You seem friendly with the desk girl," Sammie said when they returned.

"Not really. Just trying to get what we want from them." I hadn't told her I'd known Tawny in high school. "And I knew her in school." I figured that was something I didn't need to keep hidden.

Compassion softened Sammie's features. "Does she know who you are?"

"She didn't when I arrived."

"But now that I used the Lane surname, she might, right?"

"Or she might be too polite to say anything."

Sammie sighed. "I'm really sorry, Evan. This isn't good. How long are we going to stay here?"

"I'm not sure. Not too much longer, I think."

It had taken some time getting used to but I loved how whenever I was around Sammie everything became *we* or *us*. Paige nudged my shoe and I hunkered down to the ground to stroke her fur, warm and velvety under my fingers. "How are you?" I said, and she pressed her wet nose to mine.

*

Sammie settled into my room. She didn't unpack her suitcase, and neither had I. We kept our luggage atop the dresser to dig out of them. Paige sat on the unmade bed, watching us. I'd hung the 'Do Not Disturb' sign on the door handle outside so the cleaning people wouldn't interrupt us.

"I'm glad you came," I said to Sammie. "But I wished you'd called me before you left so I could have had time to prepare."

"Prepare for?"

"For example, I could've sorted things out with the front desk before you arrived. But it's okay. I'm glad both of you are here with me now."

"I didn't say anything to you because you would've told me not to come. It's always like you, Evan, to not want to make a big deal out of anything, but some things *are* a big deal. This trip you took here is one of them." Sammie started for the closet. "Maybe I'll hang up some of my clothes so they don't get wrinkled."

"Don't go in there!" I dashed toward her.

Before I could stop her she'd opened the door, bent down, and picked up the whiskey bottle. She twirled it in her hand and stared at me. "Time to prepare for, what, to hide this? I thought you looked slightly hungover when I first saw you, but I gave you the benefit of the doubt."

I started to gently take the bottle from her hand. "I'm sorry. I lost control a little last night after I saw . . . my mother." My voice faded.

"You *what*?" The bottle fell from Sammie's hand and clanked on the carpet. "You came here to see your mother?"

I moved Paige over and sat down on the side of the bed. "When I arrived here, I didn't know if I'd get to visit her in the prison. But after I stopped by Detective Mack's house—he's the one who handled her case—I decided it might be possible for me to see her after all. I was right, and Mack got me in to see her yesterday. In fact, I'm visiting her again this afternoon."

"Detective Mack? Wasn't he a mentor to you? Does he know who you are?"

"Indeed, I told him who I am. He had assisted the FBI with the local investigation into my mother's case. He'd treated me well and didn't act like I was a rotten apple just because I was a serial killer's kid."

Sammie sat next to me on the bed and our thighs touched. "You should have told me you visited your mother. We could've talked about it together, then you wouldn't have turned to that." She pointed at the whiskey bottle, on its side on the carpet. Sammie reached for the eyeglasses I bought at the drugstore and had left on the nightstand last night. "I *am* glad you came out to your mom. Since when do you wear glasses?"

"Never. I bought them to—never mind." If Sammie thought I came out to Alice, she wouldn't have understood why I'd disguised myself during the prison visit. "I got them for laughs."

Sammie stared at me without speaking. Was she trying to figure out what I'd been doing in her absence? Then she said, "Let me come with you this afternoon."

"It's only been arranged for me to visit the prison. Besides, who will watch—"

"Paige will be fine in the room by herself for a few hours. I left her comfy travel crate in my rental's backseat. We can bring it inside and she can rest in there while we're away. She's quiet so the lodge won't mind." Sammie pressed her hand against my leg and I held it there.

"My mother doesn't—I haven't come out to her yet."

Sammie sighed. The silence lasted between us for a few seconds. Then she spoke with vigor, "I want to be there for you today when you do."

I took my hand off hers. "You don't understand—even if I wanted to tell her, I can't now. She thinks I'm someone else."

Sammie's hold on me loosened. "Who does she think you are?"

"A journalist from Seven Sisters. She thinks I'm writing a story about the murders there."

"What are you seeking, Evan? Why are you here if not to reconnect with your mother?"

"I need to know why someone is killing again and what I have to do with it."

Sammie rose and paced about the room. Paige's gaze followed Sammie's movements. "Does that detective—Mack—know about this?"

It took me a few seconds to admit yes, he did.

"It isn't—you can't pretend to be someone you're not and enter a prison. I can't believe a detective went along with this crazy idea. You both could be in deep trouble if someone finds out. Did you give them a different name?"

"Of course."

"Which is?"

"Evan Samuels. That's the surname I've given people since I arrived. Sammie. Samuels. You know." I attempted a smile. "Too many people in this town associate the name Lane with my mother. That's why there was confusion at the desk downstairs when you came in and told them you wanted to see me."

"Yeah, but what about at the prison? They must've noticed your identification has a different last name."

"I told them I left my ID in the car. They didn't make me go get it. Mack helped me get inside. They know him at the jail. It's a small town."

Sammie ceased walking and looked at me. "Are you planning on lying to them this afternoon too?"

"I'm sticking with the story I've given them, yes."

"You're not going to tell your mother who you are?"

"No. I'm not here to—to deal with that. I'm here to find answers about the Seven Sisters murders and the deadnaming messages. This has nothing to do with reuniting with my mother."

Sammie sat by me again and Paige walked over on the bed and stretched across our laps. "I bet the next thing you're going to say to me is, you don't want me to come to the prison with you, am I right?"

"Would you mind terribly if you didn't?" I said.

Sammie embraced me with Paige still between us. "I only want to support you." She rested her head on my shoulder and her breath warmed my skin through my shirt.

"Thanks for coming," I spoke into her neck.

Sammie sat up in my arms. "I didn't feed Paige before I left, and I didn't feed her during the trip because I didn't want her getting carsick." She unwrapped herself from me and walked to a tote bag she'd set on the floor when we entered the room. "I'll feed her now. Of course, it'll throw off her schedule a bit."

I rose to assist Sammie, and Paige stayed on the bed, viewing us with little interest. "Do you think she'll eat?" I asked Sammie.

"Probably not." Sammie couldn't restrain her tears and I wiped them away with my thumbs.

"Here, let me."

I removed Paige's food and water bowls from the bag. I filled one bowl with cool water from the bathroom tap and put her food into the other bowl. Then I set them on the floor near the bathroom, and Sammie walked to the bed to gather Paige. She placed Paige down in front of the dishes, squatted to the dog's level and whispered encouragements for Paige to eat. Paige looked at Sammie and then at me, behind them.

"Come here," I said to Sammie. "Give her some space and let's see if she eats then."

She rose to her feet, backed up, and stood by me. Paige glanced at us again, with her ears pulled back. She seemed to not like us watching her. I took Sammie's hand.

"Let's see what she does if we don't pay attention to her," I said.

We strolled over to the television and I turned it on.

"Have *you* eaten?" I asked, sitting down with Sammie on the bed to watch TV. I found a news program and left that on.

She kept stealing looks at Paige. "On the way up I carried Paige inside with me at a rest stop and had breakfast," she said. "What about you, have you eaten today?"

As if on instinct, my stomach grumbled. I shook my head.

"And you're hungover? You must have one hell of a headache." Sammie gave me a reproachful look.

"I'll get something to eat later. I have to see my mother at noon."

"Later? When's later? It's well past mid-morning and you're going to visit your mother at noon. Does the lodge have a restaurant inside?"

Sammie's concern made me grin. "No. There's a diner in the village. I've been there a few times. It's pretty good. The front desk receptionist recommended it."

"The girl downstairs?"

I nodded.

"The diner, that's the one you told me about?" Sammie asked.

"Yeah."

"When you were on the phone with me, you didn't mention who recommended it to you."

"I said someone from the lodge had."

"Yes, but you didn't say who."

"Does it matter?" I gently took her by the shoulders. "You're the one I love, Sammie."

She looked down at her lap and then at me. "You're right. I acted crazy. I trust you."

She wrapped her arms around my neck and pulled me into her chest. I outlined the soft warmness of her inner mouth with my tongue, and she pressed her lips deeply into mine. Sammie had the Chinese character for strength tattooed on her shoulder, and I pulled down her shirt a little and traced it with my finger.

"Do you hear that?" I asked.

Chewing and lapping sounds came from Paige's food and water bowls behind us. I peeked over my shoulder to find Paige eating her food and having sips of water. Sammie couldn't conceal her smile.

"What a relief! Do you think she'll stop eating if we get up?" Sammie asked.

"Let's not find out, shall we? She's not very big. Her meal won't take her too long to finish."

"Why do you think she started eating all the sudden, here of all places? Was she stressed at home like we were?"

"They do tend to sense those things," I said.

"Let's return to where we left off," Sammie said, and nibbled my smiling lips.

*

Shortly before noon, I left Paige and Sammie in my room at the lodge and started out for the prison. Sammie had her rental car and could venture outside if she needed to. I found relief in knowing that Sammie and Paige were near me and, thus, safe.

I passed Tawny at the front desk on my way out of the lodge to the parking lot. I'd hoped to avoid her but she called my name and I stopped. I turned on the heel of my shoes and walked to the desk.

"Hi, Tawny." I thought of a question to deflect her. "Is your manager around?" I set my hands on the desk.

"He's on his way in. I spoke to him on the phone about your guest and he said that was fine. There'll be no extra charge for our guest of honor."

"Who?" I said.

"You. You're our guest of honor because you're a famous journalist," she remarked.

I smiled. "Not exactly but thank you."

Her gaze fell to the shiny desk in front of her. "I know who you are—what you are."

The mood in the room had darkened. I smiled to put myself at ease. "I beg your pardon?" I tried to throw her off and took my hands off the desk to signal I wouldn't be staying to chat.

"After your girlfriend arrived, I figured out how come you look so familiar to me. I think I used to know you. Evelyn?" Tawny's once-warm eyes cooled. It took all the strength I had for me not to bolt then. "I realized it when your girlfriend came in and said your name was Evan Lane, not Evan Samuels. Evelyn doesn't have a brother."

Someone—not the manager—walked into the lobby, and Tawny lowered her voice to speak privately to me. "I didn't tell her I know what you are, in case she doesn't know. But I know what you are, and it's my belief that it doesn't make you a real man. I hope you get help." She spoke as though I was a *thing* and not a person.

I turned away from her and walked to the parking lot. I wasn't going to ask her not to say anything to others in town, because I wasn't going to hide. Initially, I'd hid for my own safety, but I wouldn't permit anyone to shame me. One matter remained uncertain: Would I tell Alice Lane I was her child?

In the car I locked the doors and texted Sammie to tell her what Tawny had said. Sammie replied straight away and I read her text as I started the engine.

*She really said that? I don't like her tone. I hope you told her to go to hell.*

*Not quite.* Then I wrote, *Mack won't let anything happen while I'm here*, to appease her.

*I'd still like to slap the smile off that little witch's face. Paige wouldn't let that woman pet her when we came in, did you know that? Our Paige must've known the woman was an asshole.*

I feared somewhat that Sammie would run downstairs and confront Tawny. *Relax, Sammie.*

*I can't. What if she Googles you and that Crime Man thing comes up? Think she'll tell them your whereabouts?*

They would have been interested to hear that Evan Lane was back in his hometown. And if Em, who I'd considered a friend, had sold me out, who knew what Tawny might do?

Then, Josh texted to see how I was and I responded to him. His note put a smile on my face.

It appeared Em had taken my hint because she'd stopped reaching out to me. Josh sent another text to say she'd written to him to apologize to me through him.

I replied to Sammie and dodged her concern.

*Text me if you need me. I'll write too. Love you.*

I tossed my phone to the passenger seat and drove out of the parking lot. Leaving Sammie and Paige behind in the room had me feeling guilty and I fretted on the drive over to the penitentiary.

# Chapter 14

A different guard managed the entrance booth but I went through the same routine to enter the prison grounds. Karl and Eddie awaited me when I stepped through the visitors' check-in area and we chatted as they administered the protocol of yesterday. I wore my nametag.

Karl greeted me with, "How are you? Wearing contacts today, sir?" He smiled.

"Yes, right. Better for my looks, you know." I chuckled. I'd forgotten to don the eyeglasses. "I'm well, thanks for asking. How are you guys doing?" I didn't actually care to know. I had plenty of other things on my mind, but being polite to them wouldn't hurt, although I disliked Eddie.

They remembered me from yesterday and didn't ask to see identification. I was lucky the prison was small enough to let a thing like that slide, and, who knew, maybe Mack had put Eddie in his place. I liked to believe he had.

"We're good, thanks," Karl said.

"You're back already?" Eddie said to me. "Thought you would've had enough of the crazy bitch." He didn't give any indication he was suspicious of me from yesterday. He *did* seem to take genuine pleasure in the fact that his tasteless remarks irked me. I ignored him and he pressed on. "I always wondered if she ate the dicks of the guys she killed." He guffawed and waited for Karl and me to join in.

Karl didn't laugh, but if he didn't intend to correct his colleague, then I would. "No one knows if she truly ate her victims," I said, using my clout as a 'journalist' to amend Eddie's assumption.

"For real?" Eddie's mouth hung open and made him look like more of an imbecile than, in all fairness, he probably was.

"Yes. Her cannibalism was only speculation by the press because a few parts of the victims were never found."

That piqued Karl's interest. "So what do you think she did with them, did with the parts?" he asked me.

"No one knows. They were never found," I said.

"See?" Eddie said. "She ate them."

"Or she collected them, stored them somewhere that the police didn't know about."

"How come you know so much about this?" Eddie smirked.

I didn't plan to answer. "Regardless, I don't find your brand of humor entertaining." I stared at Eddie directly.

He frowned. "Oh, well, excuse me," he muttered.

I ignored him and interacted with Karl. "May I go through now?"

Karl nodded and escorted me down the halls. The keys on his belt jangled as we strode. "I'm sorry about my partner," he said.

His apology surprised me. "That's all right, it isn't your fault." I smiled at him to convey we were on good terms.

He stopped walking and I ceased in my tracks just ahead of him. "You're not really a journalist are you?" he asked and gave me an uncertain smile.

"How come you would think that?"

"I don't follow those kinds of things. It's my wife, she writes for the newspaper in town. I told her about you and she got curious, said she searched for Evan Samuels online and couldn't find you. She said if you're a writer, you would've been all over the internet. A detective arranged for you to come so it's none of my business, but should you be here?"

I weighed my answers. I could tell him I used a pen name, I could stop the fabrications right then, or I could strike a balance between the two. "I hope this will be my last visit to your facility," I said, aware I wasn't admitting fault. And if it wasn't my final visit, why should I have expected him, someone who didn't owe me anything, to cover for me? Nonetheless, I had.

He stared at me for quite a while, as though to determine what should be his appropriate response, and then he nodded and resumed walking. I trotted after him, the sounds of our footsteps beating on the tiles the only noise in the corridor until a pack of similarly uniformed male and female guards led a young woman prisoner, shackled at the wrists and ankles, past us. The girl was so startlingly beautiful that she looked like she belonged at a cocktail party in a cosmopolitan city instead of being lugged around a small-town penitentiary.

"Where's she going?" I asked Karl. "I'm assuming you don't bring prisoners through the visitors' entrance."

"I'm afraid I can't disclose that, sir." His jaw hardened and it erased any trace of approachability from a few moments ago.

"What's she in for?" I attempted a smile to win him over. "I promise not to tell anybody." Why did I expected him to disobey procedure by answering my questions when, less than a minute ago, I'd ignored his enquiry?

Karl stayed quiet and didn't look at me. He followed the system from the other day of unlocking doors and leading me through into different corridors.

It occurred to me that I didn't know anything about him except that he worked at the prison and, as far as I could tell from the exchange at the front desk, appeared ethically superior to his counterpart. His wife worked for the local paper but I didn't recognize him from my youth so I reasoned it'd be harmless to ask, "Are you from around here?"

I'd caught him by surprise by asking him something personal, and he paused for a moment.

"No, but my wife is," he said. "That's how come we settled here. I was in the service with her brother, that's how we met."

I figured it would be safer not to ask for his wife's name so that if it turned out I knew her I wouldn't risk a spark of recognition appearing across my face. "Navy." I jabbed my thumb at my chest.

Karl seemed surprised. "Is that so?" His face brightened and his tone warmed. "I'm Army myself."

"That's too bad," I joked, and he chuckled. "Have you always been a prison guard? Did you begin here straight after the Army?"

Asking about his occupation could have been risky considering I hadn't denied his accusation about my being an imposter journalist, and might have prompted him to pursue the matter further, but my interest got the best of me.

The color rose in Karl's face and he shook his head. "I wanted to be a cop after I left the service but I didn't pass the test. This was second best."

I admired him for disclosing a fault not many people would have. Speaking with him mildly appeased my trepidation and my misgivings about my pending visit with Alice. "Do you like working here?" I asked. We had something in common after all: our jobs consisted of managing, hands-on, some of society's less than desirable aspects.

"The pay's pretty good," he said.

I took the answer to mean Karl didn't enjoy his employment. I could relate to him a little since it wasn't too long ago that I'd gone to work each day looking forward to what awaited me. Albeit the grisliness of it all, I believed I made a difference in the lives of people affected by tragedies, thus making a small amends in honor of my mother's victims. Now, I dreaded returning home and facing my old life. Making a connection with a man who'd held my murdering mother prisoner helped to humanize him, and her.

"What more can you ask for?" I said light-heartedly to Karl, as he led me inside the visiting area.

*

"What did you do when you left me yesterday?" Alice asked.

Karl had exited the private room and Alice and I were alone except for the surveillance camera in a corner of the ceiling, which was something I hadn't noticed the other day. She wore the same red jumpsuit, and her hair looked greasier than it had the day before, as though she hadn't washed it that morning.

"Tell me already, don't keep me waiting. I can't live life myself in here so I have to live through anyone who'll talk to me. Today, you have the honor," she said. Her pale lips—in my childhood she'd always used a bright lipstick—curled up into a grin.

"I had something to eat and then I went back to my hotel," I said honestly, sitting in a different chair than yesterday. It felt odd holding back personal details of my existence, such as Sammie, to my own mother.

"You didn't stay for long yesterday. And, with all that time on your hands, that's all you did?"

"Excuse me but what are you getting at? Yesterday, you wanted me to leave and so I did."

"I believe you promised me something." Alice raised her eyebrows. It appeared like she was cuing me to recall what I'd said without giving me a verbal hint.

"Yes, I'm making progress on that."

"You'd better be." She grinned. "Now, please elaborate a bit. I don't like all this secrecy."

I couldn't see whether she crossed her legs behind the glass window, as that part of her was blocked by a table, which came out of the panel itself, and which she leaned on, but I imagined she had. I knew her well.

"I reached out to contacts who can help locate your daughter," I said. "It won't be easy," I added for effect. "But I think I just might be able to find her."

"That's all you have for me?"

"So far, yes. You only gave me your request yesterday. I haven't had much time."

"Her name's Evelyn, don't forget that. Last I heard, she had the same last name."

"Right, I remember." Alice gave me a long glance in silence and I considered she might question me. I didn't give her the opportunity to do so and said, "And you promised you'd help me in exchange."

"Do you really believe this is a fair exchange? I've already given you more than you've given me."

I didn't believe she had but I insisted, "What you're asking for is more complicated. You probably already have the answers I seek. I have to find the answers you want."

I moved my bag from my lap to the floor. I'd become indolent about keeping my cover and hadn't removed the notepad and pen from my bag. Thinking about it at the time, I reasoned I should have recorded our conversations. Then again, some people objected to being taped by a journalist. My mother would have been the type to nitpick over such a matter.

"Maybe I don't have more to say than the little I gave you yesterday." Alice looked toward the speaker she'd used the other day to escape me.

"Please, don't end this," I said, and reached out, as if I could stop her.

"You seem very eager."

"I've traveled far," I answered calmly.

Alice showed me her hands were in her lap. "I won't leave at this moment. I'll leave when I feel like it, and now is not the time."

I thanked her. At times, it wasn't difficult to see why the press had labeled her manipulative. What they hadn't realized, however, and what I'd grown up with, was that my mother's attitude was part of her frosty disposition. In itself that didn't make her a cold-hearted murderer, although for some it had been enough to deem her so.

"Are you sorry for what you did?" I asked.

"Don't you mean, am I sorry I confessed?" She smiled.

"Are you sorry for killing those young men?" I persisted.

"I'm sorry I hurt my daughter."

I found her answer to be both heartless and comforting.

"Aren't you going to take out your notebook?" she asked.

Her flirtatious tone gave me pause, and I sought to put an end to that notion of hers before the circumstances became twisted. "I'm surprised you noticed yesterday," I said in an oh-so-serious voice.

Alice touched the glass. "Why don't you move your chair closer so I can see you better? I can hardly see your eye color from this distance. I want to see if you have nice eyes." She winked at me and chuckled at what must have been my red face.

Without rising, I picked up my bag from the floor and walked my chair toward the glass, close enough that I could have pressed my hand to its surface.

"That's much better," Alice smiled. "Did Mack find a way to get you in here again today?"

"He helped, yes."

"I bet I've been looking forward to news about my daughter more than you've been looking forward to coming here, am I right?"

I took my bag from my lap and set it on the floor by my feet. "That's not true. I've been looking forward to our visit. We have a lot to discuss," I said, determined not to let her ruffle me.

"Don't you mean, *I* have a lot to tell *you*? You don't seem to have much to tell me yourself, except that you're working on finding my Evelyn's whereabouts."

"I thought we'd agreed—see, what you're asking me for is more difficult. It will take time. The difference between our respective promises is that you might have the answers I'm seeking. I have to find the answers for you."

Alice used her hand to wave away my defense. She stared at me and lowered her voice. "I hope you keep your promise, Mr. Samuels."

"I will."

"I hope so. Evan. Evelyn. It's kind of funny, isn't it, that your names are similar?"

I couldn't tell what she was getting at, or if she was implying something, if anything. "Not really. Both are common names."

"I guess," Alice said. She sat up in her chair to stare at something behind me, and I glanced over my shoulder and saw that she was looking at the clock on the wall. "They're serving lunch soon."

Figuring a little friendly small talk couldn't hurt, I asked, "Do you know what you'll be eating?"

Alice grimaced. "There's a set schedule. Hamburgers today."

I lurched at the reference to meat. Had she considered the victims she allegedly devoured food, fuel, or was it that the only way she could entirely *consume* them was by eating them? "That doesn't sound so bad."

"Ha. You try eating the same thing every goddamn week and then you can tell me how you feel." She released a throaty laugh and watched me from the other side of the glass, like she sought to have me join in on the joke.

I managed to chuckle a little. "Do you ever get to sit with your friends in the cafeteria?" I asked. The glimpses she gave me into her life comforted me in a small way.

"My friends? Cafeteria? You make it sound like I'm in high school. I mostly eat in my cell. I think they're afraid one or two of the other gals will try to stab me because some of the other women don't like what I'm in here for. Can you imagine after all these years no one's tried?" She seemed to find it humorous that the prison would be concerned about *her* safety. "My only friend is a gal whose wife-beating husband deserved what he got." Alice gave me a wry grin.

My heart beat faster. "Do you fear for your life in here?" I thought of the crude joke that guard, Eddie, had made yesterday when I arrived.

She shrugged. "They only let me out of my cage—it doesn't look like a cage. There's no bars. It's a metal door with a narrow opening at the top for shoving my food tray and my mail through, which I know they read—for an hour a day. That's a lot of time I can spend thinking about and fearing for my life, but that doesn't present many opportunities for someone to hurt me."

"The staff, do they treat you well?"

"What do you care?"

I held up my hands in a defensive gesture. "I'm trying to picture your life."

"For the article you're writing?"

"Of course."

"I'm flattered. And most of them, the guards, are all right," she said. "You're not wearing your eyeglasses."

"I have contact lenses in today."

"Or perhaps you don't have poor eyesight."

After all those years of isolation from one another, the part of my relationship with my mother where she could read me clearly—like she did then—hadn't changed.

"I wore them as part of a disguise, is that what you're hinting at?" My voice lifted a notch, and I didn't bother to downplay my nerves.

"No, not at all," she said coolly. "Some people wear eyeglasses because they believe it'll make them look more intelligent. You're a journalist and you might want to distinguish yourself and that's why you wore them."

"And do I look smarter with them than without them?"

"With them," she said, and I laughed with her. "That's quite a noble gesture on your part, to be a stranger and share a laugh with a convicted murderer," she said.

"If only you knew the truth," I murmured.

She placed her hand over her ear. "Come again? I couldn't hear you through the speaker."

"It's not important."

"I don't like missing out on anything so please tell me what you said."

"I said I don't care who I'm laughing with. If I find it funny, I'll laugh."

"That isn't what you said. When you spoke what you *really* said, you didn't use as many words as you did right now."

Clever, as always, I'd thought. Alice succeeded in manipulating others, whether she wanted them to tell her the truth, reveal a secret to her, or sway someone to decide a matter in her favor, and it was a trait that a serial killer would have greatly benefited from.

"It's not important," I said. "I can't remember what I said."

"That's convenient for you."

She wanted to play a game with me? Well, then, I would play. I stood up and retrieved my bag from the floor. "If you plan to waste my time here, then I might as well leave."

Alice looked aghast. "Please don't leave, Mr. Samuels. Please, we've barely started." Her voice thinned out with panic.

I paused before I spoke, "I don't think I've ever heard you use the word please more." I smiled, hung my satchel over the chair, and sat down again. It took some time getting used to and conquering the rhythm of her manipulation but in that instance, I'd believed she had a genuine desire for me to remain there with her. Then I corrected myself before she could reflect, ponder, and ask me to elaborate on my observation, seeing as I'd supposedly met her only once before then. "I don't think I've ever heard you use the word more, since we met yesterday, that is."

Alice watched me with interest. "Are you going to write anything down today? You didn't take notes yesterday."

"You have a good memory, and so do I."

"You should ask them for a copy of the tape on your way out. They record everything we say in here, I'm sure. Did you know they do that?"

I shook my head but didn't let her see my reaction either way. I had thought of that before coming there. Being recorded was another reason to avoid disclosing my relation to her, as anyone could have been listening in on the meeting and could have used what I said against me or for their benefit.

"That must be hard for you," I said to Alice, softening my tone. "It must be difficult to get privacy around here." If we could form even the most delicate, tentative buds of a friendship, maybe she'd open up to me—in a moment or two.

"Yeah, sometimes it is," she said. "I'll admit it's not as hard as it had been when I first came here. I've adjusted."

"Have you always—lived?—at this prison." I didn't know if 'lived' was an appropriate term to use for a person housed somewhere involuntarily. But I *did* know Alice had always lived there.

"Yes, I have. I nearly pissed my pants when the car pulled in and dropped me off," she said, and I instinctively pulled back in my chair at her severity. *Pissed.* I'd never known her to have been so crass. She must have picked up the language on the inside. "I got the royal treatment. Most inmates in here got dropped off by a bus. Never thought I'd live to see the word 'freedom' paired with 'prison'."

My mother laughed faintly. She seemed more contented behind those unbreakable walls than I recalled her being inside our home. Had prison served her well? It certainly hadn't ruined her spirit.

"I thought the same thing about the sign when I drove inside this place," I said.

"Driving," Alice said. "I miss having wheels. There's nothing like the feel of the open road and the power of an engine. Trouble is, you don't value it until you don't have it any longer. Did you drive here?"

I'd never known that about my mother, that she liked to drive. "I did," I said.

"Why do you own a car if you live in the city, or did you rent one, is that what you did? Isn't that the whole point of living in a city, so you can walk everywhere?"

"My girlfriend likes having a car. We both do, actually."

Alice smiled. "I knew a young man as handsome as you are had to have himself a lady.

What's she like? It's none of my business but I'd love to hear. Is she smart? Pretty? It's better for a woman to be smart than pretty. Most men don't realize that until it's too late and they're stuck with an idiot with fading looks."

Her last remark took me off guard. Did she believe my father left her because she lacked something, beauty or intelligence?

"Sammie is smart and beautiful," I said.

"If you marry her and she took your name, she'd be Sammie Samuels."

I chuckled, and then realizing I gave her Sammie's name, a very personal detail of my life, I stopped short.

"Is something the matter?" Alice asked.

"No. I realized we don't have that long to talk. I wouldn't want you to miss lunch."

"Would you like me to shut up and get on with it?"

I wasn't sure whether a smile was appropriate. "Yes, I would be grateful."

Alice folded her hands on the tabletop and then seemed to be anticipating how to proceed. "First, you need to know something. It's regarding me. Something very important that could change how you feel about me and our interview and about what I'm going to tell you."

I nodded at her dramatic, drumroll-inspired technique and wondered how many writers she used that line with before me.

"They're recording us," Alice said, "but they've already caught their killer and are satisfied. At this point, it'd be a pain in the ass for them to reopen the case. The police are happy to have their killer and the case closed. Even someone as noble as your acquaintance Mack wouldn't bother anymore. I—we—fooled them all. After the years that have passed, I'm sick of putting on this act."

*We?*

"I don't understand." I walked my chair closer to the glass plate. This close, her blue-green eyes shone softly and beautifully.

Alice watched her hands. "You see, I was diagnosed with breast cancer, and the doc gave me a few months to be left here on this damn earth because I've asked them not to treat me."

Overwhelmed with so many emotions, I couldn't gather my thoughts to speak coherently. But her disclosure warranted an immediate response from me, so I asked, "Why are you telling me this?"

Alice smiled. "I feel a connection to you?" she shrugged.

How had the revelation made me feel? It affected me but I couldn't show how much. Alice hadn't received the death penalty but cancer would take her from me. My mother. My mother, the murderer. My mother, the murderer, was dying.

A tear wet my cheek and I stared down at my lap to disguise my reaction, quickly cleaning my face with my hand. I thought of all the things we would never get to do together and all the things we hadn't done because she was locked in there. In a way, a small part of me had clung to the threads of hope that she'd be exonerated and released from the prison. Now, that couldn't happen. She'd be released upon her death, in the form of her body, but she wouldn't get to walk through those gates of freedom to meet me, her child. I breathed deeply and struggled to preserve my equilibrium. Alice wouldn't have understood my display, and losing control of my emotions would have raised her suspicions.

"Are you all right?" Alice looked toward me. Her expression appeared as though she didn't comprehend my reaction. Why would a stranger have become so emotional over her news?

I sat up and spoke quickly. "I'm fine. My allergies are acting up."

"This time of year?" Alice lifted her eyebrow. "I may be stuck in here with minimal contact with the outside world except a quick walk around the courtyard once in a while, but isn't it a little cool this time of year for allergies? You came here wearing a jacket." She gestured to my coat. "It looked like you were crying. Because of what I told you? I'm touched." Alice gave me a slight smile.

"People can get allergies this time of year. I do." Then I altered the direction of the conversation to throw her off guard. "The other day, you asked me about the weather. Why did you enquire about that when you must know about it yourself from your walks?"

Alice lifted her hands and shrugged. "It was just something to talk about."

I'd taken my phone—the guards had checked it when I arrived— in with me and it rang in my pocket. A text from someone. I touched my pocket to quiet it. I didn't want to go through the trouble of removing it from my pocket in front of Alice, who'd almost surely ask me questions regarding the caller.

She asked anyway. "Was that a phone I heard ringing? Do you have one of those computer phones I read about? Don't look so surprised. I'm allowed to read magazines in here. And I've seen my lawyers using them."

"Yes, it's a smart-phone."

For a moment I forgot about her illness. Then another matter occurred to me. Alice had raised me and I had never suffered under her hands during my childhood, but she'd also managed to hide from me the fact that she was a murderer. What if she was, simply, a versatile liar and was dishonest in general?

"You aren't lying about your illness, are you?" I asked, feeling miserable for asking, yet wondering if that could have been a way for her to pull my leg.

"Lying to you, for, what, attention?" Alice frowned. She didn't like that I'd mistrusted her. "No, I'm not lying to you. Why would I invent an illness? I may be sick but I'm not *that* sick." I refrained from responding, and she said, "I'm surprised you'd doubt me. I thought we were friends. I know you won't believe me but I've tried to be a good person in here and outside."

"Fine, if your definition of good is murdering people. You hid your crimes from your community for years so I don't think it's so surprising that I'd have some doubt about the things you say. You don't have a reputation for being straightforward about who you are."

I was angry. Angry that she was dying and that I hadn't known, but how could I have, when I'd isolated myself from her? Angry that she hadn't really been the loving mother who I believed she was during the time she raised me. She'd been an ideal mother, and when I learned she wasn't truly that, it had shattered me.

"If I'm wrong, I'm sorry," I added, in a humbler tone.

"That's in the past," Alice spoke quietly. "If I said prison's changed me, would you believe me?"

"I've known you for two days," I spoke cautiously. "And with your past, I honestly don't know you well enough to trust anything you say." Alice looked around for her escape plan, and I said fast, "But, Alice, I'm willing to listen. I hadn't meant to upset you, Alice." I emphasized her name to win her over.

Silence from her. And more silence. I considered she might ring for the guard and that I might have to collect my belongings and return tomorrow, assuming she would see me again. I was pretty sure they couldn't force her to talk to me. To Mack, yes, but not to me. Then Alice began to speak.

"They, the prison, didn't seem to have a problem with my decision *not* to seek treatment for my cancer," she said. "Why should they care if I don't want to be treated? They figure I'm a murdering scum so what do they care if I die? Better sooner than later, is what they're thinking."

I couldn't stop myself from saying, "You shouldn't deny yourself treatment."

"Why should you care, either?"

I'd made her suspicious and I struggled to correct myself. "If you want to get treatment, you should," I said. "You shouldn't let their feelings about you prevent you from doing what's best for your health."

She smiled and I felt myself blushing. "It's nice of you to care," she said. "But I'll pass."

I almost stood up, and I didn't know what to do with my hands or how to control my emotions. "You're just going to let yourself die?"

"Yes."

"Why?" I demanded.

"Because that's what I want."

"What about what your family wants?" I rose from the chair.

She shrugged and I wanted to scream at her.

"Do they know about your illness?" I said.

"They know what they need to. I know what's best." She spoke with confidence. "Please sit."

"You're giving up, just like that?"

"I'm not talking about this anymore. Please sit down."

As a stranger, I could only push her so many times before she shut me out again. I took a few moments to collect myself—Alice watched me the entire time—and then I sat.

"Once I'm gone, no one will find out about her unless I tell you. Once I'm dead, you bet you can forget about anyone finding out." Alice made a gesture of slitting her throat and I recoiled. "Sure, there's a chance that on my death, someone in my family will spill their guts, but if that doesn't happen, I want you to tell my story."

I flinched at the image of guts spilling over. Someone in her family. I was someone in her family and I didn't understand what she meant, so, then, what had she meant?

"I'm giving you permission that upon my death you can write about what I'm going to tell you today," she said. "I promise you this will be a big, career-making story for you. Everybody's going to know your name when you write this story."

"I see." I was unable to curb my disbelief. "And you've chosen me to write it, why?"

"You help me, and I help you in return. As I said, I feel a connection to you." Alice smiled as though she had a secret she wanted to disclose, which, evidently, she had. "I've protected her for long enough. I went to prison for her. Now, when I die, I want you to tell my story so you can let Evelyn know I'm not a killer like everybody thinks. I want Evelyn to have some peace."

"You are a . . . " You *are* a killer, I'd almost uttered. Then I reminded myself that she had been declared insane. "Why don't you tell Evelyn yourself when I find her and bring her to you? Isn't that what you want?

"You might not find her before I die, even I know that. That's a sacrifice I'm willing to make in order for you to get my story out there. Even if I don't see Evelyn before I die, as long as I know she'll be reading the truth, then I'm fine with that. She needs to know about her. It's time."

*The truth.*

"I'm sorry but who is this *her* you're referring to?" I asked. "Is she your daughter, Evelyn? Are you talking about your daughter?"

"No, there were two." The tears made Alice's eyes appear larger. "Two daughters. They're identical twins."

I nearly fell back in my chair. "What did you—I don't understand what you—"

"Evelyn isn't my only child."

"But I'm—"

"I'm discussing my children. This isn't about you, handsome."

Had Alice somehow figured out who I was, and did she, my own mother, get some sort of pleasure out of fucking with my mind? She had never been cruel to me but what if she'd suddenly revealed her true nature to me? I swallowed and planted my feet firmly on the floor to keep myself upright. If I was wrong and she was telling me the truth, she wouldn't understand if I keeled over.

I looked back toward the call-button. Leaving and never hearing what she had to say could have been regrettable later on. On the other hand, staying and hearing that my life wasn't what I'd thought, that as complicated as I'd thought it was, it was even more complex, could have been equally as traumatic. My mantra had always been that bad things happen but you can't let them ruin you. You simply find some way to move on. I wasn't sure I could move on from what she might tell me.

"I don't understand. You mentioned one daughter," I said.

"Mentioned one, but have two," Alice corrected me.

"You're pulling my chain, aren't you? Making a fool out of the reporter because of all the nasty things we've said about you in the past, aren't you?" I spoke fast. If she wasn't jesting, then the revelation would have been unfathomable.

Alice shook her head. "I'm a dying woman, why would I waste what little time I have left by fooling you? I've kept up this ruse for too long. It's not easy pretending to be insane. In fact, maybe I *am* a little insane. You don't do what I did if you're normal. None of my therapists over the years figured me out but I believe a few came close." She zeroed-in on my eyes. "This seems to be upsetting you. I'm sorry."

She reached up as though to touch me, to comfort me, then seemed to remember the glass that separated us. I would have liked to have felt my mother's caresses, which had been soft and patient during my youth, and I wondered whether her touch would have felt the same, or if prison and time had hardened her skin, and her spirit.

"Please, don't apologize," I said. "I'm not upset. It's my allergies."

"Oh, right, your allergies. I forgot." Cynicism didn't sour her tone. She spoke as though she sensed the discomfort of the moment and wanted to assure me there were no strange vibes among us. The feelings passing between us through the glass were such that if we hadn't been physically divided, she would have leaned over and patted my hand.

"Why are you telling me this?" I said. "It can't only be because—"

"I'm dying? No." Alice tilted her head and her gaze traveled over my form in the chair. "You remind me of Evelyn. Isn't that funny, because you're a man?"

I sat up in the chair and didn't smile like her. "I don't see how that's possible. I'm, you know, and she's . . ."

I sought consolation in something familiar and reached around in the chair to touch my bag and ground myself in reality. I breathed in and comforted myself. *This is happening. I'm here visiting my killer mother in prison, and I might have a long-lost twin sister.*

Alice smiled and slapped her knee. "Heck, I didn't say you *were* her, just that you remind me of her, or of how she was when I knew her. I have no idea what she's like today. I do bet that she's as pretty as you are handsome." Her eyes brightened with admiration. "Let me explain because this is a strange story."

# Chapter 15

As complex as my life had been up until that point, it was about to become even more so.

"Evelyn didn't—doesn't—know she has a sister out there," Alice said. "My other daughter, Evelyn's twin, isn't the type of person you'd want to meet, if you catch my drift."

I took my grip off my bag. "No, I don't 'catch your drift'." I should have removed my notepad from my satchel to make it look like I was genuinely interested, hence my questions. I didn't, though. "You hid Evelyn's sister from her? Why would you do something like that to your daughter?"

"Rachel, that's my other daughter, isn't of a sound mind."

"Rachel." I slowly repeated the name. My sister? My sister. "You're embarrassed by her?" Outrage increased the volume of my speech. "You're going to insist you did this for the benefit of both your daughters? Shouldn't you have let Evelyn decide for herself whether she wanted to meet her sister?"

"I kept—keep Rachel a secret out of concern for the safety of others," Alice said. "Including Evelyn. Even my lawyers don't know about Rachel."

"I'm sorry, but I'm not understanding you. What does this have to do with you being in here?"

"I took Rachel's place."

"What do you mean you 'took her place'?"

"If the law knew what I did, then Rachel and I would be changing places."

"You—how is that possible?"

"I confessed so she wouldn't have to."

Somewhere out there, it was possible I had a sister, a twin, and if Alice told me the truth, then my sister was a cold-blooded murderer. "You're saying your daughter Rachel is the—"

Alice nodded before I could finish with 'killer.'

"I'd kept Rachel hidden for so long I felt I owed her my going to prison for her. She never got the kind of life Evelyn had," she said.

"You're not suggesting Rachel is committing the killings in my city," I said.

"I couldn't say. I don't know what is happening exactly."

"If she is, if you are telling the truth, you could be implicated in the new crimes because you haven't gone to the police with this information."

"Go ahead, tell them. I'm a dead woman, what do I care?"

I couldn't tell whether the *master manipulator*, as the media had portrayed her, was manipulating me right then. In the prior years, her confession and arrest had led me to believe she'd fooled me enough already. I wasn't about to let her fool me twice, and as an adult no less.

"I'm going to get this off my plate, and because we don't have much time, I'm going to do it fast," Alice said.

I looked behind at the door and considered escaping. "I . . ."

"Can you just sit back and listen?" she said.

If she was authentic, hearing her side of the story could change my life in unexpected ways. And if she was lying, then I had little to lose. After some thinking, I faced her and nodded.

"I couldn't choose between my children," Alice said. "I worked so hard to have children in the first place. My husband—he left when my girls were very young—and I, had trouble having children."

At the mention of my father I felt as though I had been swallowed whole by something so brutal and powerful it had eviscerated my body and taken my soul as it devoured me.

"We went to a specialty clinic in the city, and the doctor there prescribed a fertility drug for me to take," Alice spoke. "At the time, it was an experimental drug. The doctor warned me of the risks but I was so desperate I took it, regardless." She cleared her throat and took a break. "Aren't you going to write this down?"

"I'm recording it in my memory," I said, partly in jest.

Alice frowned, and for a moment it felt like we were mother and child again. "Are you sure you'll remember all of it?"

"I'm confident I'll remember most of it."

"Yes, you have a good memory," she acknowledged. "I intended to protect Evelyn, you see—"

"You thought that having her mother go to prison would help her?" I'd tried not to make my question sound too personal, and failed.

"I'll explain." Alice seemed more composed than I expected someone in her situation would be. "I had a hard time getting pregnant so I took this drug. After Rachel and Evelyn were born, it was clear from the start, after a year or so, that Rachel was troubled. She wouldn't stop crying. Even as an infant she had terrible fits. Evelyn was fine, she was normal."

I hadn't recalled having a sister but I'd been too young to remember.

"After their births, the doctors concluded that the drugs had a negative effect on Rachel but *not* on Evelyn. They—they determined that Rachel was—psychotic, in some form." She stammered through the admission.

I didn't take offense because I knew myself well enough to know that some drug hadn't made me the way I was.

"My husband left when neither of my girls was old enough to remember," Alice said. "After he took off, my family paid for Rachel to leave my home and be cared for by a local woman in the town. Anyone who knew Rachel existed knew she was ill and that her illness couldn't be cured. When Rachel left my home, those who knew her assumed I sent her away to an institution. But I would never have allowed that to happen to her at such a young age."

I felt it was safe enough to remark, "No one in the town has mentioned her to me."

"People in the town don't talk about it. Folks don't like discussing unpleasant things, as though my bad luck might rub off on them. Once something's hidden, it stays hidden. I was unhappy with the plan but Rachel was too much for me to handle by myself, and as she got older, it became clear . . . let's just say my family thought she'd be an embarrassment to their image. The irony is I ended up being an embarrassment." Alice laughed softly to herself.

I didn't believe her yet, and I wanted to listen and not speak but I had to make myself appear like an interested journalist might, and I had to pose questions that one would have asked. "And your other daughter, Evelyn, did she know about her sister?"

"No. But Rachel knew about *her*. And she knew more than her sister's name. I wanted Rachel to have some grasp on normalcy so I kept her informed about Evelyn's life as they aged. She got to see Evelyn grow up through photographs and videos. We talked about their father as well. That part was painful for me to discuss but I wanted Rachel to know where she came from. The more I consider it, the more I think it wasn't a sound idea. You see, I think Rachel became resentful of her sister's freedom."

Jealousy burned my skin's most tender spots because Alice had told me so little about my father. Right then was my chance to ask her a question that had been on my mind for years, a question that, when I was a child, she'd refused to answer the many times I asked her.

"Did your husband have a reason for leaving? It's none of my business but I'd like to hear your opinion. You don't seem like a woman a man would walk away from."

Aside from her committing murder, that was.

"Are you joking?" she said.

"No."

Alice became very self-aware and blushed and patted her hair. "Thanks for the compliment, I think. Emotionally, Clayton, that was my husband's name, went through everything with me during the period we couldn't conceive. He loved our girls, but I think that, after everything we'd gone through, in some way he viewed

Rachel's problems as a failure on his part. He couldn't handle the idea of going through life with her the way she was. Clayton developed his own problems, drugs and drinking, after Rachel was born. He never had a real career, and my family had made it quite clear to him that they didn't approve of him. That, plus Rachel's condition—I think it ruined him."

I flinched at the revelation but I didn't judge my father. He'd abandoned us but his personal struggles had been vast. "Has your husband tried to contact you since your conviction? To see how your daughters were doing perhaps?" Expectation softened my tone.

Alice looked off to the side. "He hasn't."

The disappointment I had in him felt heavy on my shoulders.

"We can't divorce legally because I don't know where he is," Alice said. "I don't know if he's even alive."

I kept talking to prevent myself from shedding a tear. "How would you say it came about, how did you end up going to prison for Rachel?" I asked.

"During one of my visits to see Rachel at her caretaker's house, I found something—a ring—and I asked Rachel about it because it didn't seem like something she'd own."

My attention to her intensified. "What did the ring look like?"

"It was such a long time ago, I'm not sure I remember correctly but I believe it was a wide band, made of brass. On the large side. A gentleman's ring."

Based on Alice's description, that sounded like the ring Ben's father said he had given him, the ring they'd never found on or around Ben's body, or inside his house after his death. He'd loaned it to me a few times when we were kids. It had Ben's initials carved on the inner part. "I . . . " She trapped me in a vulnerable place and I stopped myself before I revealed too much.

"I asked Rachel about this ring and she said that it didn't belong to her and that it belonged to a boy who'd died. Evelyn's friend and our neighbor, Ben, had been killed recently and I told this to Rachel. Rachel said she already knew that Ben had been killed. Then I asked her how she came about having this ring. That's when Rachel said she'd killed Ben. Your child comes to you with something like that, how could you *not* help them?" Her suffering raised her voice.

I recited the publicized facts of her case. "Ben Palmer was the first known victim. But you were accused of murdering several young men."

"I'll get to that in a moment. When the police interviewed me because I lived next door to Ben, I confessed to all the deaths. Mercifully, the killings stopped from then on."

"Why did she kill him—kill Ben?" I felt tears coming but couldn't dry them without revealing my sentiment. Then I realized I'd spoken as though I was familiar with Ben, as though we were close, which we had been, but that was something I couldn't express because Alice thought I was someone else. I rectified the situation with, "Why did she murder the first young man?"

"It was never quite clear to me. But I believe it was out of jealousy. Initially, that's why she killed. In some twisted way, she wanted to hurt Evelyn. Rachel didn't have Evelyn's life with me, a life with school and friends. Her caretaker, who was a single woman, a retired nurse and a teacher, tutored her as best she could. The woman had been paid by my family to keep Rachel hidden from the town. The town is small, so it wasn't an easy task. But the woman was very careful."

"How much did she—Rachel—know about her sister?" I asked cautiously.

"After she confessed to me, I looked back and realized that she'd been pulling more and more information about Evelyn's life out of me during my visits to her."

"When did you visit her?" I hadn't recalled my mother being absent for long blocks of time.

"During my lunch hour mostly, in secret because my family didn't like me seeing her. They wanted Rachel to forget about me and me to forget about her. But I couldn't forget. Her caretaker felt sorry for me and would let me into the house. I worked as a schoolteacher but if you've done your research you already know that." She smiled in a nostalgic manner. "Rachel told me she'd started to watch Evelyn around the town. Rachel knew what her sister looked like, you see, because they're identical. When her caretaker would go to the market and to run errands, apparently, Rachel would sneak out and pretend to be Evelyn."

"Pretend to be m—her?" I said.

"Yes." Alice looked at me in a new way.

"There were others besides the boy, Ben Palmer," I said, flustered.

"Yes. Rachel started with Evelyn's friend and then she killed the others."

"Why on earth would someone—why would she do that?" My voice cracked and I couldn't disguise my emotions.

"This part is hard for me to say." Alice sighed and stared at her hands. "Rachel said she planned to blame Evelyn for all the murders so that I would let Rachel come home to live with me when Evelyn was in prison. Rachel told me that she would replace Evelyn. My daughter's—Rachel's thought process doesn't make much sense, but there you have it. She's smart, but she isn't well. Rachel can be devious. She can appear to be quite normal when she wants to be. She intended to take Evelyn's place in my life. In her twisted mind, that's what she thought. In some crazy way, I thought that going to prison for Rachel would show her I loved her as much as I loved Evelyn and get her to stop killing and leave Evelyn alone. She let me, and so I went."

"You just assumed she'd stop killing if you went to jail for her?"

"No, I . . . I haven't thought of it that way before." Alice's voice softened, and her face paled. "Oh, God, you don't think . . . Do you think Rachel's started killing again, in your city? Why would she go there and do that?"

I could have told her the truth right then, all of it, but I didn't answer. "There were rumors—it was well publicized that you consumed your victims."

"You want to know if I'm a cannibal?" Alice smiled.

"Yes, did Rachel?"

"Eat those boys?"

"Yes," I said. "If you didn't, did she?"

"She must have if they said she did." The tips of Alice's ears turned red. "The truth is, I'm not sure. That wasn't something she talked about, and I certainly never asked her. It was hard enough to get anything out of her. You'll have to leave here without an answer to that gruesome question, handsome."

"Are there victims the police don't know about?" That was something I'd wondered.

"I believe that, with my help, they found them all. I don't think Rachel kept any from me. These weren't the kinds of young men you wouldn't miss, so someone would've noticed if they were gone."

"Unlike the ones being killed today," I said.

"Is that so?" Relief softened the lines on her face.

For all I knew at the time, all the words, the entire confession, that flowed from her mouth, was bullshit. Yet, the material seemed too intricate for even someone as imaginative as her to have invented.

"You'll have to understand that I'm a little confused. I'll admit I have a great deal of doubt about what you're telling me," I said regardless. "I'm sorry but that's the way I feel. You have to understand how this looks to an outsider, it looks like you're making someone up to blame them for your actions, or if she does exist, you're trying to blame her for your crimes so you can potentially be released from jail."

I intended to make Alice own up to her crimes if she should have, but would it have been any less painful for me if she hadn't been lying?

"Why would I blame my own daughter?" she paused. "But there's no need to apologize. Let me explain better. I imagined the way Rachel viewed her actions was, if her sister was locked away, then she, Rachel, would be the child I loved."

"I need proof, something to go on."

"Do you want to see her, do you want to see Rachel?"

On the one hand, she didn't know I was her child and I wasn't so foolish as to believe a sociopath would have any sentiment for me, and therefore wouldn't care about what happened to me. Alice might lead me into a trap if I agreed to meet my alleged sister. On the other, my lifelong wish to exonerate her could come true. I needed to confirm whether Rachel was out there, no matter how dangerous she might be. It came down to my potential death or to possibly freeing my mother. It was a simple decision.

"Her last name's the same as yours?" I asked.

"Yes. Rachel Lane."

"Does she live in town?" Then I cut myself short with, "Here's the thing I don't understand, if your daughter is unable to care for herself as you've suggested, then how have you managed to provide for her financially while you're in prison?

"My family's been estranged from me since my imprisonment but they do arrange for Rachel's comforts. They took complete control of her wellbeing after my conviction."

I nearly lost my cool. "And they managed to keep her a secret? Don't you think it would have been courteous to notify your other child about their sibling?"

"Yes, I thought about it. But it was clear to me that Rachel was—is—dangerous. It wouldn't have been safe to connect Evelyn with her twin. It still isn't safe, I believe."

"Shouldn't you have let Evelyn decide that?"

"If I could speak to her today, perhaps I would tell her, now that she's older. But, like I said, she cut me from her life a long time ago."

Alice scratched at her cheeks. She must have had an itch. No, she was wiping her eyes. For the first time since I'd started visiting my mother, she'd physically expressed remorse. Why would a serial killer have retained so much emotion inside them that they couldn't have regulated their feelings in front of a stranger? Unless, of course, she wasn't a monster.

Perhaps my mother's estranged family, my estranged family, *had* kept my twin a secret from me. Regardless of Rachel's malice, I had to see if I really had a sister out there. A twin, who, if she existed, would have been an undeniable part of me.

"My family felt it would be better to keep Rachel hidden from Evelyn, to protect Evelyn and her future," Alice said.

I sat up. "They continued to hide Rachel despite knowing her crimes?"

"No, they weren't in on my plan to take her place for her role in the crimes. They don't know what Rachel did. They really do think I'm a murderer. They think Rachel's a victim of my actions, like Evelyn was. I didn't give a rat's ass what they thought." She smiled to herself. "I wanted to protect my children."

"You must love your daughter very much to have accepted life imprisonment."

"I do love Rachel. I love both my daughters, even if one of them doesn't love me any longer."

"You don't know what Evelyn's thinking. Maybe she has her reasons for not communicating with you. Maybe she doesn't hate you."

"Oh, and how would you know the inner workings of my daughter's mind?"

Her cynicism stung me all over. "I don't. But, truthfully, maybe she doesn't hate you. You don't know what she's thinking until you ask her."

"And you'll help me with that, you'll help me see her." Hope reddened Alice's cheeks. "And if you don't find her before I'm gone, then you have to send a copy of your article to her when you do find her. I'm not worried about what'll happen with Rachel. The police will know what to do from there. It's time I put Evelyn first."

"Yes, I'll try to, but first, where is Rachel living at present?" I spoke carefully. "Does she reside in Freedom?" The thought made me feel quite ill.

"The last I heard my family had to move Rachel out of the cottage they'd bought for her. They're estranged from me but they did have the morals to tell me that much. The place was deep in the woods outside town and very hard to find if you didn't know it existed. Rachel lives in a facility now. The caretaker had aged some, you see, and she couldn't continue on with the arrangement.

My family had paid her a lot of money to keep Rachel a secret, and so the woman was very comfortable with everything. I believe my family still owns the cottage but they haven't used it since Rachel lived there, but I can't be sure."

Which explained why the crimes had stopped occurring in Freedom after Alice's arrest and imprisonment, and why Mack and the local police thought their job had been finalized for good. Still, I wasn't confident about the idea that Rachel, if she was real, was murdering again, and in Seven Sisters, but that was the one strong lead I had.

"Do you know what became of Rachel's caretaker?" I asked.

"If you're wondering if Rachel killed her, you're wrong. I believe she moved away. I could tell that Rachel didn't hate the woman, but the only reason Rachel didn't hate her was because the woman respected Rachel's space. Perhaps she respected Rachel's privacy too much. She'd told me Rachel spent a lot of time in a woodshed on the cottage's property. The woman didn't go in there, which I thought was odd, but, as I said, she gave Rachel some freedom at home. I think she wanted to pacify Rachel."

"Did you ever go in there?" I asked.

"Into the woodshed? Yes. Nothing stood out to me."

"Did anyone from your family go inside?"

"I don't think so. Why?"

"It's a bit odd, isn't it, her spending time alone in that shed?"

"I never saw anything out of the ordinary." After a moment Alice said, "At the facility, Rachel had been writing to me here under a different name but I stopped writing back when her letters became . . . disturbing."

"You didn't feel it was your obligation to inform someone of her condition?"

Alice smiled sheepishly. "I'd thought Rachel would stop acting so strange if I went to prison for her and showed her how much I cared."

"Perhaps you should have let her go to prison, where she could have received the treatment she needed."

"A mother would do *anything* to keep her baby out of jail," Alice retorted.

"Even if that meant subjecting your other daughter to the loss of her mother?" I'd spoken before I comprehended what I was saying.

Alice gave me a long, hard look, and then she said, "I hope you never have to make a similar choice someday, Mr. Samuels."

I brushed aside my growing emotions. "Let's get back on track. Do you know which facility houses Rachel? Since she wrote to you from there, do you have an address for her?"

"Let me see if I remember."

I allowed Alice plenty of time to mull it over.

"No, I don't remember the name of the facility," she said. "My memory's not as sharp as it once was." She mumbled a few street names and cursed under her breath. "No, none of those were it. Hold on a minute. Let me think."

A moment of time went by before she sat up in her chair and recited a post office box number in a triumphant way, the way a game show contestant shouts the winning answer to a tricky question. "That was the address on her envelopes when we were still exchanging letters," she said.

The box was in Lamont. I didn't imagine I'd find Rachel inside the post office at any given moment, but I couldn't see another place to try. Perhaps the mail office would have the name and address of the person who rented the post box. But, I wasn't officially the law, and would they readily give such information out to an ordinary citizen like myself?

Could I get up and call for the guard, leave without letting Alice know she was my mother and that I wasn't just another striving young journalist, that I was her son?

Her words collided into my thoughts. "I still expect you to uphold your end of our deal, promise me you'll try your very best to find Evelyn before my death. I don't need to see Rachel again."

"I promise I will try," I said.

The irony left a bitter taste in my mouth. According to Alice, Rachel was a murderer but she was also my sister, my twin, and I couldn't help but feel a bit sorry for someone who shared my blood, someone whose mother wanted nothing to do with her. Then the idea that Alice might be untruthful surfaced again in my mind, and I thought of a question to catch her with.

"What did you end up doing with the ring you found in Rachel's room?" I asked.

"I chucked it into the river, same as I told the police."

"It never was mentioned in any of the articles written about the case."

Alice shrugged. "They never found the ring."

I received another text and Alice glanced at my shirt pocket. "Your phone's making noises again. Someone wants you out of here real bad, handsome. You have places to be. I understand."

"I'll call the guard to let him know we're through here." If they'd been listening in on us like Alice suggested, I considered they might not allow me to leave the building until I spoke with someone.

As if reading my mind, Alice said, "They record the meetings between prisoners and guests but don't listen to the tapes unless they suspect something. So if you don't say anything to them when you leave this room, and I don't say anything, we should be fine."

"How do you know what they do with the recordings?"

"Word gets around in this place. It's real cozy." She beamed. "Go ahead, call for a guard to come collect you. I know you'll be in touch if you can. You know better than to break a promise to me." Alice gave me a sly wink. "It's best you write to me with any news. It's hard for me to get phone calls in here as you can imagine. They read any letter that comes to me, so if you'd like, we can use a code word for our little mission."

"What will the code word be?"

She appeared pleased that I was letting her decide. "Molasses. You're working on finding me molasses." Alice smiled. "I always liked the taste of the stuff. Haven't had it in years."

I almost said I never knew that but caught myself. "Molasses it is, then."

Alice pressed her hand against the glass separation wall. "Come here, let me look at you. I don't get many visitors."

I only needed to move an inch to crouch and place my hand on hers through the glass. Our hand size matched palm-to-fingertip.

"Would you look at that," she said. "Your hand's not much bigger than mine. Do you know what they say about a man who has small hands?"

I warmed at her innuendo.

"Perhaps your feet are bigger." She tried to peer down at my feet from where she sat. "Doesn't matter. Anything you'd lack you'd more than compensate for in charm."

I laughed and moved my feet so that she couldn't see them.

"We get along," Alice remarked. "Feels like I've known you for years." She sat back and looked me over. "Perhaps we knew each other in another life." She smiled. "You can call the guard using that there," she said, pointing at the button on the wall behind me.

"I know," I said.

Given what she'd disclosed to me, I should have been running out of there and traveling to Lamont to see whether she told truths or lies, but I didn't want to leave before Alice did. I wanted to hang on to my mother until the last possible moment, until they hauled her away from me.

"Why don't you call first?" I said. "I need a few moments to organize myself."

"You haven't even taken your notebook out of your bag. Will you remember what we talked about?" Alice stared at me, waiting for me to flinch, and there was that side of hers again, the side that, as an adult then, led me to believe she could still have been a killer.

"I'll be fine." I patted my phone through my pocket. "Someone tried reaching me and I'd like to check my messages before I go."

"You can do that on your way out, or in the parking lot."

Alice took control of someone without them realizing. She ordered you around without it feeling like you were being commanded. She'd done the same to me as a child as she was doing to me, seemingly a stranger to her, now. She could be manipulative, but that in itself didn't make her a killer.

I turned my face to the side so she couldn't see my eyes. "I'll check them when I want, thanks." I used a defiant tone.

"Keep in touch, handsome."

Some moments later, I didn't watch her leaving but I heard the guard collecting her from the room. Seeing my mother, older, frailer, and, in many ways, defeated, had made me question my decision to avoid a connection with her for so many years. She wasn't the monster I remembered reading about in the newspapers of my youth. She was my mother, and she'd declared her innocence, and she was never getting out of prison unless I assisted her.

What I wanted to come true for years, and what I never in my life imagined would, had happened: I'd heard her say she hadn't murdered those young men. And while I should have felt relieved, I didn't feel I could begin to accept her words as the truth unless I validated her innocence myself.

In the parking lot, I sat in the car and read Sammie's texts. I hadn't started the engine. The guards hadn't given me peculiar looks on my way out so I assumed Alice was correct in thinking they didn't listen live to the prisoner visits.

*Wanted to check on you*, Sammie had written. *I think you're in too deep, love. I'm calling Mack if you don't write me or call soon.*

How easily could Sammie have obtained Mack's number? I texted her back.

*So it turns out I might have a twin my mother hid from me named Rachel. She lives in Lamont. Heading there now. I'll be fine. Don't worry about me. Love you.*

*What??* *Call me NOW. You can't go there yourself. Wait for your detective friend to go with you. Please, Evan. Promise me.*

I would never have been able to reassure someone as protective as Sammie was. I wrote her again.

*I can't wait. I have to go now. I'll be ok. Don't worry!*

*Love, I always worry. I'm calling you now.*

I loved Sammie with all my everything but I'd already decided that when she did ring, I wouldn't answer. There might have been a murderer out there who looked like me. At that time, I wouldn't have allowed anyone or anything to stop me from finding out, not even our love.

# Chapter 16

In the town of Lamont, I parked a short walk away from the post office.

"Do you know when the person who owns box 293 usually comes in to collect their mail?" I asked the clerk at the front.

"I can't give out that information unless your name's registered to the box, too. Are you registered?" she asked.

I wasn't and it would have been pointless to have lied. "I'm not."

"Then I'm sorry, I can't help you, sir." The clerk, an older woman, returned to sorting through the letters in front of her.

I glanced at the line forming behind me but didn't leave the counter. I rubbed my face and ruminated over some ways to pry the information out of her. I decided I'd try desperation. The name stitched to the front of her shirt said Beth. "The thing is, Beth, and I'm going to be completely honest with you—the box I'm asking about belongs to my sister.

She isn't well, and my family and I are very concerned for her safety. I'm trying to track her down for our mother."

I'd managed to hold Beth's interest, and at some point in my explanation, she'd stopped going through the mail and looked up at me. "This is a pretty big city," she said. "Do you really think I have time to pay attention to everyone who comes in here to collect their mail?"

"No, but—"

Beth cut me short. "Hold on." She held up her finger for emphasis. "I understand first-hand what it's like to have family troubles, so I'll tell you that a young woman usually comes to collect mail from the box today."

"Today?" I didn't want to sound too eager. "Has she already been in today? Have I missed her?" I became aware that I was resting my elbows on the counter, and I stood up and retreated slightly.

Beth smiled, and to think I'd assumed she couldn't. "She hasn't. She's due to come in today, in two hours or so. Looks like today's your lucky day. I'll be on my break then, but I'm sure you'll recognize your sister when she comes in. Come to think of it, you two do look alike. That's why I remember her, because she's very pretty. Even with all the people coming in here all the time, she stands out."

"We're twins." I thanked her.

"You can wait in here if you'd like, but I need to assist the customers in line." She waited for me to move.

"Thanks for your help," I said, and stepped out of the way. "I'll go outside for a bit and then come back in." I would have surely piqued the interest of the security guard by the entrance if I loitered for hours.

I left the post office to see if I could manage to get something to eat and then planned to return closer to three in the afternoon, when Rachel was due to arrive. I felt guilty shutting off my phone to avoid Sammie but I wasn't leaving Lamont without an answer or two and it wouldn't have felt right telling Sammie lies about my whereabouts, so I avoided her for the time being.

I bought a plain bagel at a corner café. I couldn't sit still inside the café so I walked around the city in the clear, crisp day as I ate. I threw the bagel away after only a few bites.

I started for the post office again, and with more than a few minutes to spare, stopped inside a community art show happening in a little building off to the side of a police station, which I found quite fitting at the time. I'd been trying to soothe myself and prepare but I didn't pay much attention to the amateur, yet surprisingly decent, mostly urban landscape paintings housed within the makeshift gallery. My mind was on whether

Beth had remembered Rachel's routine correctly and whether I should make haste and haul my ass over to the post office. I didn't know exactly what I would do if I saw Rachel.

In the end, I decided to return early. Well before three, I re-entered the building to find that, as promised, Beth wasn't at the counter. A rather glum seeming young man stood in her place and assisted the customers before him as though the task annoyed him. Beth hadn't been the friendliest person, but I'd got the impression that she enjoyed her job.

I read the advertisements for postal products posted on the wall by the entrance door and kept an eye on the people entering the post office. Around three-thirty, Beth had retaken her place at the counter and I began to worry Rachel, or whoever collected her mail, wouldn't make an appearance.

Beth waved me over to the desk when she had a lull in customers. "I saw you frowning over there. Your sister will turn up, I'm sure of it."

I half expected Beth to point Rachel out to me when she entered the building, but if my sister looked as much like me as I, and everyone else, thought, then it shouldn't have been too difficult for me to spot her.

"Give her a few more minutes," Beth said.

"Does she arrive later sometimes?" I inquired.

Beth's eyes deepened with sympathy. "I'm afraid not but maybe she's had a slight delay of some sort."

I nodded, although I didn't believe a half hour counted as a 'slight' delay. I went to return to standing near the door in case Rachel showed.

A well-dressed woman entered the building and though the only thing I went on was her uncanny likeness to me, albeit with longer hair and a smaller frame, there was no doubt in my mind that she was Rachel. My mother had told me the truth. I felt doubly betrayed by her, for hiding my sister from me and then going to prison for her. But what if Alice was still telling tales and Rachel was my sister but not a killer? There was only one way to find out.

Beth caught my eye and nodded at me. Rachel kept her hands in her pockets as she strolled toward the brass boxes along the wall at the back of the lobby. She didn't carry a purse and stopped in front of one of the boxes and removed something from her coat pocket, presumably the box key. I didn't want to alarm or startle her so I observed from afar and didn't approach her.

I felt Beth watching me from the counter, probably wondering why I didn't speak to my sister. The door opened at my left and Rachel glanced over her shoulder in my direction and I pretended to check my phone.

She walked past me with a few letters in her hand and I followed her outside. Beth shouted, "Hey . . . " at my back. Rachel took her time moving down the front steps to the sidewalk, and the concern that she might have sensed me trailing her evaporated. If she had felt my presence, her manner gave no indication.

The day had cooled more and I tugged my jacket around me as I walked a few paces behind her. She paused briefly to look in a shop window at a display of plump chocolates in neat rows, and I slowed down behind her so I wouldn't have to pass her. I breathed more easily when she continued down the street and I could track her without my intentions being apparent. I still had my phone off and I wondered what Sammie was doing and if she had called Mack.

Rachel rounded the corner and came to a halt. She walked into the lobby of what looked like a very nice doctor's office and I casually kept an eye on her from the building's wide glass door that faced the sidewalk. Rachel chatted with a woman at the desk inside and signed herself in. There wasn't anyone else inside the lobby, and if I entered then, I'd stand out. I stared up and read the business name displayed in gold letters on the brick façade. *Facility for Mental Health.* The place seemed much too posh to have been government-run and most likely had to have been a private facility paid for by my estranged family.

A young man in a dark blue uniform exited the building through a side door, stood on the pavement, and lit a cigarette. A facility worker on his break. The city was large enough that he minded his own business and didn't pay attention to me, a stranger loitering outside.

When he put out his cigarette and I knew I had limited time left to approach him and ask if he knew Rachel, I stepped close and described Rachel to him, fully aware I'd look suspicious. Again, I pretended to be a relative of hers and the man's posture became less threatening.

"You're a relative? All right, then. I was going to say how you look a lot like her," he said.

"Everyone tells me that." I managed a smile. "You do know her?"

"Yeah. I'm one of the attendants they have working with the lunatics in there." He chuckled, and had the hacking laugh of a lifelong smoker. "Joking. I'm joking. Rachel's not as mad as the others. That's why she's allowed to come and go."

"She can come and go, isn't that an odd privilege for a patient? How well do you know her?"

"I know her pretty good. Better than you it seems. She's an adult and what we call a voluntary patient, so she can leave when she likes but she hasn't wanted to move out entirely. I think she has nowhere else to go. I don't think her family wants her to move in with them."

The irony of her having been declared mentally stable enough to enter and exit as she desired didn't elude me.

He looked at me askew. "Shouldn't you know all this since you're her relative?"

"I haven't seen her in a very long time," I said.

The orderly nodded but I could tell he didn't quite trust me any longer. "Like I said, I get the sense she stays here because she doesn't have anywhere else to go, no family who are willing to deal with her. But all that will change now, won't it, with you here?"

"It should, yes." I thought up a question a relative would ask. "Do you know how she's been lately?"

"I know she has a fellow. I figure her brother would want to know that." He grinned.

"What's his name?" I asked.

"Don't remember his name. A-something I think, or maybe that's his nickname. Yeah, that's it—she calls him *A*. Rachel told me he's a friend of her family's and that he travels a lot, to France and places. Apparently, he has more than one apartment in more than one city, due to his work. I get the feeling her family are rich folks. Judging by how they treat Rachel, they're not very nice people, I'm sorry to say. I have hope you're a better person." He stared at my clothes as though he wondered how the hell I fit into the picture. "My name's Brian, by the way."

We shook hands.

"What's her fellow's line of work?" I asked.

"I'm not sure. Something that requires him to travel a lot, she said. He comes to visit her once in a while, more than her family, that is. They hardly ever come." Brian gave me a judgmental glance. "I've finished my break and can take you upstairs if you'd like to see if she's around."

I didn't want to tell him that I'd seen her go inside but hadn't approached her.

"I know she leaves for work at some point in the late afternoon," Brian said.

"She has a job?" My surprise became exposed through my voice.

He watched me closely. "Yeah, she's a cashier at the department store down the street. The store's one of our work program sponsors. I have to head in, so do you want me to take you inside with me and tell her you're here to see her, or what?"

I pretended to check my pockets for my phone. "You know what, I left my phone in my car. Is it all right if I run and fetch it first? I'm parked a few blocks away. I can come inside when I've retrieved it."

I wanted to check out where Rachel worked, as though understanding her life could have aided me in comprehending her motives and why she'd done what she might have done, and continued to do. I still hadn't decided where I wanted to confront her, or if I even wanted to confront her. I'd caught a glimpse of her but that wasn't enough, possibly. I had to attempt to speak with her, although I comprehended the hazards of doing so solo.

Brian's demeanor hardened, and his eyes clouded over with disappointment. "All right. Just let the lady at the desk in the lobby know you're here to see Rachel. I'll tell her also. I have to return to my shift and I won't be able to wait for you."

That was what I'd hoped he'd say. "Thanks," I said. "I'm grateful."

"My pleasure," he muttered.

I found the department store down the street from the facility like Brian had mentioned. On the outside it seemed like the kind of place you went to when you wanted to purchase something for a large discount, and the décor was rather drab and outdated. Rachel couldn't have begun her shift yet but I browsed around without asking the other employees questions about her.

The department store was vast, and by the time I exited I'd learned little of Rachel's life besides the fact that her occupation seemed surprisingly ordinary. It was the early evening and I passed a woman standing outside in an adjacent alley, smoking by a dumpster. Rachel, having a cigarette before her shift.

Aware that my face might startle her, I didn't cease walking to stare at her, and continued forward. I did feel her look my way but when I glanced back, it appeared she hadn't come out of the alley onto the sidewalk. At some point, after walking a couple more blocks, I turned and walked with a determined stride back to the alley. The dumpster was far enough inside the cobblestoned alleyway that my heart gave a start at the isolation from the public street.

She was staring at the ground when I approached her with caution. I had nothing on me that could be used as a weapon.

"Do you have a light?" Rachel asked, looking up at me. She'd been standing there with an unlit cigarette in her hand.

"No," I said.

She watched me with anticipation. "Well, then?"

"Rachel. I'm . . . We're related." I didn't waste any time. "I've spoken to our mother."

She gave me an odd, wistful smile and tucked the cigarette into her jacket like she wanted to save it for later. "I know who you are. I knew who you were when you walked by. I'd been waiting for you to turn around and talk to me.

The receptionist where I live told me Brian told her that my brother was looking for me."

I couldn't read her expression. Her eyes were warm, not glassy like how I'd always believed a murderer's would appear in person. "How did you . . ."

"I've been following you, Evan. The uncanny thing is that I found out about you—you know—by accident. I was on the web one day—this was years back—and I saw a story your college newspaper had done on you. They called you their 'gender pioneer.' I'd lost you for years and then I found you."

I remembered the article well: *From the Navy to College Student and Gender Pioneer.* I'd been genuinely touched by the journalism students' enthusiasm and so I reluctantly participated in the interview.

Rachel moved a step toward me and I backed up into the cold, damp brick of one of the walls that formed the alley. She had me cornered and we were far enough away from the sidewalk that passersby couldn't see us. Rachel continued. "I recognized your face as mine."

She'd found me again by random, by chance. Oh, what luck I had. I grabbed at her jacket and pushed her away from me. Rachel stood aright and leaned against the brick. She gave me a shot at escaping but I didn't move. For a reason I didn't know, whether I was frozen in fear, or it was morbid curiosity, or because even though she was a bloodthirsty maniac, she was still my twin, my blood, and therefore the closest visceral connection I would have to anyone, I stayed. Though she wasn't pinning me against the wall and I could have fled right then, I didn't move. I craved the answers only she could give me.

"You killed Ben," I said.

Rachel crossed her arms. "He thought I was you. It was the wintertime, I tucked my hair—it was longer than yours—under a hat."

*Too much to bear*. What a cliché. But that's how I felt. It was too much to bear. I shouldn't have let Rachel see me crying but I couldn't hide the water swelling in my eyes and the steady, warm flow of tears down my cheeks. The tears burned my face and the revelation about Ben's death thrust me closer to the edge of a breakdown more than I ever had been before. How betrayed he must have felt before he died.

She seemed to anticipate a verbal reaction from me, for me to curse her aloud, but I held back my words, for anything I could have said to her would have been spoken too late.

"You shouldn't have come here," she said, moving out from the wall. Her tone implied the chain of events unfolding between us wouldn't end well for me.

I jumped a step toward the sidewalk but only made it halfway when she backed me up against the wall again.

"I don't know why I started again." Rachel sounded in awe of the horrors she'd committed. "I don't know what came over me."

Compulsion, like Mack had said about Alice.

"She—our mother—stopped exchanging letters with me. That upset me." Rachel wiped her eye. "Don't worry. I haven't told her what you are now. I wonder what she would think if she found out you aren't so perfect," she threatened. "I promised the boys—the recent ones—to pay them money to fuck me, that's how I got them to come with me. They were convenient. Before Mom stopped writing to me, I felt that her going to prison for me showed how much she loved me. That's why I'd left you alone, because I thought she loved me more than she loved you."

Despite her pleasant appearance, Rachel wasn't of as sound of mind as she looked. I slumped forward, away from the wall.

"We don't write each other, either," I said with desperation. "My mother—our mother—doesn't write to me. Why are you doing this to me?" I had trouble seeing her through my tears. I cursed myself for crumbling in her presence. You can't rationalize with a serial killer and I should have known that better than anyone. "Rachel, please, I'm your brother . . . "

"I never wanted you," Rachel said. "When I looked you up again recently, I read about how you won that award from your city for your work. I left the bodies so you'd find them. I forgot to say congratulations—your girlfriend—or is she your wife?—is beautiful. I saw a photo of her with you when I went to your apartment. Your little dog's sweet, by the way. You're so successful, no matter who you are, and Mom always loved you more than she did me, that's pretty clear."

Her erratic speech alarmed me. "Rachel?" I spoke softly.

"I thought I could get her to love me a little more than she loved you, or at least notice me."

"She does love you. She went to prison for you." I reminded her of the good things she had, a boyfriend, a job, and a family who were paying for her to get better, and how I, too, was estranged from our mother.

"How do you know all that about me?"

For a second I thought I'd disarmed her.

Then she said, "I live in a fucking mental hospital. I'm never going to get better, and I know that. As for my boyfriend, our family pays him to keep me company, that's the only reason he's with me. He's a male escort. That's how come he travels so much. I hate men. I killed those boys before they could become like our bastard father who abandoned us. No one really loves me. Not our mother, not you. No one."

"Our mother's dying," I said carefully, so as not to startle her. "She has cancer."

Rachel gave me a withering sneer but her eyes appeared melancholy. "It's what the bitch deserves." She spoke like a sullen child, and such malice from even the likes of her surprised me. "You want to know something interesting? I'm not going to kill another man after you, I've decided I'm going to kill a woman, someone close to you, someone you love very much."

Rachel knew what Sammie looked like and where we lived. Rachel had an evil smile then. Her eyes shone. She seethed and her face reddened. Part of me felt for her. After all, it was *Evelyn* who Alice wanted to see, not Rachel. But I wasn't going to let her stop the love Sammie and I had, and I wasn't going to allow Rachel to ever hurt Sammie, for if I let Rachel kill me, then she'd be able to get Sammie.

Rachel's frame, not much smaller than mine, surrounded me. "I'll slit your wrists right here to make it look like you ended your life over your guilt that *you* killed those people, *Evelyn.* Like mother, like son. I'll use your phone to text your suicide note to the media beforehand. Who'll protect your woman then?"

I hadn't seen a weapon on her. She looked into my eyes and all I saw in hers was my demise if I permitted it. I wouldn't allow her to hurt Sammie. I might not have lived myself but the chance that Sammie might was worth the peril. I pushed against Rachel's chest and shoved her out of my face.

She bent backward, swayed, and then found her balance. Then I noticed the small knife in her hand, its blade rusted and glinting faintly. Had she used that to carve the messages on the boys' flesh and take souvenirs or eat them? She must have taken the knife out of her pocket at some point as she regained her footing.

I shouted for help and bounded for the sidewalk. Something caught my arm. Rachel had a piece of my shirt clenched in her hand. I'd underestimated her strength, and every time I tried to shake her off me, she grabbed more of the cloth material. I kneed her in the groin, which didn't affect a woman like it did a man, and her face barely registered pain.

She yanked me around to face her and came toward me, forcing me to back into the brick wall. Rachel held the blade lightly against my throat, and even at that distance I felt its coolness and its power.

I risked a joke. "Whatever happened to cutting my wrists?"

Rachel spat in my eyes. "Fuck you. I'll decide what'll happen to you."

I blinked and her saliva trickled down my face. I began to call for help again. Rachel shook her head and pressed the blade against me a little more. I breathed heavily. I looked down and saw that the blade had become dulled over the years she owned it, but it still looked sharp enough to slice into my neck where my muscles throbbed in panic through my flesh.

My skin burned from head to toe, but the spit had cooled me, surprisingly, and the movement of her softly touching the blade across my neck was so vigorous and constant that I *heard* it. That was one thing I hadn't learned throughout the many years of my job: that you felt more alive than ever the moment before you died.

She pressed the blade more to my throat. Panic rose up within me and I swallowed. Rachel rubbed her other hand across my neck and showed me the faint smudge of blood on her fingers. She'd cut me but not deeply, and I grasped that if I didn't hurt her myself she would kill me. A strange thing it is, to realize you have to kill your sister to save your life.

"Get the hell away from him," a voice said.

Mack, and he sounded near enough to help.

Mack stepped farther into the alley. He held a gun in his hands, pointed at Rachel. "I've called for backup. They'll be here any second. Once they come, you won't stand a chance," he told her. "Put down the knife. That'd be the best thing for you to do, or else I can't promise it'll end well for you."

Rachel glanced his way. "Lose the gun or I'll slit his throat." When Mack didn't reply she said, "I mean it."

"Okay. Take it easy. Don't do anything stupid." Mack dropped the gun and I felt defeated at the sound of it hitting the cobbled ground. He held up his hands.

"Don't lecture me on stupid." Rachel laughed. "I'm not the one who sent the wrong woman to prison."

With the knife constricting my throat, I barely managed to whisper to Mack, "I'll explain later."

"No, I'll explain when I feel like it," Rachel said. "How about right now?" She'd stopped looking at me and focused on him.

Mack nodded at me and I knew he was checking to see how I was coping. I smiled weakly at him.

"I killed those boys," Rachel said. "The recent ones, too. That's how come the killings started up again. Our mother went to prison for me for the first killings."

I'd expected to see surprise on Mack's face but it was clear he already knew. "It's over, Rachel," he said in a soft voice. "Put down the knife. Let him go."

"It isn't." She dug the side of the knife deeper into my throat and I cried out in pain. "It's not over unless I want it to be."

Mack made a gesture with his hands as though to calm her. "Okay." His tone implied he'd handed control over to Rachel. "Why don't you let him go and then the two of us can talk? How does that sound?"

Sirens blared and their distance between us lessened. Going by how Rachel increased the pressure of the knife on my throat, she heard them also.

"It's done," Rachel whispered to me.

I winced and braced myself for the end. During what seemed like a mere second, she stepped back from me and dragged the knife across her own throat. The knife fell from her hand to the cobblestones and echoed in the quiet alley. Blood shot out of her and decorated her pale throat with a bright smear. Rachel touched her throat and looked at the blood covering her hands, as though shocked by what she'd done.

Mack reacted before I did and ran toward Rachel.

"She can't die," I screamed, and reached for her, because although she would have had no problem killing me, she was still my sister, my blood.

He kept Rachel upright in his arms and tried to lessen the blood spilling out of her by pressing his hand to her throat. As I touched the cloth of her jacket, her knees buckled and she fell out from Mack's arms to the ground, and landed on her side.

Blood continued to pour from her throat and formed a small pool by her mouth. Mack and I knelt by her and covered her neck with our hands to try and cease some of the blood coming out of her until the other police arrived. She blinked in and out of consciousness.

"I'm helping her because she's my sister," I told Mack. "Why are you helping her?"

"It's my job."

I'd never thought of it that way before; Mack nabbed killers, but it was also his duty to save them if the need came about.

He rang again for an ambulance while I continued to press my hand around the brutal rip in Rachel's throat.

"Be careful with her neck," Mack said in between talking on the phone.

I'd seen enough of death to conclude that Rachel's life would end soon regardless of help arriving. What could I have said to a dying murderer? A sister I had never known? Cold sweat dampened my back.

"You're going to be okay," I whispered.

And maybe she would, finally, be at peace.

Rachel opened her eyes briefly, long enough to see me there with her. She closed her eyes and smiled and shook her head. She knew my words were only to comfort her.

Many police arrived and blocked off the alley from the street where a line of onlookers had formed. Rachel had stopped breathing. One of the officers checked her pulse, made eye contact with Mack, and shook his head. He politely asked me to move out of the way and Mack helped me stand up. We watched as the officer gave Rachel CPR but he couldn't get her to breathe.

One cop asked another if she should put handcuffs on Rachel.

"You really think that's necessary?" Mack snapped at the woman. "She's not going anywhere."

The paramedics arrived in an ambulance shortly after and took over for the officer trying to save Rachel's life. They stopped the bleeding and tried to get her heart to start up again. After what seemed like an hour, one of them, a young red-haired man, stood up from working on Rachel and approached me. Mack put his arm around me.

"I'm sorry," the man said. He patted my arm and retreated.

The police officers stood around as the paramedics reversed the ambulance, which bleated a backup signal, and proceeded to load Rachel's sheet-covered body onto a gurney, and roll her into the back of the ambulance.

"You don't have to watch this. Come with me," Mack said. "I'm parked nearby. I'll drive you to the hospital so you can get that checked out." He pointed at my neck.

"I'm okay, really." I took a tissue out of my pocket and wiped the cut. The blood had stopped coming out, and there was only a few spots of red on the tissue.

"You still might want a doctor to look at it in case the blade was dirty."

"I'll worry about that later. Right now, I want to return to the lodge to see Sammie. I can't explain it but I have to see her now." It wasn't enough to text her to confirm her safety, I had to see her in person. I pulled out my phone and turned it on to let her know I was on my way there.

"She's fine. I spoke to her recently," Mack said.

"You did?" I waited for him to elaborate but he didn't. "I'm parked close by as well," I said.

"Where, exactly?"

I told him.

He signaled to the officers and strode with me out to the sidewalk, moving past the crowd that had accumulated, to cross the street. We washed our hands in a public restroom.

"I'll drive you back to your hotel. We can get someone to pick up your car later and take it to Freedom," Mack said, outside again.

"No, I'll drive myself. Thanks anyway."

"You're sure?" He raised an eyebrow.

"Mack, I'm not a kid anymore."

He smiled. "You really aren't. I'll walk with you to your car. That's the least you could let me do. And I'm sorry about your sister."

"It's not your fault." I'd never get to discover if Rachel had any good in her but I had no more tears left for someone I hadn't known.

"It's not yours, either," he said.

I couldn't appreciate his words then but knew that someday they would be valuable to me.

"The police here are going to need you to come back at some point before you return to Seven Sisters. They'll want to take your statement on what happened today."

I nodded. "Sammie and I will take a detour and stop here on our way home. You don't think it'll take more than a few hours, do you? It won't take days, right?"

"I wouldn't think so," Mack said.

I told him about the cottage where Rachel had lived with her caretaker. "What will happen to Rachel's body when they're finished with her?" I asked.

"Either someone will claim her or she'll linger."

"My mother's family will take care of the arrangements." I was certain they would. "How'd you know where I'd be today?"

"As I said, your girlfriend called me. She wanted to drive to Lamont herself and look for you but I advised her against it. She told me she was worried about you coming here. She said something about a Lamont connection to the murders in Seven Sisters. I promised her I would help. After she called, I went to speak with your mother at the prison." My concern must have showed on my face because Mack said, "Don't worry, I didn't disclose your relation to her. I conveyed to her that I received a call that the journalist she spoke with could be in danger, and I asked her what she'd told you. That's how I found out about Rachel. She was surprisingly cordial to me—I believe you've had a good effect on her—but it took a lot of effort on my part to pull the information out of her. She was *very* reluctant. You know how stubborn she can be."

"That's a damn understatement," I murmured.

"When I went to the facility where Rachel was staying—there's only one place like that in Lamont—she'd already left for work. The orderly I spoke with mentioned Rachel's brother had been there looking for her. Figuring you might have gone to the store where she worked, that's where I went, but you weren't there. One of Rachel's co-workers told me she liked to smoke in the alley before her shift."

I listened on and off as he spoke, and before long he'd walked with me to where I'd parked. We stood on the sidewalk alongside the car.

"Were you aware my mother has cancer?" I asked.

Mack looked at his hands and then at me. "Yes. I withheld her condition from you because I didn't want to worry you. I didn't want you to have to hear it from me. I wanted her to tell you."

"She did, but she doesn't know she's my mother."

"Yeah, I guessed that much."

"Thanks, Mack," I said. "I know you saved my life. I thought about giving you a hug, but a pat on the back will do."

He grinned and opened his arms. "Come here and give me a hug, buddy."

"One more thing. How'd Sammie get your number? I never gave it to her."

"She called the station and asked to speak to me. I promised her I wouldn't let anything happen to you. About your mother—we got it wrong. I'm sorry."

"She confessed. You couldn't have known." I embraced the big guy right there on the street.

# Chapter 17

The night after Sammie and I returned to Seven Sisters, we sat on the couch in our apartment, wineglasses in our hands and Paige nestled between us.

We'd driven home from Freedom together and had left Sammie's car behind for the rental company to pick up from the hotel parking lot. I hadn't spoken to Tawny when we checked out of the lodge and I doubted I'd ever see her again. Some places and people were best left in the past.

My neck was healing fast but my heart needed some more time.

The Seven Sisters police were working with Sammie's organization to notify the families of Rachel's unclaimed victims.

"It's good to be back to normal," Sammie said to me. "But I know that nothing will be normal again after what you've endured."

"It's a new normal," I said. And I wanted the new normal to be Sammie and me forever.

We'd had the TV on earlier but turned it off after a few minutes. Both of us had to return to work tomorrow. I'd received a call from Chief Gilani upon arriving at home, letting me know that, unofficially, my suspension would be revoked and my absence at the hearing could be overlooked. He hadn't said that the change of heart had stemmed from my help solving the recent killings, but I liked to think of it that way. The chief would also get to keep his job.

Before we parted ways, Mack had assured me Alice's conviction would be reopened and reconsidered in an expedited manner because of her illness. "I'll be talking to the DA tonight," Mack had told me. He'd said the DA would arrange for Alice to have time served for covering Rachel's crimes by taking her place.

The police wanted to interview Rachel's companion and a warrant had been issued for him.

I'd promised Alice I might reunite her with her child, and perhaps I would try. With the limited amount of time Alice had left, I'd have to try soon. And maybe I'd bring along a jar of molasses for her.

I found out through the chief that Em had admitted to selling the story to *Crime Man* and that she'd resigned from the clean-up team. When I'd asked Josh if he heard from her, he welcomed me back home and texted that Em hadn't contacted him since her resignation. I never heard from her again, but I liked to believe that she and her son were faring well.

Paige moved down to our feet and I cradled Sammie's head in my lap. "It does feel good to be here," I said, reaching over her to set my wineglass on the coffee table. "Let's get married."

I took Sammie's wineglass from her and put it next to mine on the table. The ordeal of the past few days and her support throughout everything made me realize how much she meant to me.

I beamed at the stunned look on her face. She moved off my lap and sat up. I got down on my knees in front of her, and Paige wagged.

Sammie hid her face in her hands and laughed. "You're proposing? Now? After everything that's happened? That's one of the things I've always loved about you, Evan, your spontaneity." She took her hands from her face and smiled at me.

"Will you marry me?" I asked.

"Where's the ring?"

"I don't have one yet. We'll go shopping tomorrow night after work."

Sammie laughed. "Oh, you're something else. But I love you. And I'll marry you."

"You will?"

"Yes." She touched my hands.

"Maybe my luck is beginning to turn around." We stood up and kissed, with Paige barking behind us like she was in a celebratory mood.

A text came through. It was for me.

"Aren't you going to read that?" Sammie asked.

"No, I'll look later. Let's celebrate tonight. Just us."

"All right, but what if it's for work?"

"It can wait."

"I better check for you." Sammie grabbed the phone from me before I could stop her. I waited as she read. "You should see this." She handed the phone to me.

There'd been a stabbing at a bar earlier in the day. "What about celebrating?" I said. "I don't have to go. My job doesn't mean more to me than you do."

"I know. But go." Sammie put her hand on my chest. "We're getting our rings tomorrow. That's good enough. I know how important your work is to you."

"Okay, but I love you more than work."

"I know you do." Sammie's eyes shone when she smiled.

I texted Josh to let him know I'd be getting the van from the garage and picking him up at his house. Our job was, sadly, never done.

ENDEAVOUR PRESS

Endeavour Ink is an imprint of Endeavour Press.

If you enjoyed *Carved in Blood* check out Endeavour Press's eBooks here: www.endeavourpress.com

For weekly updates on our free and discounted eBooks sign up to our newsletter: www.endeavourpress.com

Follow us on Twitter: @EndeavourPress